The Way It's Supposed to Be

April Garner

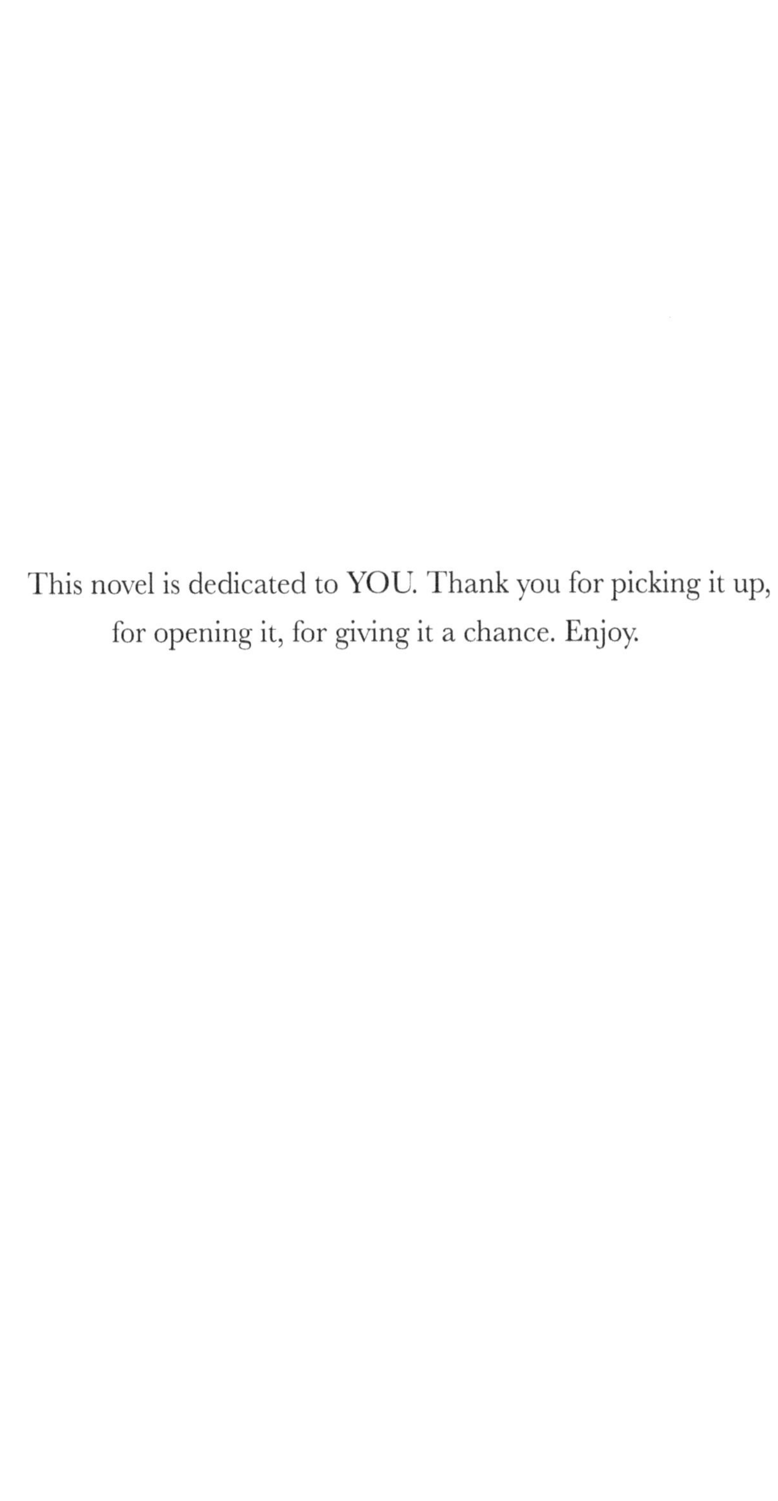

This novel is dedicated to YOU. Thank you for picking it up,
for opening it, for giving it a chance. Enjoy.

CHAPTER 1

Day 1

Mitch was late again. He banged through the front door of the house, gripping his briefcase in one hand, a bag of groceries in the other. He'd told Allie he'd be home an hour ago, but he got caught up talking to a coworker at K&S Properties and lost track of time. After stopping by the market, traffic had been bad. No worse than usual, though. He didn't know why the bumper-to-bumper on the ranch roads always surprised him. They were built for ranchers moseying to town to buy dry goods now and then, not for the modern sprawl of suburbia's commuters that now crowded the roads.

Mitch dropped his briefcase by the couch next to a teetering stack of Allie's books and headed to the kitchen to stash the few things he'd picked up for dinner. He didn't know what they were having, but Allie'd asked for Swiss chard. He'd also picked up some mixed nuts for pre-dinner snacking and a six-pack of Blue

Moon.

"Allie, You home? I got that Swiss chard you wanted…or I think I did."

He studied the greens in his hand. They'd all been jumbled up, not in their properly labeled places at the store.

"Is it the same thing as kale? Shit, this might be kale," he muttered, then shoved it in the fridge anyway. He wasn't going back to the store. Greens were greens. He pulled a beer off the plastic ring and shut the door, leaning against the fridge as he popped the tab but then froze mid-sip.

His gaze fell upon the cutting board by the sink — the big bamboo one Allie's aunt had given them when they moved in together. Chunks of carrot had tumbled haphazardly across it; some had rolled onto the counter and floor. A glass salad bowl sat at the ready next to the cuttings. But none of that was what got his attention.

It was the puddle; it oozed over half the cutting board and onto the counter, just like the carrots. Like the carrots, it had spilled onto the floor as well. Mitch slowly approached the mess as though it might bite, placing his beer on the island as he passed it. As he drew closer, he could see their large paring knife, with its wooden handle, lying in the sink, spatters of the same oozing dotted around it in the sink. They were red, those spatters, and they looked very much like blood.

––––––

"Allie?!"

Mitch turned from the sink and called out. He leaned into her little study off the kitchen, but she wasn't there. He took the stairs two at a time, calling her name, looking in all the rooms. He expected to find her in the bathroom, doctoring a sliced finger. It would be no wonder; she had a careless tendency, and Mitch couldn't stand to watch her cut anything; it made him nervous. But it was an awful lot of blood for a cut finger.

There was no sign of her anywhere. Maybe the cut had been bad enough to send her to the emergency room. He fished his phone out of his back pocket. No missed calls. He held the home button down and shouted, "Call Allie!" into it.

Straight to voicemail.

"Shit!"

She was always letting her phone battery run out or leaving it somewhere. What was the point of having a mobile phone, Mitch wondered frequently, if you didn't have it with you? He did admire her, at times, though. She lacked that need to be connected that most modern people had. She felt no sense of panic whatsoever if she happened to reach for her phone and found she'd left it at home.

Mitch clomped back downstairs to the kitchen, pausing at the door, scanning the room for…clues, he guessed. He was about to turn around and check the garage when he noticed the oven. The dish towel with the hand-painted butterflies, the one

Allie wouldn't let anyone use that had a permanent place over the oven handle, was gone.

His eyes shifted back to the cutting board, and he crossed the room to it. The carrot pieces were listing right and left, vegetable sailors drowning in a sea of ooze. One of them, a piece about an inch-and-a-half long, was lighter colored than the rest. He leaned in to peer closer. A fingernail!

Mitch stumbled backward, catching his left hip on the edge of the island and let out a yell. As he regained his footing and stared back at the thumb, he saw Allie's silver braided ring still on it. The contents of his stomach lurched. His lunch and that one sip of Blue Moon threatened to come back up. His nausea quickly morphed into fear.

———

He felt panic – a furious, nauseating swarm of butterflies – begin to work its way up from his belly to his throat, gunning for his head where it would wreak havoc. He forced it back down, making himself think clearly. He opened the pantry and pulled out a ziplock bag, turning it inside out over his hand. He went to the cutting board and, gingerly, grimacing, picked up the thumb.

He started to hold it under the ice dispenser on the fridge but thought about freezer burn. Not sure if that was a thing with severed thumbs, he fetched a second baggie and filled it with ice, placing it in the first one, covering the thumb, exhaling with relief now that it was out of sight. When he found Allie, there'd be a chance it could be reattached.

As he stood in the kitchen, sealing the bags, he noticed the pattern of blood splatters on the white tile floor. There was a puddle by the cutting board and sink and droplets over to the oven with the missing towel. He scanned the floor and saw more droplets by the backdoor. She'd wrapped her bleeding hand in the dish towel, which wasn't very absorbent. It must have started bleeding through the cloth at the door.

Why would she go out into the backyard with a bleeding hand and missing fucking thumb?

His gaze shifted from the backdoor to the garage door. He pushed it open, and sure enough, Allie's car was there, next to the boxes she had yet to unpack from when she moved in eight months ago.

He opened the backdoor, carefully stepping over the blood on the tile. He found more of them on the wooden deck outside, leading down the steps into the St. Augustine grass. It was half brown, half green. It had been a mild winter in Central Texas, and the grass hadn't gone completely dormant. There was a cool breeze, but it was still warm for February. The sky overhead was gray, and rain clouds threatened in the distance.

Mitch looked out toward the woods. This was Allie's favorite part of the house. She couldn't care less about the ridiculously large main bathroom with soaking tub and walk-in shower or the butler's pantry. It was the greenbelt that made their property special for her.

He scanned the grass, looking for more blood drops, and he saw them, leading away from the house, harder to see in the grass but definitely there. Then, halfway across the lawn, he saw an odd-looking piece of wood. Jogging toward it, he realized it was Allie's faux-wood phone cover. When he turned it over, he saw blood smeared across the screen and the battery completely dead, as expected. He shoved it into his back pocket next to his own. The blood droplets continued, clinging to the blades of grass, toward the greenbelt path at the end of their yard.

He took off in a dead sprint.

———

Mitch ran down the path, still clutching the baggie with the severed thumb.

"Allie, are you back here?"

He scanned the trail's edges for anything indicating she'd come this way. Still jogging, he spied what he thought was a piece of clothing but turned out to be one of those orange tags they tie around trees indicating they should be cut down or saved — he couldn't remember which. Not keeping his eyes on the path, Mitch caught his foot on a tree root and fell hard on the packed dirt, pain shooting through his left ankle.

"Aaaah, godamnitshitmotherfucker!" he cried out, rolling to sit up, rocking, clutching his throbbing leg. As the hurt slowly subsided into a dull throb, Mitch got to his feet and proceeded down the path more slowly, testing his ankle. He could put a little weight on it, but the lingering pain forced a limp.

As his body slowed down, so did his thinking. Panic began to subside. It made no sense to him that Allie would accidentally chop off her thumb, then run off into the woods. Unless, maybe she lost so much blood, she wasn't thinking straight? What if she were passed out somewhere out here? His urgency began to return just as he approached a widening of the path, a clearing, the kind of place Allie imagined fairies or ancient people gathering for ceremonies.

The light that broke through the trees fell upon large limestone boulders which looked purposefully, yet erratically, placed. The smaller ones in the shadows wore bright green moss. Allie had dragged him away from his computer and new listings one Saturday to show him this place. She'd been excited, hiking fast ahead of him, talking. His mind had been on work.

Mitch limped over to the large, flat rock they'd rested upon that day. There was more blood – a small, congealing puddle on the rock as if she'd stopped and rested here, then more droplets leading toward where the path picked up again on the other side of the clearing. He followed them, his speed limited by his injured ankle that he could now feel swelling inside his work loafer, but the drops petered out.

Had the bleeding simply stopped, and she continued down the path? Had she doubled back, trying to get back to the house?

As he stood, slowly rotating in place, considering his options, he caught a flash of red out of the corner of his eye. He turned, but it disappeared like a frightened animal, with a rustling of brush.

He turned to sprint after it but was tripped up by the pain in his injured ankle and pulled up after a few steps, limping heavily. He'd lost it completely. Mitch finally pulled out his phone and dialed 911.

—————

"911, what's your emergency?"

Mitch was still limping down the path through the greenbelt, hoping for some sign of Allie. She had a red sweater she liked to wear. Had she been wearing it that morning when he left for work? They'd both been rushing around, trying to get out the door after oversleeping the ancient clock radio by their bed. He hadn't had time to pay attention to details. He didn't even know if the glimpse of red he'd seen had been her.

He saw it again, a flash of red, and he began to hobble faster.

"Goddamnit!" he hollered, phone still pressed to his ear.

"Sir, what's your emergency?" the operator repeated.

"It's my wife." Mitch was panting between words, branches swatting his face and scratching at his slacks, as he tried in vain to catch up with what he'd just seen.

"She's missing, and I think…Christ, I found her thumb in a pool of blood in our kitchen! I don't know what the fuck is going on. Can you send someone out here?"

Mitch slipped on some loose rocks where the ground had begun to slope gently toward the creek, but unfortunately, he caught himself from falling with his injured leg. Pain shot through him as he crumbled to the ground and dropped his phone. He sat, clutching his ankle, trying to get his brain to think around the pain. As he came back to himself, he heard, at a distance, the 911 operator calling to him.

"Sir, are you there? Are you there? Stay on the line…"

He scrambled through the rocks and dry leaves and retrieved the phone. "I'm here. I fell. My ankle, I think it's sprained. Just send someone please. She's hurt, and she's missing."

"Sir, I'm going to need your location."

"I'm in the fucking woods behind my house! I'm right next to this fucking tree and that fucking rock! Don't you have GPS or something? Part of my fucking problem is I don't know where the fuck I am!"

"Calm down, sir. We're having a hard time getting your exact location."

"Don't tell me to fucking calm down! I'm sitting in the middle of the woods behind my goddamned house; my wife is missing and hurt. Just send someone to find her!"

"What is your address?"

"18 Hilltop Road."

"I'm sending EMS and police. Are you able to go back to your house and meet them?"

Her air of authority was doing what it was supposed to do — calming him down and getting him to think more clearly. He realized he wasn't finding anyone out there by himself in his condition. He could feel his shoe getting tighter, his ankle swelling. He didn't want to look at it.

"Yeah, I can do that," he responded, taking a deep breath.

"Walk back toward your house and stay on the line with me."

The operator talked to him all the way back to the house. He didn't remember exactly what she said but recalled she asked some questions, which he did his best to answer. He could tell she was just keeping his mind busy, keeping him talking.

As Mitch limped up to where the woods met the yard, he could hear sirens in the distance. He'd been distracted from the pain in his ankle by the mission to get back to the house and the operator's steady voice, but now it came roaring back with a vengeance. He crumpled to the half-dead grass and rolled onto his back, sweaty and exhausted in his realtor's suit.

"Sir, are you still there?"

"Yes, I hear the sirens." He felt a fat raindrop hit his forehead.

———

Mitch was parked on the couch in his living room, foot propped on the table, with a ziplock full of ice resting on his throbbing ankle. They'd given him a painkiller, but it didn't seem to be working on his ankle so far. His brain felt a little numb, though. He turned his head to peer through the kitchen, out the full-length glass in the backdoor. He could see lights bobbing out in the woods. They were looking for Allie. It was dark and raining hard.

The detective was sitting across from him in the old, brown recliner. She wasn't reclining, though; she was perched on the edge, notebook in her lap, looking at Mitch expectantly. She'd been interviewing him for the better part of an hour. They'd already been over what had happened when he got home several times. She seemed especially interested in how he'd followed the trail of blood to the woods.

Mitch was tired of talking.

"I'm sorry, did you say something?" He shook his head to clear it.

"Do you want something to drink? Coffee?"

"Can I make it Irish?"

The detective grinned a little. "Of course. Hey, Jason!" she called into the kitchen. "Can you rustle up some coffee in there? And give it a little kick?"

"Sure thing," Jason called back from the kitchen.

Mitch hadn't realized anyone else was still here. He'd passed off the thumb, reluctantly, to one of the investigators processing the scene, though he was assured it wouldn't be far if they found Allie. After that, it seemed everyone was out in the greenbelt looking for her.

What was this Jason doing in there? Surely not just kickin' it at the kitchen table, waiting for short-order coffee instructions.

"There's whiskey in the pantry on the top shelf," Mitch called. His voice sounded far away to him. None of this seemed real.

As the bubbling sound of the automatic drip maker drifted into the living room with the familiar and comforting smell of coffee, the detective turned back to Mitch. "So, has Allie ever left like this before?"

"You mean chopped her thumb off and taken off into the woods?" he responded sarcastically. "No, can't say that she has."

"Easy. I have to cover all the bases."

"Sorry…What was your name again?"

"Murphy."

"Sorry, Murphy. It's been a strange night, and it sucks being stuck in here with my leg on a table when I could be out looking for her."

"I know, Mitch, but plenty of experienced officers are searching for her out there. You can help by answering my questions, so we can find her faster. Has she been acting odd lately or under any stress?"

"Um, well," He was loathe to get personal, but with what was at stake, he felt he had no choice. "She had a miscarriage."

Mitch reluctantly launched into the story. It had been a little less than a year ago. They'd gotten lazy about using protection; pregnancy no longer sounded like a death sentence since they were committed to each other. When Allie missed her period, they'd been surprised but happy. They'd shared the news with immediate family and even started talking about names.

"She was still living in Austin then," Mitch noted.

"Y'all weren't living together…when was this?"

"About eight months ago. That's what prompted her to move in finally."

"The pregnancy."

"Yeah," he paused as Jason entered with two cups of coffee.

"Here you go!" Jason said. "One spiked, one regular." He handed them their coffees, smiled at Murphy and returned to the kitchen.

Mitch continued, "Yeah, I'd thought it was a good idea for a while. I moved out here because the real estate market is booming, and it's all the better to live where you work — makes getting to clients easier.

"When I moved, Allie was still working as a journalist at the *Austin Globe*, so she stayed. Then, she got laid off. She was trying to find something else but was spending all her weekends in Lime at my house. When she got pregnant, I finally talked her into moving in with me."

Mitch paused to sip his coffee, then set it back down on the side table next to one of Allie's piles of books. "Two months later, she…there was blood. She miscarried," he said with a hitch in his voice.

"I'm so sorry. That must have been hard on both of you."

"Yeah, well…" Mitch stared at the pile of books to his left, so he wouldn't have to make eye contact. "Funny thing is, she had mentioned it a couple of times, miscarriage."

"Like how?"

"Like, she just said she was a little worried. She said she knew it happened a lot, and she…you know, worried. I guess that's normal, though." He shook his head.

"Look, I don't see how this is going to help. She's out there, somewhere, bleeding, and I ought to be out there looking for her." He leaned forward, trying to catch another glimpse of the bobbing flashlights outside, but the storm was picking up, and visibility was low.

"Look, Mitch. I don't know what happened here. I'm just trying to put together who she was, what her state of mind might have been, so we can narrow our search area."

"But this doesn't make any sense! Why would she do that, cut off her thumb, and just, what, leave? Wander off in the woods. It makes no sense!" He was getting agitated.

"None of this makes any sense right now. That's why we have to consider every possibility. Any piece of information could point us in the right direction…What do you do again?"

"Real estate. I'm an agent with K&S Properties."

And Allie's a writer?"

"She's published a couple of short stories in local magazines. Her day job's at *The Hill Country News*, but the pay is shit. It's a sinking ship."

"Like all print media, huh?"

"Yeah, I guess. Look, are you interviewing me for a job? I don't understand why any of this is relevant."

Murphy was unflappable. "Listen, it's late, and we're going to call off the search pretty soon, but they'll be back at it by first light. Try to get some sleep, but if you think of anything or if something happens, don't hesitate to call me, even if it's the middle of the night."

She handed Mitch her card. "That's my cell at the bottom there."

"Okay, thanks…."

"Murphy."

"Right."

"What about the…um, her thumb?"

"It's been bagged for evidence. We'll have to make sure it's hers first."

"But her ring's on it."

"I know. I don't think it's not hers. We just have to confirm. We'll keep it cool, but a thumb usually can't be reattached after about eight hours."

It had been almost four hours since Mitch got home and discovered Allie was gone. Saving Allie's thumb didn't look good if they were calling off the search soon.

Mitch, sheltered from the downpour by his small front porch roof, watched Murphy and Jason get in their car. He stared down at his hands. He thought about the ring; he'd bought it for her at a mall kiosk when they first started dating. It had cost five dollars, and he was shocked it had lasted so long. He'd wanted to get her something better, but she was sentimental about it and rarely took it off.

Looking at his thumbs, he began to imagine what it could've been like to sever one. Allie's ring had been on her left thumb, so…*shit!*

Mitch took off through the yard, headed toward Jason and Murphy, who had backed onto the street and were preparing to leave. He rapped on the driver's side window, and Jason rolled it down.

"The thumb," he was breathing hard from his sprint. "It was her left one."

Murphy leaned forward to make eye contact with Mitch around Jason. "So?"

"She was left-handed."

———

Murphy'd made a note of it before she and Jason had taken off into the night, but she didn't seem to find the fact that Allie'd lopped off her dominant thumb as significant as Mitch did.

He wandered back into his kitchen, stopping to pick up the two coffee mugs in the living room. Murphy had drained hers, and presently, Mitch finished his off, too. Someone, probably Jason, had cleaned up the blood and the spilled vegetables.

Mitch loaded the mugs into the dishwasher and noticed a thin film on the countertop. It looked like flour. He stared at it momentarily, put his finger in it and examined it. He couldn't imagine why Allie'd have flour out if she was making a salad. He didn't even realize they owned any.

Mitch's head felt leaden as he dragged his bum ankle up the stairs. It still really hurt. Maybe the EMTs were right; maybe it needed an X-ray. It really could be broken. He peeled off his dirty clothes and dropped them onto the bathroom floor, then stepped into the shower and let the warm water pour over him, rinsing away the sweat and dirt he'd accumulated in the green-belt.

He thought he wouldn't be able to sleep, but as soon as he was horizontal in bed, his mind and body gave way to exhaustion.

CHAPTER 2

Day 2

Mitch awoke to sunlight streaming in from the east-facing bedroom window. Allie loved that window, but Mitch hated how it woke him up every damned morning before he was ready. They hadn't gotten around to getting a shade for it.

As the fog of sleep cleared from his head, the previous day's events returned to him — the blood, the thumb, the detectives. He swung his legs over the side of the bed and got up to take a piss, but pain shot through his left ankle, and it refused to hold him. He went down with a thud and a steady stream of expletives. Maybe it really was broken.

Mitch hobbled to the bathroom and relieved himself, intent on getting back in bed to think some more and wait until the pain subsided. But just as he was lying down again, his phone buzzed on the nightstand.

"Hello?"

"Mitch, this is Detective Murphy. How are you doing this morning?"

"Shitty, actually. I think my ankle's broken. Allie's still gone, so not great, but how the hell are you this fine AM?"

"Good," she said briskly, ignoring the crap he'd just dished out. "You should probably get your ankle checked out first, but could you meet me for coffee this afternoon? I'd like to talk a little more, see if anything comes to mind."

"Yeah…yeah, that's probably a good idea. Is there…will there be a search team again today?"

"As we speak. They've been out there since dawn."

"Oh. Maybe I should go help --"

"You just take care of your leg and come meet me at that little coffee place on 5th and Live Oak at one o'clock, okay?"

"All right. What's the place called?"

"Cuppa Coffee, Cup o Joe, I dunno. Can't remember. But it's the only one at that intersection."

"See you then."

––––––––

Mitch struggled into his clothes with his left ankle now swollen the size of a large softball, and he headed out the door to the urgent care clinic at the front of his subdivision. He was impatient, eager to get this over with, so he could concentrate on what to do next. How to find Allie.

Soon enough, he found himself sitting on a paper-covered table behind a curtain at the clinic. An intern, who looked younger than Mitch, was admonishing him. "You really should have come in last night. If it is broken, the bones may have moved around with you walking all over the place on it."

"Yeah, coming in last night wasn't an option."

"Man, I know how it is, out having a good time, and you don't want to ruin anyone's night with a trip to the ER, but if the bones have moved out of alignment, it could mean it'll need pins. It's worth skipping the last couple beers of the night to avoid surgery, don't you think?"

Mitch's eyes met the young physician's unblinkingly. He suppressed his irritation at the presumptuousness, reminding himself that getting out of here expediently was his priority. "Can we just get it x-rayed please, and go from there?"

It turned out Mitch had a small fracture, but nothing a few weeks in a boot wouldn't fix. The intern seemed almost disappointed he wouldn't need surgery. They'd had to wait a long time for the x-ray machine to be available and then for the clinic staff to dig up a boot that was the right size, so by the time Mitch wobbled to his car, he was running late to meet Murphy. Grateful for the automatic transmission, he pulled himself and his leg into the car and sped off toward downtown Lime.

Mitch lucked out with an empty parking spot right across the street from the coffee shop. It was no wonder Murphy couldn't remember the name; the place didn't have one, per se, just a temporary-looking banner with the word "Coffee" on it next to a big stock image of a steaming cup. This was the third establishment he'd seen in this spot since he moved to Lime a year and a half ago.

Looking up and down Live Oak Street, which functioned as the main drag in Lime, most stores were well-established, having been there for years. They served locals and tourists alike. There was a hair salon, candy store, several restaurants and souvenir shops. Visitors came from Austin or other larger cities to cool themselves in the chilly waters of Limestone Springs or for their annual holiday festival in the winter. It was the surrounding native limestone that gave both the spring and the city of Lime their names. Despite the many signs on Live Oak Street that featured ripe, green fruit, there wasn't a real lime tree to be had in all of downtown. You wanted garnishes for your margaritas, you had to hit up Brookshire's.

As Mitch approached the transient-looking coffee shop, his realtor cogs started turning idly. He wondered what was wrong with the space. It had an ideal corner location, plenty of traffic, decent parking. Why did the smoothie shop that was here a few months ago fail? What about the doughnut store before that? Some spaces were like that, he knew, and no one could tell why.

As he entered, he spotted Murphy at a back corner table and clumsily maneuvered himself with his booted foot across the room. She pushed a cup of coffee toward him. "Thanks for coming."

Mitch took a sip from the paper cup and winced. It was lukewarm and fairly bitter. He wondered who'd move into the space next.

Murphy started right in: "I just wanted to know if you thought of anything else that might help, maybe something she mentioned in the past couple of weeks, odd behavior."

"No. I wracked my brain the whole time I was waiting at urgent care. She seemed completely normal, for her anyway."

"What do you mean 'for her'?"

"She's just different from most people. Kinda weird… but in a good way," he said, as if defending Allie against his own assessment.

"Like how?"

"Well, you know we're not actually married, right?"

"No, I didn't. On the 911 call, you said she was your wife."

"I just said that because I thought they'd take it more seriously. A girlfriend disappearing doesn't sound as…important."

"Severed body parts are usually taken pretty seriously, no matter your relation," Murphy said pointedly.

"True. But I feel like we're married. We live together, she was pregnant. 'Girlfriend' doesn't do our relationship justice."

"I get it. Were you planning to be married?"

"I wanted to, but Allie didn't like the idea. She says marriage is a tool of the patriarchy used to keep women subservient to men. Plus, she doesn't think we need the government to tell us we're committed to each other. I see her point. I don't disagree, but I can't let go of wanting something official to connect us."

They sat for a minute in silence until Murphy changed the subject. "What about a journal? Did she keep one?"

"Why?"

Murphy shrugged. "You said she's a writer. They usually keep journals. It might help us out."

"I'm not sure. I see her write all the time, but it could be anything — notes for work, story ideas, grocery lists…"

Murphy studied Mitch silently.

"What?" Mitch felt like he was failing some sort of test.

She shook her head. "Nothing. Listen, I found some things. They might help us find her, and if I tell you, maybe it will spark some memory so we can work together on this."

Mitch began pushing some spilled powdered creamer around the bare metal table, which reminded him of the powder on the kitchen counter from the night before. He suddenly realized his kitchen had been dusted for prints. He sat back in his chair. "You mean you're not going to arrest me as a suspect?" He stared as if trying to bore holes into the back of Murphy's skull. He was feeling pissed and smug at the same time. But Murphy didn't flinch; in fact, she smiled a little.

"Found the fingerprint powder in the kitchen, huh? Jason's so bad at cleaning that shit up. No, I don't think you forcibly cut off Allie's thumb, chased her into the woods, came back, didn't clean up and called 911. It's absurd."

"Sounds like you've had that same argument recently."

"Some people have seen too much CSI. Anyway, we weren't just looking for your prints. The knife showed hers on the handle, consistent with vegetable chopping and none of yours or anyone else's.

She paused and grinned, "You ever help out in the kitchen, man?"

Mitch remained unamused. "So, what did you find?"

"Several things, which may not be of any consequence, but did you know Allie was arrested when she was twenty-two for public intoxication?"

Mitch shifted uncomfortably in his seat. His face began to feel hot.

It had been in Austin. Allie had drifted away from a party west of UT campus, drunk, and was found wandering down Lamar in the middle of the road. A car almost hit her, and the driver called the cops. She pleaded that she just wanted to go home, but she'd been walking in the wrong direction.

Murphy paused and eyed Mitch, looking indecisive for a moment. "There's something else, too. Did you know Allie was married?"

Mitch stared at her uncomprehendingly. "That can't be right."

"There's a marriage license to someone named Chris Hammond from ten years ago."

"I know that name. They dated, but they weren't married. That has to be a mistake."

Murphy passed a file folder across the table, flipping it open to reveal a photocopy of a marriage license.

Mitch stared: *Allie Burke and Chris Hammond, on this day…*

He snapped the folder closed. He couldn't believe Allie would've lied to him about this, but he saw no other explanation for the document. His world, which had always felt solid to him as an adult, began quaking and slipping sideways underneath him. He closed his eyes and pushed the folder back across the table. "Fuck," he muttered under his breath. "Why are you telling me this?" His voice was tight, belying barely-restrained anger.

Murphy leaned close to him. "Because I want to find her. I want to help you. As much as I hate telling people shit they don't want to know, the only way we'll find her is if we work together.

"The search team isn't going to stay out there forever. There's no evidence she left by anything but her own accord, no sign of struggle or breaking and entering, no enemies by anyone's account, and she is an adult. Maybe she doesn't want to be found."

"Mitch slumped in his chair and rested his forehead on the table. The coolness of the metal felt calming. He wasn't sure how to feel — relieved Allie hadn't been kidnapped or scared she'd treated a suddenly-severed limb with a walk in the woods. "What if she's hurt too badly to get home or lost or…just not well..or dead?"

"Those are all possibilities," Murphy responded quietly. "But if that's the case, I have confidence the search team will find her. The fact that they haven't makes me think she's alive and relatively well, just…"

"Hiding?"

"Maybe."

What if she's lost it?

Mitch was starting to lose it a little himself. He could barely stand the fact that Allie was gone, and he was sitting on his ass in a coffee shop. The heat of anger had left him, and now he felt a cold tremor work its way into his hands.

"Mitch, whatever her reasons for being gone, we'll find her." Murphy reached across the table and briefly rested her warm hands on his.

They left their mostly full cups of cold coffee on the table and parted ways after Murphy promised to stay in touch. As Mitch drove home, it started to rain again.

———

Back at home, Mitch wandered around the house, halfheartedly searching for something that might tell him where Allie had gone. The mundane clutter of their first floor seemed ridiculous in the face of the seriousness at hand. He picked up a months-old magazine from a stack on the floor by the couch, stared at the cover a moment and sat it back down. The coffee table was cluttered with mugs, TV remotes, and Allie's crossword puzzles.

His ankle ached, even in the boot, and dragging it around was tiring. He finally poured himself a whiskey and slumped into the couch, propping his injury on the table. He sat, staring at the wall, sipping a drink he wasn't tasting, until he heard his phone buzzing in the dead quiet of the house. Shit. It was in the kitchen. He hauled himself off the sofa with a groan and got to it just before voicemail picked up.

"Hello?"

"Mitch, it's Murphy. They've found something."

He gripped the phone and closed his eyes, remembering what Murphy had said about no news being good news.

"Mitch, you there?"

"Yeah," he rasped.

"Look, it's not a lot, but they found a cave where it looks like someone slept last night."

His heart began hammering. "What else? Did they find any sign of Allie? How long ago was she there? Was there blood?"

"They just found the cave, and there's not much there, like I said, but it's something. If it was Allie, she was doing all right as of this morning."

"I'm going out there. I think I can find it. Allie mentioned a cave once —"

Murphy cut off his yammering, "Don't be stupid. Your ankle's broken."

"Look, I can't just sit here doing fucking nothing. I've got to —"

"I know, I know, " she cut him off again, "But there's a road that runs not too far from there — about a mile. Let me come get you, and we'll drive."

————

Murphy pulled the car over onto a wide spot in the dirt road. Dusk was settling in. The two walked down the road until Murphy directed Mitch into the trees at a stake with orange reflective tape around the top. She had a flashlight, and they followed orange stakes, making slow progress with Mitch's lame leg until he could see roving lights through the trees. Murphy stopped and made a phone call.

"They're expecting us," she said.

Mitch had trouble navigating the cave entrance's upward slope, but once inside, he could almost smell Allie – that curious mix of lavender and tea tree with something earthier, like a freshly-planted garden. Maybe it was all in his head.

The cave's wide opening tapered quickly to the back, where

leaves littered the floor. Several crew members were poking around. Mitch could imagine her there, curled up against the storm outside, hand wrapped in that butterfly dish towel, shivering. His chest ached. What had been going on in her mind?

"You said she mentioned a cave before?" Murphy asked, jarring him out of his reverie.

"Yeah, it was a while back. She can go on and on about the woods and," he paused, looking sheepish, "sometimes I'm not totally listening."

Murphy smiled perfunctorily. "You've never been here before?"

"No. What have they found?"

Murphy walked over to a technician filing labeled samples in a tackle-box-like container and spoke to him briefly. Then, he handed her something, and Murphy returned to Mitch with a baggie in her hands. Mitch realized he was holding his breath and made himself exhale.

"Not a lot; just the leaves matted down and these."

Murphy handed the baggie to Mitch, who saw it contained several hairs. His heart began to beat faster as he held them up for a better look, sure if he looked closely enough, he could tell if they were Allie's. They looked decidedly unremarkable, three brown hairs pressed between the thick plastic.

He stared at them, trying to divine Allie's whereabouts as if they were tea leaves. But he couldn't even tell for certain they were hers. He handed them back to Murphy and sighed, deflated.

"We'd better get going," Murphy said, "It's getting dark."

———

That night, Mitch didn't sleep well despite his earlier physical exertion. He tossed and turned, tangling the sheet around him. He dreamed. He could hear Allie in the house, the rustle of movement, her faint voice. He tried to follow the sounds, but each time he rounded a corner, sure he would see her, he'd face an empty room. He called out to her, but she didn't respond, yet he could hear her talking to an unheard person as if she were on the phone. He went through the whole house only to discover an endless maze of previously unseen rooms had sprouted off the kitchen, her movements and voice hidden within.

He started through the maze, but there was something in his eyes. His vision was blurry, and he began to feel dizzy. He fell to his knees but could still hear her, just ahead, around the corner out of reach. He woke up sweaty and frustrated, needing to pee, sun streaming into his face.

———

Murphy called Mitch later that morning. He'd been sitting at his desk, not working, mostly staring off into space and yawning. She said the search team had been called off. All the evidence pointed toward Allie having left voluntarily. They couldn't tie up resources and taxpayer money for a woman who didn't want to be found. They were needed elsewhere. As much as Mitch hated to admit it, it made sense.

He paced the living room floor after the phone call, dragging his boot, trying to think of what to do next — where some clue of Allie might lie. He scanned the living room, trying to see it with fresh eyes – the piles of books and magazines on the floor by the couch, on the coffee table. He always had to move them to set his drink on the table when he watched TV. That was, of course, after an exhaustive search for the remote, which Allie was forever hiding in a drawer.

They were at odds that way. Allie was always in the middle of five different books, but she considered TV remotes "clutter" and books "works-in-progress." Mitch argued her "works" took up a lot more space than his remotes.

No clues here, just the detritus of daily life. He wished he could go for a walk to clear his mind, but he parked himself on the back porch and stared at the woods instead. Eventually, the gears in his head started grinding.

Work, he thought. He should call Hunter at the *Hill Country News* office.

Her sister. He should call Jamie in Minneapolis. Despite living states apart, they were close.

Chris Hammond, the apparent ex-husband. Maybe Mitch could track him down. It was a total long shot, but he felt like the fact that Allie hadn't told him the whole truth about Chris was significant. And he had to admit to himself, he was curious. *Is that why she doesn't want to marry me? Did she think I wouldn't understand if I knew? What else hasn't she told me?*

Mitch dragged his brain off the spiraling path of unanswerable questions and tried to focus. One task at a time. He pulled his phone from his back pocket and called Hunter.

It rang for a long time, but just as Mitch was about to hang up, Hunter picked up the phone. Mitch was surprised he was answering it himself. He wasn't in the mood for small talk and didn't want to get into all the details, so he gave Hunter the Cliff Notes version of events. When he said that Allie was missing, Hunter was predictably shocked.

"Shit, Mitch. That's awful. I'm sorry. How can I help?"

"Have you noticed anything about her lately, anything different about her behavior or demeanor? I know it's a weird question, but, well, she was injured, bleeding, when she left, and I'm not…100-percent sure about her state of mind."

"I'm the wrong person to ask. I haven't seen her in two months."

"Huh?"

"She hasn't been to work in two months." Hunter paused. "You didn't know?" Mitch was silent, so he continued. "I guess it was more like six weeks ago. She came into my office and said she was thinking of quitting. She said she wanted more time to focus on writing her book. She had a lot of time off saved up, so I talked her into taking it and getting back to me at the end. As much as we could use her salary, financially speaking, I can't run a paper without reporters, and she is the best we have. I didn't want to lose her permanently."

"And you haven't heard from her since then?"

"I called her just last week. Left her a voicemail, but she didn't return my call."

Her phone, Mitch thought. "Hunter, thanks; I have to go."

Mitch hung up and looked around wildly. He remembered finding Allie's phone in the yard, the battery dead. Then what had he done with it?

CHAPTER 3

Day 2

Allie awoke with a start, face down at the mouth of the cave. Her breath caught. She peered anxiously down from the edge. The rocks below were slick with last night's rain. He was gone.

She stayed that way, stock-still like a deer alert to danger, for a long time, scanning the ground below, only her eyes moving. Then she realized she hadn't checked the cave and, in a panic, flipped herself over, leaning back on her one good hand to keep from tumbling over the edge behind her. No one was there. Had she dreamed him?

She rearranged herself, cross-legged, facing out toward the forest. She wasn't willing to accept that she was safe just yet. She was still, gazing out over the trees, listening and watching for any sign of him. To an observer, she'd have looked like she was meditating, but her muscles were tensed tight as guy wires, ready for fight or flight.

Slowly, she began to relax. As she did, the orange fire of the sun began to show itself over the horizon. The eastern sky was a moving kaleidoscope of pinks, oranges, and yellows. One of her favorite things about her home state was the big, endless sky, unadulterated by skyscrapers or mountains. Whatever the weather, it was all on display up there and ever in motion. And today, she could savor it as long as she wanted.

Her left hand still throbbed where it was missing its most useful appendage, that opposable thumb that separates person from beast. It pulled her attention away from the sky. The bleeding had stopped, and the butterfly towel, soaked in crimson, had done its job. She was afraid to unwrap her hand, though, afraid to see. She knew she needed some first aid to avoid infection, and it took her only a moment to know the place. She scrambled out of the cave, dropped to the rocks below, and headed back toward civilization, cradling her injured hand, trying to ignore the pain.

———

Allie came to the edge of the greenbelt just a few lots from the house she was looking for. She followed the fence line. When she came to the Buckmans', she hoisted herself over the wooden slats with difficulty, favoring her hand. The Buckmans were gone a lot. Lianna always texted her when they went out of town and asked her to keep an eye on the house. They had no pets, so she never had to do much — take in the mail and water a few plants at most.

She let herself in with the backdoor code and disarmed the alarm as Lianna had shown her. The Buckmans were avid campers and hikers, so she hoped to outfit herself with some useful gear along with some basic medical supplies.

She found some hydrogen peroxide and bandages in the downstairs bathroom. She unwrapped the dish towel and dropped it in the sink without looking at her damaged hand. She drew a deep breath and braved a glance at her ruined hand. It was less disturbing than she thought it'd be. There was about a half-inch stump where her left thumb had been; blood congealed at the edges. It was a fairly clean cut; she'd been using the big paring knife and, not used as frequently as the others, it was plenty sharp. She could see white bone, which ended abruptly, in the center.

Allie fumbled the cap off of the peroxide bottle with her right hand and poured it over the wound, holding her left hand over the sink. Pain blossomed in her hand and found its way to her head, bringing tears to her eyes. With her good hand, she gripped the wrist of the injured one, squeezing tightly. She closed her eyes and inhaled sharply, rocking back and forth, trying not to scream.

When the bubbling of the liquid subsided, she blotted it with a tissue and re-wrapped the stump with gauze, finishing with a layer around her hand for good measure while trying to get her breath to return to normal.

Inhale, 1, 2, 3, 4. Exhale, 1, 2, 3, 4...

She was finally calm enough to examine her bandaging job. She peered at it, and decided it would do, then went in search of gear to take her mind off her hand.

She hit pay dirt in an upstairs closet. She found sleeping bags, three tents, four sleeping pads, a water purifier, and even a few freeze-dried backpacker meals. Behind all of that were several backpacks. She chose the green one for its camouflage. She shook it out to see how big it was and heard something clunking softly in the bottom. She reached inside and her hand closed on something smooth and hard. When she pulled it out, she saw a red Swiss Army pocket knife. Perfect, she thought and slipped it into the front pocket of her jeans.

She began loading the green backpack with provisions, including the smallest, one-person tent. The only stove was a large one designed for car camping — not practical for her to carry — so she left it. She toted her bag back downstairs and returned to the main suite. She found some hiking boots in the closet that probably belonged to Lianna. They looked brand new. They were a size too big, but with a thick pair of socks she found in Lianna's drawer, they would be a damn sight better than the soft, water-logged moccasins she wore now. She also grabbed a spare pair of socks, knowing it was essential to keep her feet dry.

Her dad was an avid backpacker, and he'd taken her and her sister on trips when they were young, even though they sometimes didn't appreciate it and complained.

In the kitchen, Allie found nothing much in the refrigerator — some expired milk and one shriveled vine of cherry tomatoes. But there were cans of tuna and beans in the pantry, so she added them to her pack. She grabbed a ziplock bag from a drawer and circled back to the bathroom, where she put together a few first aid supplies.

She wasn't sure what to do with the bloody dishtowel. She didn't want to leave it to alarm the Buckmans, so she rinsed it out best she could and tied it to the outside of her pack to dry. When she saw her sodden moccasins lying on the bedroom floor, she tied them up as well.

Allie stood by the backdoor and hoisted her pack, carefully threading her left hand through the strap to avoid jostling it. She paused, scanning the downstairs, making sure she'd left everything more or less as she'd found it. She felt guilty. The Buckmans didn't want for anything, and they might not even realize their camping gear was missing. They were generous people who certainly wouldn't stress over losing a few cans of food, but Allie didn't like taking without asking. She returned to the kitchen and dug through drawers until she found a dogeared notepad and a stubby pencil. She was clumsy writing with her right hand, but it was serviceable.

Dear Buckmans,

I was in desperate need, so I took some of your camping gear and a few things from the pantry. I'm sorry. I hope I can repay you one day.

Thank you for always being so kind.

She didn't add her name. The idea seemed somehow incriminating, though they were sure to realize before too long that it was her. She left the note on the counter by the coffee pot and headed to the backdoor.

Reaching for the handle, she paused again and looked back at the interior of the well-appointed house. *This is it*, she thought. "Goodbye," she whispered to no one, then reset the alarm and left. She threw her new pack over the fence and scrambled over after it. Backpack fastened on her back, she set out at a brisk pace. A few steps from the house, she began to feel much better.

CHAPTER 4

Day 6 or 7

It's amazing what people throw away, Allie thought as she hiked. She'd been staying out in the woods for six or seven days now, she thought. She'd been wandering vaguely west, away from her house and the tiny-but-growing town of Lime where she lived. She didn't think of it as home yet. Eight months ago, she'd moved to Lime to live with Mitch, who'd moved there because it was the next trendy place on the edge of the Hill Country to turn itself from a sleepy rural town into an overcrowded suburb, which meant a bustling real estate market.

She'd held out for a long time, not wanting to leave Austin. Her grandparents had died several years ago, and her sister had moved to Minneapolis. Despite those things, or maybe because of them, she'd felt compelled to hold vigil there, pin the city down for her family with her presence. And she loved it — the live music to be had for the price of a couple of drinks any night of the week, the festivals, the history, the funkiness that refused to completely die despite the monolithic condos emerging from the skyline all over downtown. But…

She'd been spending most weekends in Lime since Mitch moved there. They'd been together four years then, and it was as if she were missing an appendage after he left. Mitch wanted her to move in with him, but she resisted, citing her job at *The Globe*. Then she was laid off and began spending more weekdays in Lime wallowing in her unemployed misery and avoiding the indignity of searching for a job. With all those extra hours in bed, it was no wonder she got pregnant, especially after she forgot to refill her birth control pills. Unemployed and knocked up, she couldn't seem to coerce a logical argument against moving in with Mitch. So she had.

Over the past days in the woods, Allie's lack of hunting knowledge had compelled her to, grudgingly, visit civilization twice more since her first forage for supplies at the Buckmans'.

On the first, she'd tentatively crept up to the back of a strip of stores, hoping to find something worth eating. She'd been lured to the spot by the smell of baking bread. Sure enough, she found some day-old croissants still in their protective plastic cage. She was too nervous to stay longer, but just before she scurried back to the woods, she spotted a squashed Saint Louis Cardinals baseball cap on the ground, forgotten, next to the dumpster. She picked it up — a little worn but functional, with faded black markings on the bill where its previous owner had graffitied it with what looked like a heart with now unreadable initials inside it. She hurried back into the security of the trees.

During the day, she hiked, lounged, and taught herself things like how to make rope out of bark, delighted with what she was learning. At night, she made small fires, like she'd learned to do in Girl Scouts as a kid. She had no trouble sleeping, and the vague, underlying malaise that always lay just under the surface of her psyche had subsided. There was no one in her ear making "gentle suggestions" about her career choices, no mother on the other end of the phone line with thinly-veiled inquiries as to why she'd taken another job as a reporter, and in a rural town, at that.

Her mother was an account executive at a marketing company. She prided herself on climbing the corporate ladder, one busted rung at a time, etching a door in the interminable glass ceiling. She didn't understand why her youngest daughter wasn't more ambitious.

There was no one to look at Allie with pity when someone else gave birth to a healthy baby, the way all her Lime neighbors had. They'd treated her like a sick child ever since the miscarriage.

Mitch wasn't there either, and she didn't have to be faced each day with the notion she was somehow failing him with her damaged womb, her lack of ambition, and her aversion to marriage. She felt free, light, despite the pack's weight on her back. She did miss reading books and writing. Next time she ventured into civilization, she'd have to do something about that.

———

Two days later, Allie had to return to the city. The croissants were delicious but not very filling. Knowing she'd need provisions soon, she hadn't ventured more than a mile from the line of small towns that followed the highway, hiking instead, parallel to them. She was nervous but felt better with the broken-in Cardinals hat pulled low to shadow her face. She had no idea whether or how hard anyone was looking for her.

This time, instead of looking for likely dumpsters, she headed around the main strip of shops, street side. It was a smallish town, and she didn't bother to discover its name. As she strolled, she saw few people on the street, and so many of the store windows were boarded over, it seemed deserted. She half-expected a trite tumbleweed to drift across the cracked street.

She casually searched the ground as she walked, and by the time she saw the type of shop she'd hoped to find — a coffee place with public internet access — she'd collected $1.53 in lost change. Hopefully, that would be enough for coffee.

As she walked through the door to the familiar tinkle of bells over the door, a few patrons glanced her way disinterestedly. She blinked in her new surroundings, temporarily forgetting how to comport herself in a public place containing other humans. Seven or eight people dotted the cramped booths and tables, several sitting at the bar, a few clicking away with their heads bent into the phones, coffee and congealing food in front of them. One woman, haloed in smoke, was reading a real newspaper. A small TV in the corner over the bar mumbled at low volume.

Allie perched tentatively on a cracked-vinyl-covered bar stool, balancing with her backpack still firmly attached to her. She cradled her new coins in her right hand, with which she was quickly becoming more adept. Her left hand, wrapped in a fresh bandage, she held hidden beneath the bar.

The woman behind the counter pretended not to notice her for a long time. Allie waited. Then, she began pointedly staring at the woman, daring her to continue ignoring her. Finally, the woman reluctantly ambled over. "Whatcha need?" Her eyes were steely.

Allie slapped the change on the counter and asked, "Is this enough for a cup of coffee?" She met the woman's stare evenly, surprised and delighted with her own boldness. Perhaps a week in the woods forgetting how to be social was useful. The name tag on the woman's apron said, "Brandee." She looked about the same age as Allie.

"Coffee's a dollar fifty, so yeah. 'Don't leave much for anything else, though."

Brandee stared at Allie for a long second and then said defensively, "Coffee's not that good. 'Been on the burner all day."

"That's fine. I'll take a cup."

Brandee's stare softened infinitesimally, and she ambled over to the Bunn coffee machine.

Allie, feeling as if she'd passed a ritual test, relaxed a bit and asked, "Hey, I don't s'pose you have some paper and a pencil I could borrow?"

Brandee returned to the counter with the coffee. "Some's over there by the computer."

"Great. Thanks. I apologize; I don't have much in the way of a tip."

"S'okay," Brandee replied gruffly, "No one around here much does."

Allie took her cup to the computer at the end of the bar and offloaded her backpack at her feet. She woke the computer with the grimy, nicotine-colored mouse and sipped her coffee. *Not that bad, really. Nice and hot.*

It didn't take her long to find what she was looking for. She began scribbling notes with a stubby, eraserless pencil on the scrap paper beside the computer. She'd sat back to think for a moment when the local news on the television caught her eye. Her picture was on the screen — one from a wedding she and Mitch had attended last year. She quickly turned her face back to the computer screen and watched from the corner of her eye. She couldn't hear what the newscaster was saying, but the ticker across the bottom read…

LOCAL WOMAN ALLIE BURKE DISAPPEARS INTO

THE HILL COUNTRY. POLICE DO NOT SUSPECT FOUL PLAY. SHE MAY BE INJURED…

Allie felt panic rising from her belly, but she pressed it back down. As she furtively glanced around, she saw none of the patrons paying the least attention to the news or her. She drained her coffee, stuffed her notes into her pack with a few extra pieces of paper and the pencil and headed toward the small bathroom in the back to regroup. As she splashed water on her face, washed her hands, and as an afterthought, used paper towels to wipe down her stinkier parts, she caught a glimpse of herself in the mirror.

In the photo, her hair had been curled, and she'd had a full face of makeup — "warpaint," her dad would've said. Now, in the mirror, she saw a woman with greasy hair pulled back into a hasty ponytail, a streak of dirt on her cheek and twinkling, unadorned eyes starting out from underneath a well-worn cap. She grinned at her reflection. There was no way anyone would recognize her.

On her way out the front door, Allie again thanked Brandee and apologized for her lack of tip money. "For what it's worth," Allie said, a little embarrassed, "Here's my last three cents. And a quarter I found over there on the floor."

As she passed the change over the counter, Brandee looked at her and asked, "Where're you from?" with a new spark of curiosity.

Allie met her gaze; then Brandee dropped her eyes to Allie's freshly bandaged hand she'd unwittingly rested on the counter in full view. Allie felt her face go hot as she and Brandee stared at her thumbless hand. When their eyes met again, Allie was surprised to see not alarm on Brandee's face but a mild, questioning look, her head cocked to the side. Impulsively, Allie reached over with both her hands and gave Brandee's hands a gentle squeeze. Brandee smiled only slightly, and then Allie was gone.

———

Allie was relieved to be out of the coffee shop where she could breathe again. She strode down the street quickly, wanting to visit a dumpster before returning to the woods. Foraging behind a strip of stores with faded signs — a small grocery, a bakery and a modest restaurant — she gathered canned goods a little past their dates, some yogurt, also gently expired, and a box of assorted tea bags. Her last stop was the bakery, but she found nothing worth taking. Still, it was a good haul. She hoisted her pack and turned back toward the woods, preparing to rejoin the wilderness. Then, she found herself face-to-face with a large man. She froze.

His alarmed expression made her instantly nervous. She rifled through the filing cabinet of her brain for a useful response. "It's okay," she said as calmly as she could manage with her heart hammering against her ribcage, her hands up in surrender.

"I was just going."

"Here," he said.

She hadn't noticed until then he was carrying a bakery box of assorted bagels, headed for the trash. He held them out to her, and she noticed the alarm on his face had disappeared behind kind eyes. Slowly, she took the bagels from him, and they stood there in silence, facing each other.

"Thank you," Allie said softly.

The man shrugged and turned to walk back around the store, presumably the way he had come. Allie ran back into the woods, backpack bouncing behind her. She couldn't believe her good fortune.

The bagels were a boon, as was the rest of her haul. Allie happily munched on blueberry, cinnamon raisin, garlic, and "everything" bagels for days as she hiked, camped, and began to think about putting her new knowledge into practice.

On what she thought was maybe two weeks since she'd hastily departed Lime, Allie awoke with the sun as she seemed to do every morning she slept in the wilderness. She stretched and pulled herself out of her sleeping bag and tent. Her fire from the night before was still a little warm, so it was no trouble getting it going again to boil water for tea. It wasn't coffee, but it'd do. She sat against a tree, munching a bagel and studying her notes.

While at the coffee shop, she'd looked up how to catch and cook small animals using a snare. According to her notes, she'd need a couple of medium-sized sticks.

No problem with that; there were sticks big and small everywhere.

A sapling in just the right spot might be harder to find but doable.

And a length of wire or rope. Hmmm… That was going to be trickier.

She could make rope from strips of bark or the right plant, but she wasn't confident her fledgling cord-weaving skills could produce something long and strong enough. She contemplated her shoe. The long boot lace might work, and with luck, she wouldn't have to sacrifice it permanently. She broke down her tent, packed her gear, and started walking.

Allie didn't have a destination in mind so much as she was searching for the right signs — game trails or scat — something to indicate the presence of animals. It wasn't long before she came across rabbit droppings along a narrow, gently-worn path. She sat down and removed the long lace from her right boot. She was surprised at how quickly she was adapting her fine motor skills to a nine-fingered approach.

Consulting the diagram she'd copied into her notes, she fashioned the lace into a noose. Now she needed two "Y" trigger sticks, which she found with minimal search. She retraced her steps back to the scat and began looking for a sapling to bend over and set her snare.

It took a while, but it was remarkable how much easier it was to be methodical and patient out here, away from the demands of society and all the to-do lists. She finally found an appropriate tree-ling near the rabbit path. Using a rock, she drove one of the Y sticks into the ground and began setting the snare. She had trouble getting the sapling to stay bent; it wasn't as flexible as it looked, but after reseating the Y stick in the ground several times, she finally got it to stay. She stood back and looked at her handiwork. She was quite proud of herself for being so resourceful.

Allie spent the next two days camping out of sight but near her snare. On the third morning, as she cautiously approached the trap, she could see she'd caught something. It was too small to be a squirrel or a mouse, but it was furry and wasn't moving. She crept closer, feeling an inexplicable sense of nervous foreboding. There was blood. It was a rabbit's hind leg, no body attached, dangling from the noose. *A larger animal must've stolen it,* she thought, *damnit.* She'd just caught a coyote or a bobcat an easy breakfast.

Allie scanned the area around the snare, frowning, and then she saw it — the bloodied body of a brown rabbit, the side of its abdomen still heaving slowly up and down with breath; it was barely alive.

Her heart picked up its pace. She crept slowly toward the injured animal, not wanting to startle it, but the rabbit was too far gone to react. Its eyes were beginning to glaze over. She saw the bloody stump where the rabbit's leg had been. Blood stains also matted the fur around its mouth. Allie realized in horror the rabbit had chewed off its own leg to escape her trap, only to find it had lost too much blood to escape into the forest.

Allie was filled with agonizing remorse. "Ohhh…" Soft desperation escaped her lips; tears welled in her eyes. She'd envisioned finding a thoroughly dead animal in her trap, not a half-alive bunny who, thanks to her, had spent its last night on earth filled with fear and pain. Her snare had transformed from ingenious to monstrous.

She knelt on the dirt next to the dying rabbit and reached out and touched its fur gingerly. It flinched in response, just barely. Its respiration quickened in shock and fear at her approach. "I'm so sorry," she whispered. She swallowed the lump in her throat along with her tears. Then, she found a rock and hefted it into her hand. She knew this was merciful, but she turned her head away as she brought the rock down hard as she could, crushing the rabbit's skull. She didn't want to have to do it again.

Allie struggled to skin and disembowel the carcass with her pocket knife, as her hand-written instructions described, but she got the job done and tried not to think "skinning a rabbit" so much as "cut here, flay there." She roasted it over the fire. It was lean and gamey-tasting, and Allie didn't enjoy eating it, but she knew she needed the protein.

When she finished eating, she walked a little ways from her fire and dug a small hole with a sharp rock and her hands. She dropped the rabbit bones, fur, and entrails into it and covered them with dirt, marking the small gravesite with the rock she'd used to dig. She thanked the rabbit for nourishing her and apologized again. Then, for reasons unfathomable to her, she crossed herself like a Catholic. She blew the rabbit a forlorn kiss and went back to put out her fire. She was eager to be away from that place.

CHAPTER 5

Day 3

Mitch hobbled out into the yard, stopping where he'd remembered finding Allie's phone in the grass before he lit off into the woods after her. He closed his eyes, trying to remember what he'd done with it after he saw the faux wood case in the grass and picked it up.

Picked it up. Looked at it. It was dead…Didn't have it in my hand when I went into the woods…back pocket.

He about-faced and went upstairs to the bathroom, where his jeans were still on the floor, right where he'd left them two days ago. He found Allie's phone in his right back pocket. He plugged it into an outlet in the bedroom and waited impatiently for it to charge enough to turn on.

When it did, he saw she had thirty-seven unread texts and

two voicemails. He scrolled through the texts first — nothing of consequence, just irrelevant group threads with her mother and sister. Then, he checked the voicemail and found the one from Hunter that Allie hadn't even bothered to listen to. The other was from a neighbor, Lianna Buckman, earlier that morning.

Hi Allie, this is Lianna. We got back late last night, and this morning I found a strange note that I think is from you? Give me a call, will you, as soon as you get this? Hope you're all right.

Mitch hit "call back," and Lianna picked up almost immediately.

"Allie!"

"No, this is Mitch. I'm calling from Allie's phone.

"Mitch! I wanted to reach you, but I didn't have your number. I got this strange note, and I think it's from Allie."

"I'll be there in ten."

"Wait, the house is a mess. There's laundry everywh–"

When Lianna answered the door and invited Mitch inside, he first noticed how clean the place was. Nothing was out of place save a basket of neatly-folded laundry sitting by the stairs.

"Pardon the mess," said Lianna, flapping her head toward the spotless white laundry basket. "Have a seat."

Mitch parked himself on the couch while Lianna bustled into the kitchen to make coffee.

"What happened to your leg?" she asked, still shouting from the kitchen.

"I was hiking, and I fell, twisted my ankle. It's just a minor fracture." He'd accepted the coffee to be neighborly, but he didn't want to get into telling stories. He wanted to see the note and be on his way.

Lianna returned with two steaming mugs. "You know, I did something similar just last year. We were backpacking in the Canadian Rockies, and I had to hobble all the way down the mountain to get out. It was ridiculous. I hope you weren't too far from home when you did yours."

"No, I was pretty close. Listen, Allie is missing, and I'm worried about her. Could I see the note?"

"Yes, of course!" She hopped up and walked into the kitchen again with an ease Mitch envied. When she returned with the note, she handed it to him and plunked herself back on the couch, watching him, waiting for his reaction.

Dear Buckmans, he read silently, *I was in desperate need, so I took some of your camping gear and a few things from the pantry. I'm sorry. I hope I can repay you one day. Thank you for always being so kind.*

"She didn't sign her name," he mumbled.

"But is it her handwriting? It's so shaky, but she's the only one who would've been in the house. I hope she's okay."

"Yeah, I think it is." The handwriting looked like a second grader's, but he still recognized how she formed her letters. With no thumb on her left hand, she was probably writing with her right, he surmised.

"I checked, and we're missing a sleeping bag, a tent, and a few other little things," Lianna offered.

"I'm sorry; I'll pay you for them," he said, more out of duty than remorse.

Lianna waved him off, "No, no, not necessary at all. I just wanted you to know that wherever she is, she's got some protection from the elements. Is she…camping?"

"Maybe," Mitch muttered. He might be able to convince himself she'd done just that — gone off on a spontaneous trip — if it weren't for the thumb. He didn't need to get Lianna all riled up by telling her about it, either. "Can I keep this note?" he asked.

"Of course, honey. I'm sure she'll turn up or get in touch soon. 'Probably just took off for a bit of alone time."

"Yeah…" he trailed off.

"Listen," she said, a little brighter, "I know everything's fine, but just in case, I have the number of a detective who might be willing to help you."

"Oh, that's okay —" he started, but she had already gone back into the kitchen where he could hear her rummaging through a drawer. She returned with a card.

"I ran into her at The Chamber of Commerce luncheon last month, and she seemed like good people. Give her a call. Maybe she can help."

Mitch glanced down at the card, already intent on tossing it when he got home, and the name caught his eye. His eyes widened, and Lianna noticed.

"What? Do you know her?"

CHAPTER 6

Day 16?

Two days had passed since the rabbit. Allie had been hiking aimlessly and stopping to rest a lot. The lean, gamey meat had given her the runs, so she spent a lot of time digging quick holes and squatting over them.

Her treasured bagels had run out, as had her dumpster finds, and she now felt true pangs of hunger. The creek she was loosely following, along with the water filter, ensured she didn't go thirsty. Feeling tired, sick, hungry, and — she hated to admit — a little lonely, Allie was beginning to think it was time for another visit to the city. After pumping her canteen full, she hiked away from the creek towards civilization.

———

The community she found was larger than the last one with Brandee and the coffee shop. It was something between a large town and a small city. *Better for resources*, she thought, feeling uneasy.

She wandered the streets cautiously, picking up the occasional forgotten change. She passed several establishments that might have promising dumpsters out back. There were a few people on the street, running errands or hurrying to work. Others were milling around on cigarette breaks, and one older man pushed a curly-haired toddler in a stroller, slowly meandering down the sidewalk.

Allie passed another man sitting on the ground slumped up against a building; he held a dirty styrofoam cup with a pittance of donated change. She'd watched him shake the cup at several passersby who ignored his plea, but when Allie walked by, he just croaked, "Hey."

She circled around behind the shops and counted stores back to the diner she'd passed. In their trash, she found a bag of slightly-bruised apples. She wiped one on her shirt and bit into it. It was a little past ripe, but Allie was ravenous. She didn't stop until she'd consumed most of the core. She stashed the rest of the apples in her pack.

Next door, behind a convenience store, she found some expired hard candies. *Do they actually go bad?* she wondered. And then she found a real prize — a personal-sized pizza someone had left in the toaster oven too long and then shoved back in the box for the trash. It was cold, but Allie thought it was heavenly.

As she licked the last few crumbs of burnt pizza off her fingers, her stomach began to cramp. The rabbit meat was not yet done with her. She hoisted her pack and scampered around to the front of the stores in desperate search of a bathroom. The diner.

She stumbled through the door and was making a beeline for the back, when a woman's voice called out to her from behind the counter. "Toilet is for payin' customers only!"

Allie ignored her. She was about to shit her pants.

"Hey, ya can't take that pack in there!"

She was speed walking down the narrow corridor to the door with the woman sign on it when someone grabbed her from behind by the pack. She spun around. The yelling counterwoman was in her face.

"Ya can't take this big-ass pack in there! You gotta buy somethin'!"

Desperate, Allie shoved the pack at the woman and said, "Watch it for me!"

She made it behind the locked door to the one-hole toilet just in time. As she sat there in relief, she could hear the woman grumbling loudly outside the door, her voice fading as she walked to the front of the diner. "Damned freeloaders, never buy nothin'. Think they can just stink up the toilet. Then who has to clean it, huh?! 'Steal all the toilet paper…"

When Allie's bowels had stopped cramping, she washed her

hands and left the bathroom, anxious to retrieve her pack. She approached the yeller behind the counter. "Can I have my pack, please?"

"S'by the door. I don't have time to babysit yer stuff."

Allie glanced at the door. No pack. She felt a twinge of panic. "It's not by the door. Are you sure you don't have it back there?" she asked, peering over the counter.

"No, it's not back here. I tol' you I put it by the door!"

Allie looked around wildly. The place wasn't big. She hurried around the perimeter, looking under tables and behind chairs. No pack. She turned her attention back to the yeller who wore a tag with "Rose" on it.

"Listen, Rose" Allie said, beseeching the woman for some sign of humanity, "That's all the stuff I have in the world. I NEED that pack. Did you see someone take it?" She'd have been angry at Rose if she hadn't felt so desperate.

"I didn't see nothin'. I'm busy here, can'tcha see? Some of us have to work for a living — can't just go around expecting handouts from strangers. Serves you right."

Allie looked around at the few other patrons in the diner, hoping someone would offer some help. None of them would meet her eye. She bolted out of the diner into the street, scanning it for some sign of her pack or the person who'd taken it. She stepped off the curb to cross the street, but it was higher than she anticipated, and she fell hard onto the asphalt on her hands and knees.

She picked herself up. She felt numb but was dimly aware of the throbbing pain in her knees and palms

She limped to the other side of the street where a railing separated her from a river — the Pedernales maybe, she thought — and sank down against the wall. Her jeans were torn and bloody at the knees, and her palms had deep scrapes embedded with asphalt pebbles. *At least I don't need thumbs to catch myself,* she thought bitterly.

Allie stared down at her knees, and they started to go blurry. The tears welled up and overflowed. She cried on the street in broad daylight, not caring who saw. One trip to the bathroom, she had nothing.

———

Several people walked past her as Allie sat there, arms wrapped around her knees, head bent, tears dripping, but none paid her any attention. Was it because she was sitting on the street, dirty and bleeding, that they gave her a wide berth or just the natural discomfort people have with a crying stranger?

When she felt cried out, she wiped her face with her t-shirt and stood up. She took deep breaths, trying to figure out what to do next. First, she needed to doctor her wounds somehow. *Stealing the toilet paper…* Rose had given her an idea.

Allie remembered passing a drugstore during her earlier reconnaissance, so she headed back toward it. She observed it furtively from the other side of the street, reminding herself of a low-budget crime show. *Casing the joint*, she thought and giggled to herself.

It was around lunchtime, and there were a fair number of shoppers in the store — *good*. She could see the cash register off to the left through the glass storefront. She'd have to get in without being closely scrutinized.

She wiped her knees with the underside of her shirt, which was already filthy, and tried to pull the torn fabric of her jeans over the wounds as best she could. She crossed the street and hesitated as someone approached the register with a purchase, taking the cashier's attention. She slipped through the door and skirted to the right. No one noticed her.

Her heart hammering in her chest, she quickly found the first aid aisle thanks to overhead signs. She grabbed a box of bandaids and a bottle of rubbing alcohol and made her way to the back of the store, where, as she'd hoped, there was another one-hole restroom.

Locked inside, she dumped alcohol over her new wounds. It stung. She picked the asphalt pieces from her right palm with the middle and index fingers of her left hand. Her left hand, still bandaged due to the missing thumb, had escaped the severe scrapes of its mate.

She'd grabbed a large box of bandaids, hoping it was an assorted pack, and she wasn't disappointed. She covered her knee wounds with two large bandaids apiece and one smaller one for her hand. She took the rest of the bandaids out of the box and shoved them in her back pocket, then trashed the packaging. She took a deep breath, checked out her dirty, nervous expression in the mirror and readied herself for the trip back out of the store. Then she saw it, just to her left over the toilet. It was so grimy it barely let light through, but this bathroom had a window, and it opened. She grinned.

———

Feeling a little better with her injuries bandaged, Allie walked away from the drug store down a back alley. Now what?

It was early afternoon, and the day was warmish, but it would get chilly tonight. She decided her next task was to find a blanket or jacket and maybe a few snacks before returning to the woods. She'd find another, more friendly city tomorrow and see if there was some way she could resupply herself more thoroughly.

She began walking up and down streets and alleys, searching for anything that might provide warmth and food. Three hours later, all she'd managed to acquire was a small, ratty piece of cloth that barely constituted a blanket and smelled like dog. Her scraped knees ached, and she was tired and hungry again. It would be dusk soon.

She passed a large, nondescript brown building, and the small crowd of people milling around outside of it caught her eye. Her eyes traveled up the building to the words "Community Solutions." As she watched the people, she realized it was a shelter. The crowd was waiting for it to open up for the evening, so they could get out of the cold night and maybe have a hot meal.

She looked longingly at the door, thinking how nice it would be to sleep inside. Indecisive, she crossed the street to get a closer look but kept her distance from the fifteen or so people who'd gathered there.

CHAPTER 7

Still day 3

Back at home from Lianna's, Mitch flopped down on the couch. The short trip had worn him out. He plucked the detective's card from his back pocket and marveled. Of all the detectives, Lianna had handed him Murphy's card. Mitch had yet to get used to how the same people in small towns popped up everywhere.

He knew it was past time for him to call Jamie, Allie's sister, but he hadn't yet been able to face the barrage of questions she was going to have. He closed his eyes just for a minute. There was more there, he admitted. He'd always liked Jamie, always respected her, and perhaps for that reason, he was shying away from her judgment.

———

Mitch awoke with a jolt and fell off the couch to the sound of glass shattering. Blinking the sleep out of his eyes, he scrambled up off all fours and went to the kitchen. A large rock lay on the floor amidst broken shards of the back door's glass. He caught movement through the kitchen window, out of the corner of his eye and hobbled outside as fast as he could around the corner of the house — nothing.

He looked behind the bushes that pressed up against the house. He went out to the edge, where the yard met the woods, and peered through the shade of the trees. Nothing. He even looked up in the trees, feeling like a goddamned idiot as he did, as if the rock thrower would've shimmied one like a monkey.

"I DON'T HAVE TIME FOR THIS FUCKING BULL-SHIT!" he hollered at the sky. He fell to his knees in the grass, staring down at it, seeing every blade. A beetle made its way through its own little grass forest, struggling doggedly over each tiny blade.

I can't do this, he thought. *I don't know where she is. Does she even know where she is? I'm not a goddamned detective. Why did she leave? Does she want me to let it go? I can't let it go…*

He looked up at the sky and screamed at it, because there was no one else to yell at. He hollered nonsense syllables until his throat was sore, the stress of the past several days pouring out volcanically.

Are you done? He chastised himself. *Do you feel better now? Then get the fuck up off the grass and go find Allie. She's not out here hanging with the beetles.*

He dragged himself back around the side of the house, and then he noticed some limestone rocks at the edge of the grass, right before the start of the forest. They hadn't been there before. As he approached, he could see they were arranged in the shape of an arrow, pointing straight into the woods.

———

Mitch stood, staring at the rock arrow and then squinting into the wilderness where it led. Was it Allie? But then why not just come up to the door? Of course she chopped off her thumb, then ran into the woods. With that kind of rationality…

He walked tentatively a little ways into the greenbelt, following the arrow. It wasn't long before he spotted another, slightly smaller, more crooked arrow. He followed that one, too, until he came across a third. They curved slightly to the right and eventually spit him out in the same clearing he'd passed through looking for Allie. He glanced at the large rock and saw the blood splotches were gone — washed away by the pelting rains of the storm.

His eyes drifted to yet another rock picture at the center of the clearing, formed in the shape of an "X." *X marks the spot,* he thought. His shoulders had been hunched into his ears in tense anticipation. Now they relaxed. This was like something out of a Wiley Coyote cartoon. Definitely not Allie.

He heard the bushes move behind him — something big, not a lizard or a squirrel. But before he could turn around, a voice said, "Freeze! Put your hands where I can see 'em!"

Mitch raised his hands and slowly turned around. A man, no a kid, had a handgun trained on him. He looked to be around 17. He had both hands on the gun out in front of him, and his grip was steady, but his eyes betrayed his nervousness.

"Jeezus, Tyler, this isn't CSI. Drop the cop act, will ya?" Another kid about the same age stepped out of the brush. Then he addressed Mitch. "Hey, Mitch. How's it hangin'?"

"Not great just now," Mitch replied. The kid with the gun seemed jumpy, and that made him feel jumpy. He swallowed and purposefully slowed his breathing. It was important to stay calm..or at least appear to. "Do I know you?"

"Sorta. Steve Richardson's my dad."

"Ah," Mitch replied. Steve Richardson worked out of the same K&S office Mitch did. They occasionally crossed paths and had beers together once or twice after work, but they weren't close. Steve had been in the business a lot longer than Mitch, and he had a reputation for being able to sell popsicles to penguins. Everyone said he was a nice guy. He talked about his kids a lot. "Adam, right?"

"Close. Aiden."

"Okay then, Aiden, Tyler. Can I put my hands down so we

can have a rational conversation about what the hell is going on here?"

"Sure," said Aiden. Have a seat there by the X."

Mitch could tell Tyler was a bundle of nerves, but he wasn't sure what to make of Aiden's casual attitude. Either he was putting on an act or he was just a naturally laid-back kind of person. He hoped for the latter.

Mitch sat cross-legged by the X, and the two boys sat down opposite him, out of arm's reach. Tyler still had the gun trained on him. He looked silly sitting "crisscross applesauce" with a firearm pushed out in front of him — like a toddler throwing the ultimate tantrum. Mitch smiled at the thought, despite the tension.

"What's so funny?" Tyler asked.

But before Mitch could answer, Aiden cut in, "Tyler put that thing down for chrissakes. Relax!"

Tyler rested the piece in his lap but didn't relax his two-handed grip. It was silent for a few beats, the three of them staring at each other, so finally Mitch prompted, "So?"

"I'm sorry about your wife. That's gotta be hard," Aiden said. He had an easy confidence about him, the same kind I'd glimpsed in his dad.

"Yes, it has," Mitch answered, "but how'd you know about Allie?"

"Everyone knows, man. It's a small town."

There was another pregnant pause in which Tyler and

Aiden exchanged looks, each seeming to expect the other to take the lead, and Mitch lost his patience. "Look guys, as you know, I've got a lot of shit on my plate right now, so if you could get to the point —"

"We think we know where she is," said Aiden.

———

"Oh?" Mitch responded casually. He didn't buy it. None of it made sense. Why lead him out into the woods, train a gun on him, simply to offer information? They wanted something, and he was none too sure they actually knew anything about Allie. Neither kid seemed willing to start, so Mitch gave in.

"So what do you know?"

"Well, we were out here, just hanging out you know, um, smokin' a little weed," Aiden grinned a little sheepishly.

"It was just us," Tyler said.

Aiden turned to Tyler for a slow moment. "Yeah," he said pointedly at Tyler.

Kids are such terrible liars, Mitch thought.

"Anyway," Aiden continued, "We were just hanging out and thinking about going back home, 'cuz it looked like rain, when we saw someone aways off, through the trees. It was a woman with brown hair. She was wearing a red sweater and jeans and holding her left hand like it was injured or something."

Now Mitch was paying attention. He hadn't told anyone

about Allie's thumb, and the news had only reported vaguely that she might be injured. Maybe these kids knew something after all.

"When was this?" he asked. "Like what time? How did she look? Which direction did she go?" Mitch was struggling to keep his composure. For the first time since she disappeared, he might finally have something to go on.

"Calm down, man. We're gonna show you," said Aiden.

They had to proceed slowly because of Mitch's ankle. Aiden and Tyler, he noticed, stayed slightly behind him and steered with their voices. They didn't trust him for some reason.

"I gather you're the ones who threw the rock through my back door," Mitch said as they walked, mostly just to make conversation.

"Sorry about that," said Tyler. "We were just trying to tap on your window, get your attention, but I guess I threw it too hard."

Aiden chuckled, "Yeah, sorry about that. Didn't mean to scare you."

It didn't take long for Mitch to surmise where they were headed. After a tiresome, hour-long hike, they approached the same cave he'd been to with Detective Murphy.

"We followed her here," Tyler said.

Aiden frowned. "Yeah, we were a little high and just curious about where she was going in the woods, alone and hurt. I wanted to go up to her, you know after we reached the cave —

see if she needed help, but Tyler was totally paranoid she'd smell the pot on us and thought we might get in trouble."

Now it was Tyler's turn to scowl.

"You obviously don't know her," Mitch responded. Allie smoked herself now and then.

"Tyler always gets paranoid when he smokes. " He paused for a moment, then resumed his story. "So I wanted to go up to her, but Tyler was all scared and babbling, so I gave in, and we went home."

"That's it?" Mitch asked incredulously. "You just left her there? You didn't get help? You didn't tell anyone?"

Aiden shrugged. "She's an adult. We thought sure, maybe she cut herself or whatever, but she seemed okay."

Mitch took some deep purposeful breaths to calm himself. These boys had made a grave mistake, but they were just kids. They were still young enough to assume adults could take care of themselves. Something was still bothering him about these kids, though.

"What's with the gun? If you just wanted to tell me about Allie, why go through this whole arrow bullshit charade? I don't get it."

Something about that line of questioning got Tyler's hackles back up, and he raised the gun again. Aiden tried to placate him.

"Come on man, relax, please?" He seemed genuinely desperate to calm his friend.

Now Tyler's hands were shaking as he pointed the gun at Mitch's chest. "You can't tell my dad I was smoking!" he almost sobbed.

Mitch was alarmed at the combination of Tyler's emotional volatility and what was presumably a loaded gun. He tried for calm and reasonable. "Tyler, I don't even know your dad…"

"His dad's Big Joe Turner," Aiden said quietly.

Mitch then began to see why Tyler was so nervous. "Oh. Look, okay, I do know OF your dad, but I don't hang out with him, and even if I did, I wouldn't tell him. Promise. I'm a 'legalize it' kind of guy."

The panicky tears brimming Tyler's eyes finally spilled over their dam, and he crumbled to the forest floor, dropping the gun between his knees.

"Hey, man." Aiden slowly approached him, kneeling down, putting an awkward arm around him as if he weren't quite sure this was the thing to do. Mitch walked over to them cautiously, making sure Tyler glanced at him and knew he was coming. He didn't want to startle him with the gun lying in the leaves.

Mitch knelt in front of the kids. "Hey, it's okay. It's going to be all right."

As Tyler stared at the ground between his legs, crying softly, Aiden looked at Mitch, seeming relieved he was there. Aiden reached slowly for the gun, saying, "I'll just put the safety back on…"

He took the gun a few feet away and began fiddling with the

safety. As he did, Tyler began to blubber.

"He'll kill me if he finds out I was smokin' again. He said he would — no tuition money, and I'll be stuck in this shithole town forever. He'll kill me, he'll kill me…"

He was sobbing, and Mitch was doing his best to pat his shoulder, saying "shh, shh," like you would to an infant who couldn't settle down to sleep.

Suddenly, a loud *bang!* from behind Mitch set his ears to ringing and nearby birds into flight.

Tyler and Mitch fell back on their asses at the loud rapport and gaped at Aiden. The gun had gone off, and blood was oozing from his shoe.

"Oh, shit," he said softly and promptly passed out.

———

When Aiden came to a few seconds later, Tyler and Mitch were already at his sides. "Omigod, I shot myself, I shot myself! I'm gonna die!"

Tyler, who'd been shocked out of his sobbing, stepped in. "Shut up. You're not going to die, dummy!" Then, under his breath, "I swear, you don't know shit about guns."

They eased off his shoe and found the damage wasn't that bad. He'd only managed to graze the outside of his right foot, near his pinky toe. It was bleeding some.

"You're going to be fine," Mitch reassured him, "You just

clipped it."

Aiden sat up and looked at his foot. He seemed to decide Mitch was right and relaxed a bit. The three of them sat there looking at each other until Tyler said, "What are we going to do?"

They were both looking at Mitch expectantly. He was the adult. He was supposed to have clarity here. Mitch had questions scrolling through his mind:

Should I call Murphy? Where did this kid get a gun? What are we going to tell these boys' parents?"

He remembered something Allie always said when his mind got racing, and he rapid-fired questions at her: *One thing at a time.*

His mind turned to the immediacy of caring for wounds. "Aiden, do you think you can walk?"

He gingerly replaced his shoe and stood up to test his foot, limping a little. "Yeah, I think so."

"Good. Let's make our way back to my place. We'll fix up your foot and decide where to go from there."

Seeing Tyler's worried glance, Mitch added, "Don't worry; I'm not calling any parents." And he meant it.

––––––––

Between Mitch's ankle and Aiden's foot, the way back was slow going. Mitch asked questions to pass the time. Tyler's catharsis on the forest floor seemed to have burst his dam of defensiveness. Mitch asked, "So your dad's Mayor Turner, huh?" and both boys began to talk.

Tyler and Aiden had both been caught smoking behind the high school during lunch break. Aiden had gotten a slap on the wrist from his parents, but the Turners were a different story. They hated drugs — caffeine and alcohol notwithstanding, of course.

Tyler, christened "Joseph Tyler Turner" after his dad, had been pressured into taking AP classes by his parents. They hoped he'd get into MIT or Harvard. He had been on the debate team in middle school and had done well with it. Ever since then, his parents had been convinced he'd make a great lawyer, though he'd long since stopped thinking the same.

"It was kind of fun in middle school because my friends were in debate and stuff. I was pretty good at it, but I got tired of it. It was a lot of pressure. I wanted to quit, but my parents never could let go of it.

"I smoke because it's relaxing, you know?" he said. "At school and home, I'm always so stressed out. But out in the woods with a joint, it's like I can forget all that even exists for a while."

Aiden, who'd been quiet for a while, chuckled at that.

"What?" Tyler responded defensively.

"I'm not laughing at you, man. It's just funny how different our lives are, but we both smoke to escape them."

Mitch looked back at Aiden, who was limping along behind

him, prompting him to elaborate.

"Tyler's parents are all up in his business all the time, and I don't envy him that, I promise. It's just that mine are different. They're kinda hippies, you know? They weren't even really mad when we got caught at school, just told me not to do it on school grounds anymore. They're great; I love them. It's just…"

"Just…" Mitch prompted again.

"Sometimes I wish they'd give me more…direction? Whenever I ask for their opinion, what I should do on anything, they're all like, 'You decide what's best for you.'"

"Must be nice," Tyler grumbled.

Aiden ignored Tyler and continued. "I go out in the woods to smoke because then I don't have to think about all the decisions I have to make in the next few years about school, a career, all that. It's overwhelming, you know? I know I sound like a privileged asshole."

"We've all got problems," Mitch said. He was impressed with Aiden's mature analysis of his and his friend's situations and surprised they were both being so open with him. Maybe that was easier than confronting parents, though.

They hiked in silence after that.

———

It was dusk by the time they reached the house. Mitch was exhausted, though Aiden and Tyler looked no worse for the wear, despite Aiden's grazed toe. In the kitchen, Mitch found some gauze and tape. He had Aiden take off his shoe, and he cleaned and bandaged the toe. Cleaned up, it didn't amount to more than a bad scrape with a bruise forming around it.

"Want some coffee?" Mitch offered. He had no idea whether high school kids these days drank coffee.

"Honestly," Aiden glanced at Tyler and hesitated, "I could really use a joint about now."

"Fair enough. I could really use a whiskey."

They moved to the back porch, where the evening was pleasantly cool but still stupidly warm for February. Not that Mitch minded. The boys set themselves up on the edge of the porch, and Mitch left Aiden to his rolling papers while he poured himself whiskey and water on the rocks in the kitchen. Out the window over the sink, he could see them talking low to each other. When he returned, the boys were trading the joint back and forth, taking long, slow drags. As he sat down beside them, Tyler glanced at Mitch.

"You know that shit is bad for you, like way worse than weed," he said.

"That's what I hear, but what can I say? I like it better."

Tyler held the joint out, offering it to Mitch, but he declined. "No thanks. I never developed a taste for it."

They sat silently for a while, but Mitch could feel tension in the air as if the boys were internally debating something. Then Aiden spoke.

"We've got to tell you something."

"Okay…"

Aiden took a deep drag on the joint and passed it to Tyler. "It wasn't just Tyler and me in the woods that day. Gentry was with us."

"Who's Gentry?"

"He graduated last year, but he still hangs around. 'Never really moved on after high school."

"Man, I can't wait to get out of here," Tyler chimed in.

"Anyway, he's always got weed, so he was in the woods with us that day. When your wife passed us —"

"We're not married."

"Oh, yeah? I thought…anyway, when she passed us, Gentry was the one who wanted to follow her, so we did. I mean, I was just curious about where she was going."

Aiden had Mitch's full attention now. The kid began talking a little faster and seemed nervous, despite the joint he was smoking. Something was beginning to worry him.

"We followed her to the cave and saw her climb up in it and lay down in the back to sleep, which we all thought was kinda weird. Tyler and I were ready to go back. It seemed a little creepy sitting there watching her. Gentry wanted to stay, but we talked him into walking back to town with us. Only, part way back, he stopped and turned around. We hollered at him, asking where he was going, but he wouldn't answer, so we went back on our own."

"Do you think he went back to the cave?" Mitch asked urgently.

"I don't know."

"Why didn't you tell me this before?" asked Mitch. He didn't understand why they might want to keep this detail a secret.

Tyler spoke up. "We didn't want to alarm you. Gentry…he's kinda rough and weird, you know? He's got a reputation. Most of the girls around here don't trust him."

"What do you think he meant to do?" Mitch asked through a clenched jaw.

"I…I don't know. I mean, he was really high. I don't know that he *could* have done anything."

"You mean you don't think he could've gotten it up?" Fear made Mitch blunt, and he stared into the contents of the glass in his lap, but he could almost feel Tyler's face getting red.

"Yeah, er…"

Mitch rose from his chair, feeling the need to pace, but his aching legs reminded him he'd just hiked several miles on a bum ankle, and he abruptly sat back down.

"So where is Gentry now? Where does he live?"

Aiden took the lead again. "A trailer south of town," he said, waving his hand in the general direction. "We haven't seen him since that day in the woods, but that doesn't mean anything. Sometimes we don't see him for weeks at a time."

They sat without talking for a few minutes until Mitch broke it with the part of this that made him the most uneasy. "I still don't understand why you didn't tell me this before."

Aiden babbled, "Well, Gentry's not here, and he didn't agree to this whole thing…"

"He's my brother," Tyler said glumly.

Mitch got up and made himself another drink.

———————

Mitch managed to ferret some more information out of Tyler and Aiden before they left. They'd seen Allie's story on the news and realized she was the one they'd seen in the woods. Aiden wanted to tell the police, saying it was the right thing to do. Tyler was too afraid of getting in trouble for smoking, so they compromised on telling Mitch and came up with the ridiculous rock-and-arrow plan, paranoid someone would see them if they knocked on my door. They hadn't planned to use the gun. Tyler had brought it along "just in case." He swiped it from his father's gun cabinet. Aiden had been almost as surprised as Mitch when Tyler whipped it out first thing.

The two boys stayed at the house until around midnight, then drove home in Tyler's car they'd parked down the road. After exchanging phone numbers and saying goodbye, Mitch went into the kitchen. He was already somewhat drunk, but he poured himself another drink anyway. He took a sip, and it tasted like water. As he pondered the glass, amber liquid with ice cubes tinkling inside, he thought.

They seemed like good kids. A little dramatic and impulsive maybe, but isn't everyone at that age? They'd told him some of Gentry's story. Between what Tyler had said and reading between the lines, Mitch had a pretty good picture of Gentry's last few years. He'd been his parents' golden boy until his junior year in high school — straight A's, AP classes, star hitter for the baseball team. Then, in Tyler's words, "It was like he just decided to quit life."

He started skipping school and got kicked off the baseball team for missing practice. His grades fell, and Tyler was pretty sure he was coming home drunk or high more often than not. He'd graduated, thanks to his backlog of high grades, but the Turner household had been rocky after that — lots of yelling and threats. Tyler had made himself scarce, hanging out at Aiden's house or anywhere but home, but when his parents finally kicked Gentry out of the house and wrote him off, their attentions fell on Tyler to be all that Gentry had failed to be.

From what Tyler and Aiden said, it was a good bet Gentry was selling, if not cooking, meth out of that trailer of his. Aiden had said he used to hang out with them when they were younger, pitch baseballs to them in the backyard. He was a cool big brother, and Aiden, an only child, seemed to admire him. Mitch realized it wasn't just the weed that drew them into Gentry's company. They'd instinctively been trying to protect him by leaving him out of the story. Perhaps meeting Mitch in person, seeing how desperate he was, had changed their minds.

Mitch wondered what had happened in that cave. Maybe Gentry hadn't even made it back there, Mitch thought, hopefully. But he also knew what chronic drug use could do to someone already bitter about life. It could make them moody, mean. Mitch thought of his own dad, when his alcoholism and pills had turned him into a man Mitch no longer recognized, in the final months of his life. He poured his full drink down the sink and went to bed.

CHAPTER 8

Still day 16ish

Allie milled around on the edge of the group of people waiting to get into the shelter. An older man kept taking furtive glances at her and making her nervous. She began making mental notes on how she might defend herself if attacked. She wondered if anyone would help her. Finally, he ambled over, and her shoulders tensed. "What's a nice girl like you doing in a place like this?"

Show no fear, she thought and met his gaze. He stank of urine and alcohol. He chuckled and dropped his gaze. "I'm sorry. That was a stupid-shit thing to say. I'm not real good at conversation anymore."

He began to fidget from foot to foot and turned as if to shuffle away. Allie found herself not wanting him to go. It seemed like ages since she'd talked to anyone remotely friendly. He was the first halfway civilized conversation she'd had in a long time.

"No, no. It's all right."

He turned back to her with a glimmer of hope in his eyes. Maybe he was lonely, too.

"I mean, it was a stupid-shit thing to say, " Allie laughed, "but I forgive you."

He grinned and stuck out a rough, cracked hand. "Charles."

"Allie," she responded, shaking his hand and returning his grin. His hand felt impossibly dry in hers.

"You haven't been sleepin' rough long, have you?" he asked.

Allie wasn't sure what he meant, but she said, "No."

Before he could ask her another question, she asked him, "So how's this place work, anyway?" She was relieved to have someone to ask.

"They'll open the door anytime now and let us in. In bigger places, they make you register and jump through all sorts a hoops, but here you just walk in an' find a spot on the floor. Lucky if you get a cot. Watch out, though. The others'll steal your shit if you're not real careful."

"I ain't got shit to steal," Allie said, subconsciously lapsing into Charles's speech patterns. She still had the smelly rag of a blanket dangling out of her left hip pocket, but it was hardly a treasure she'd miss.

"Sometimes that's the best way," he said and winked. "Nowhere to go but up."

"So no food in there, then?" she asked.

He laughed, "Nope, not here."

They heard the clunking of locks inside, and the door to the shelter opened. The woman in the doorway didn't speak. She just opened it and went back inside, and those on the sidewalk followed.

"C'mon," Charles prompted Allie.

———

Allie and Charles managed to lay claim to one cot, but it soon became clear to Allie that sleep would be next to impossible, exhausted as she was. There was moaning and loud, nonsensical ranting going on in one corner. Loud retorts of "Shut the fuck up!" punctuated but did not quell the noises. Allie wondered if this was what prison was like.

She and Charles decided to take turns lying on the cot but eventually gave up. Charles pulled a bottle from his ragged coat, and they sat on the cot against the wall. Charles took a swig and offered Allie some. She tipped it back cautiously. The alcohol burned her throat and her empty stomach. Tanqueray it was not.

They sat there, not talking, for a while. At first, Charles occasionally offered Allie a swig from the bottle, but eventually, he seemed to forget, which was okay with her. She'd been sitting there wondering, and finally, she just asked him, "So, what's your story?"

"My story?"

"How'd you get, you know, here?" she asked, gesturing vaguely.

He took another pull on the bottle and sat contemplating it in his lap. She was about to ask again when he spoke.

"I had a wife once. Her name was Melodie. We had an apartment in Bastrop — not fancy, but we got along. I was desk clerk at the Broadway Hotel. She was a…whatchacallit…patient technician at the hospital. We didn't make a lot of money, but we got along okay.

"Anywho, Mel got pregnant. We's worried about money but basically getting along, you know? We had a beautiful baby girl. She had the pinkest cheeks, and she smiled at me all the time. She was just starting to make those cute baby noises, y'know?

Charle's sad smile and glassy eyes told Allie he was back there with his baby girl right now. Her heart began to ache. She knew this story didn't have a happy ending.

"I was working double shifts at the hotel since Mel wasn't working cuz of maternity. I hated bein' gone from 'em so much, but we had to make rent. Then, I come home late one night after my shift, an' there's an amb'lance outside our building. I didn't think much of it, but as I walked up the stairs to our place, I got this bad feelin'. I could hear voices and crying on the other side of the door. When I went in…"

Charles's voice cracked. Tears welled up in his big, red-rimmed eyes, which were still trained on the bottle. His words were getting slurry from the liquor. Allie just waited until he shook his head to clear it, composed himself and continued.

"Our baby girl was gone. She was dead. Crib death, SIDS, they said. Mel was a wreck. She cried for days, wouldn't get out of bed, didn't eat. I asked the doctors, the coroner, whoever would listen, "What happened?" I wanted to know why, but no one would tell me.

"Mell thought it was my fault. She was always after me not to smoke in the house with the baby. I didn't do it much and always by the open window, but….maybe she was right."

"What happened to Mel?" Allie asked softly.

"I's after her to get up, take a shower, eat something at least. Eventually, she did. She found some support group she liked. I thought she was doin' better. We even talked about maybe havin' another one. Then, one day she kilt herself. She had these pills the doctor gave her when the baby died. She took the whole bottle. Must've done it right after I left for my double, 'cuz but the time I found her she was stone cold."

"Charles, I'm sorry." Allie rested her hand tentatively on his arm. He glanced down at her missing and bandaged thumb but didn't seem to register anything unusual.

"Anway, after that I just kina went downhill. I started drinkin' a lot, missed some shifts an' lost m' job. 'Weren't too long after that I got thrown out of our place. 'Couldn't pay rent. I stayed on Judy's couch for a while, then Angela's, but no one wants a stinky ol' drunk in their place. 'Don't blame 'em.

"Don't member much from that time, but one thing's clear. This one night, I'd drunk all I had an needed a place to sleep. I saw this park, not sure where it was, but the moon was full shinin' on it, an' there was this bench like a gift from God. I thought, 'seems like good a place as any to be.' An' I laid down and passed out."

Charles was silent again. Allie thought he'd fallen asleep, nodding his head into the bottle in his lap, but after a few minutes, he jerked back awake, eyes wide.

"What happened then?" Allie asked.

"Huh? Then wha'?"

"After you found the park bench and passed out on it. How did you get here after that?"

"Oh! Well, I had a wife…"

"I know, but what about after she was gone? How did you get here?"

"Don't really know. Kina drifted from place t' place an' here I am!" He threw his arms wide in a wobbly grand gesture and grinned.

Allie gave up. She stood up, eased Charles onto his side and placed his bottle on the floor. "Rest," she whispered. He was out immediately.

Allie lay herself on the hard concrete floor and wadded up the ratty blanket for a pillow. She lay on her back, staring up into the dark, listening to the ever-present moaning. She was so unbelievably tired, she actually fell asleep.

———

"Ow! What the hell?!"

Allie awoke with a sharp crack to the head. Her makeshift pillow was abruptly gone, allowing her head to free-fall the short distance to the hard floor. Rubbing the back of her head, she said up and looked around but couldn't see who'd taken it. Either they were gone or feigning sleep. The shelter was quiet, except for the woman moaning softly in the corner, curled on a cot in tortured sleep. Gray light was just beginning to filter in through the one small window. Allie noticed Charles's bottle was gone, too.

She lay on the floor, now pillowless, not sleeping. It was hot, and the still air was oppressive, smelling of sweat and bodies long gone unwashed, hers included. There was the slightest tinge of vomit amidst the other aromas. It was a far cry from waking up in the woods. Allie's stomach was cramping with hunger.

Eventually, Charles started mumbling in his sleep and then came all the way awake. He looked around. "Where's my bottle?"

"Don't know," Allie answered, "I guess someone took it."

"Godamnit, girl, you can't leave shit like that just lyin' around! I needed that!"

"There was hardly anything left in it. Maybe one swig."

"That's one swig more 'n I got now, godamnit!"

Charles's eyes were wild and bloodshot.

"It's okay, it's okay," Allie reassured, thinking fast. "We'll get you a new one, a full one, today. I'll help you, okay?"

Charles took a deep breath and let out a sigh, "Okay, okay. I'm sorry. I didn't mean it…" He squinted at her. "What's your name again?"

"Allie"

"Right!" he said, though Allie had a feeling it didn't ring a bell.

Charles surveyed the room, gaze fixing on the dim light growing brighter through the window. "'Bout time to go."

As if on cue, Allie heard the turning of locks at the door. She hadn't even realized they'd been locked in. The same woman who'd let them in again opened the door and departed without a word.

Charles stood suddenly at the sound of the door. "Gotta get goin' before the rest wake up and get ideas."

Allie didn't know what ideas he was talking about, but he was the veteran here, so she followed his lead. As she followed Charles to the door, they passed the moaning woman. She cut off her soft noises abruptly and opened one eye. "Y'all going?" she asked in a ragged whisper.

Allie had nothing left to steal, but with all of the previous night's noisy antics, this woman made her nervous. Then, to Allie's surprise, Charles nodded at the woman and said, "Come on then, Mag."

The three emerged, blinking into the light of morning. Allie squinted. Her stomach was making loud, hungry rumblings. When they'd walked two blocks from the shelter, Charles seemed to deem it safe enough to talk.

"Mag, this is…" he'd forgotten again.

"Allie." Allie supplied. She looked at Mag, whose eyes were old, tired and watery but fairly sane. Allie offered her hand. Mag looked surprised but took it and shook it briefly.

"Pleased to meetcha," Mag said and chuckled softly.

Allie was so hungry, she could barely think straight. "Do you guys know where we could get some food? I'm starving." And she thought she literally might be.

"Oh yeah," Mag said. The three began to walk again, and Allie trusted they'd lead her in the right direction. She was too famished not to. They came to an auto repair shop called "Cars R Us." The "R" was even backward, just like the toy store. Allie followed Charles and Mag around the back.

"What are we going to eat, old tires?" she joked, feeling delirious from the hunger.

"This place is a good bet," Charles said. "Everyone shops the dumpsters at the grocery an' the diner, but no one thinks a car shop's gonna have anything."

Charles boosted Mag over the side of the Cars R Us dumpster, and sure enough, she came up with a clear plastic box full of mini muffins, only two of them gone. There was also a half-full jar of generic peanut butter, a loaf of white bread with just a few moldy pieces, and half a bag of pretzels that were only a little stale.

Allie was astounded. Cars R Us was still closed in the early AM, so they sat right there in the alley and feasted. Through a mouthful of bread and peanut butter, Allie asked, "How did you find this place?"

"I look in all the dumpsters," Mag said, stuffing mini muffins in her mouth, two at a time. "Just never know where you're gonna find gold. 'Sides, like Charles said, the obvious ones 're always picked over. There's a lot of folks who stay out around here."

"Why's that?" Allie asked.

"Dunno," Mag replied. "Maybe cuz it's the only town around here with a decent shelter and the cops don't harass you for sleeping in the park near as often as some places. That's what I hear, anyway."

If Community Solutions was a decent shelter, Allie hated to think what its counterparts were like. "So why do y'all sleep at that place? Isn't it nicer outside?" Allie asked, thinking of the woods.

"We both sleep out some," Charles said. "But sometimes the weather's not so great, and it's nice to know you ain't gonna get rained on or woken up by the cops in the middle of the night. They're more lenient around here, but ever so often, they get a wild hair an' start kickin' people outta the park."

When they were full, Allie found a plastic "Thank You" convenience store bag in the dumpster, and they put the remainder of the peanut butter and bread in it. Allie hid it under her jacket.

"What now?" she asked, looking at her new friends. She wasn't ready to part ways with them. It felt good to have company.

"You promised me a bottle," Charles said, pointing a shaky finger at her.

"Right." Allie had no idea how to pull this off, but she could tell he needed it, and she wasn't one to break promises. "Any ideas?"

––––––––

Charles led them to a run-down liquor store with "LiquorsTown" over the storefront and show windows full of fancy bottles that hadn't seen a dust cloth in an eon. He pointed at it from across the street where they were congregated.

"Great," said Allie. "How do you propose I pay for it?"

Charles shrugged.

"What do you usually do?" she asked impatiently. He had a bottle last night that he'd gotten his hands on somehow.

"Sometimes I go sit on the sidewalk closer to downtown an' ask for change 'til I get enough."

"Yeah, I seen you," Mag scoffed. "You really ham it up down there with that homeless veteran shit."

"You're one to talk," he retorted.

Charles went on. "Sometimes I hang outside the Liquors Town —"

"It's 'Liquorston'" Mag interrupted again.

"It's not a fuckin' east coast uppity fuckin' city, woman! Lemme finish, goddamnit!"

Mag went silent but with a smirk on her face.

"Anyway…I hang outside, and sometimes I can get someone to buy me a bottle or give me a beer from their twelve-pack. If I'm real lucky, I find half-full bottles around back where kids leave 'em after they've snuck too much an' thrown their guts up. I was thinkin', though, a pretty girl like you'd be able to get somethin' better 'n I would."

Allie scowled at him. Using her body as currency didn't resonate well with her. Fresh out of school, she'd struggled to get herself taken seriously as a journalist, and what Charles proposed went completely against that. But he had a point; he wasn't wrong. And desperate times….Charles was definitely desperate.

She gazed across the street. "It's not even open yet."

Likely wouldn't be soon, either, she thought. It couldn't be later than 7:30 in the morning.

"Oh, it's open," Charles said. "Watch."

They stood watching the apparently vacant store, and Allie,

growing impatient, was about to ask what the hell she was watching for, when a girl walked up to the front door. She couldn't have been more than twelve. She knocked and then nodded at someone inside. The girl walked down the side of the store and just around its corner. Allie could still see her but not the wall she was looking at. The girl dug something out of her pocket and held it up to the wall. It looked like a wad of bills. A bottle in a paper sack appeared from the wall. The girl took it and hurried back down the street the way she'd come.

"What the hell?" asked Allie.

"You can get a drink any time of day here," Charles said. "You just can't go in the store."

"Is that…legal?" Allie asked.

"Prob'ly not," said Mag, "But I've never seen a cop try 'n stop it."

"So how are we going to do this?" Allie asked, mostly to herself. Now, she was a little excited. This was a challenge she could think about from a distance — not searching for food when she was desperately hungry or looking for shelter while utterly exhausted.

Allie left her two new friends leaning on the closed storefront and crossed the street. She had a loose plan, but mostly, she'd have to wing it based on who came along.

First, she circled around back to the alley, checking for the bottles Charles had mentioned teenagers sometimes left. Unsurprisingly, there was nothing — just a few empties and broken bottles.

She staked out a piece of wall on the side of the building, not too far from where she'd seen the girl make her transaction. It turned out there was a window set into the wall there, like a drive-thru but smaller. It looked like the bottom portion slid open for exchanges.

She was skeptical there'd be much traffic at this early hour, but it must've been a hard-drinking town, Allie thought, because she only had to wait 15 minutes for a new customer to appear.

A woman, somewhere between 30 and 50, walked up. Allie couldn't tell her age. She was thin with a weather-worn face, but Allie suspected by her eyes, she was younger than she looked. She eyed Allie suspiciously.

"Hi," Allie greeted her.

The woman barely nodded at her before rapping on the window and handing over a handful of bills for a six-pack of Milwaukee's Best. She walked away without making eye contact with Allie again.

Allie wished she had something to do. She felt awkward just standing there, trying to look casual, against the wall — a cigarette, even though she hadn't smoked them in years, her phone, a book, anything.

Over the next hour, two more customers came and went, but they seemed just as stand-offish and mistrustful as the first. Allie was waiting for just the right one. She could afford to be patient; it wasn't like she had anywhere to be. Then, a man approached.

As he walked towards Allie and the liquor store, she tried to gauge his age. Twenty-five maybe? As he got closer, though, she thought it was more like eighteen. Even better.

As he got closer, Allie smiled and met his eyes with hers. "Hey," she said lazily.

"Hey, yourself," he replied with a grin.

Allie watched him walk to the window and purchase a bottle of Jack Daniels. He stuffed a decent amount of change in his hip pocket.

"What's going on?" Allie asked, with a flirtatious lilt to her voice. She'd never flirted with a guy to get something before, only when she was actually interested. She had to admit, there was a certain feeling of power to it, and it wasn't all bad.

"Lil' party," he answered. "Wanna come?" His eyebrows were raised, and he was smiling. He was playing her game. She wondered why one would be partying at 9am — hangover party from the night before or just a handful of young guys with nothing to do? She supposed, for her purposes, it didn't matter.

"C'mere a sec," she said, motioning with her head.

He strode over, looking anticipatory and pleased with himself.

"Listen," Allie said, tilting her head to look him in the eye. "I need a bottle of vodka, but I left my purse at home. 'Think you could help a girl out?"

Jesus Christ, if I were a cartoon, I'd be batting my Betty Boop eyelashes at him.

Allie felt simultaneously powerful and disgusted with herself.

"Well, that depends. You gonna come party with me?" He either couldn't tell or didn't care that she was over a decade older than he was. Or that she smelled like a homeless shelter.

"I can't just now, baby, but do you think you could be a good guy and do me a favor?" She was laying it on thick with the "baby" stuff, but he was eating it up. It kind of amazed her.

"Everything costs something," he replied.

His dad probably says that, thought Allie.

Allie realized it would take more than charm to get what she wanted, but she was committed to getting Charles his bottle. She'd just met him the night before but already felt loyal to him. Maybe it was because she'd been lonely or because he hadn't seemed surprised or judgmental about her wandering the street. Either way, he needed it, and she would get it for him. She'd promised.

"Wanna peek?" she asked, teasing up the hem of her shirt.

He laughed, "I've seen plenty of tits. It'll take more than that."

She was sure he had. He was a good-looking kid in a small town where there wasn't much else to do besides drink and fuck.

Allie knew she had to be shrewd. "Tell you what. I'll show 'em to you as a preview. You can have a little more after you get me the vodka." She winked, hoping he'd bite.

"How much more?"

As little much more as possible, thought Allie, but she said, "Gotta leave a little mystery, right?" and winked again.

"Deal," he said and winked back at her.

Allie reached around her back and unhooked her bra. She pulled up her shirt, her eyes trained on him the whole time.

He shifted the crotch of his pants a little.

Allie let her shirt fall and looked at him expectantly, alluring smile still plastered on her face. He looked lost in reverie for a moment, then came to and turned to the window. He bought a cheap, plastic handle of vodka and then walked over to hand it to her in its brown paper sack.

"Thank you, baby," she crooned. She laid it on thick, but he was still lapping it up.

She reached for the sack, and he pulled it back.

"Uh uh. I want my reward for being such a good citizen first." He put the bottle down on the ground behind him and bracketed her, placing a hand on either side of her on the wall. Strangely, Allie was feeling a tingling in her crotch as well. She hadn't planned on this part. It occurred to her that she must smell pretty rank after so many nights unbathed and living outside, but he didn't seem to notice. She turned her face up to his, leaned in and kissed him open-mouthed.

He pulled her hips roughly into him. She could feel his erection poking into her, and she reached down to put her hand on it. He tasted pleasantly of Jim Beam and Marlboro reds. His hands climbed up her skin to her breasts, squeezing and massaging, then pinching her nipples. She moaned. This kid was surprisingly good.

She moved her hands up to the back of his head, entwined her remaining nine fingers in his hair and pulled his head back, exposing his neck to her kisses. He reached down her jeans, fumbling with the button and zipper along the way. His hands went to pussy, where she could feel it was wet and warm. As he massaged and rubbed, she began to feel the crescendo building.

Well, what the fuck do you know? Allie thought in wonder.

He started to pull his hand out, but she shoved it back down with her good right hand until he finished the job. She came fast and hard, sniffling a moan as she peaked and then let out her breath as her body relaxed.

She slumped into him, marveling that someone so young could be so adept. He must've had a lot of practice…or a good teacher.

"I'm not done yet," he said, a confused look on his face.

Oh. Maybe it was just luck.

"Listen, my friends are waiting for me," she said, rebooking her bra, but maybe I'll come by that party la—"

He slammed into her, knocking her head against the wall and began roughly fumbling with her jeans again. She saw stars and felt a sharp ache bloom across her skull.

Shit. Time to get the fuck out of Dodge.

Allie didn't think. Adrenaline flooded her veins. Her knee came up, connected with his hard crotch, and he went down. She stepped around him, snatched up the brown bag and sprinted across the street, leaving him in her wake, wheezing. He hadn't even had the breath to yell after her.

As Allie approached Charles and Mag on the other side of the street, her legs pumping furiously, they registered her alarm, and their eyes went wide.

"Go, go!" Allie shouted.

Without question, they started running, and Allie followed, down the sidewalk, shoes slapping the pavement behind Charles and Mag. She felt exhilarated.

She felt free.

———

When it finally seemed safe to stop running, Allie saw they were in a park. Slowing to a walk and panting for breath, they passed an old wooden playscape that had been painted once upon a time. It was deserted. Charles glanced at a guy nodding out on the park bench as they passed.

C'mon. He motioned them away from the occupied bench into the trees on the park's edge. They plunked down on the ground, out of sight, relieved to rest. When he'd fully caught his breath, Charles asked, "What the hell happened back there? D'you steal it?"

"No," Allie replied, handing him the paper-wrapped bottle. Then, she regaled them with the tale of flirting with the kid and kicking him in the nuts when he wanted more. She left out some details.

"Wow," Mag said. "You've got some nerve!" She was grinning in admiration.

"Yeah, well…" Now that the adrenaline was wearing off, Allie felt less exhilarated and more uncomfortable. She felt a heaviness in her gut like she'd swallowed an anvil. What she'd just done wasn't exactly her mother's brand of feminism. That anvil felt a lot like guilt. She changed the subject.

"So, Mag, can I ask you something?"

"Fire away."

"Well, you don't seem…I mean, I don't know if you're aware, but you were moaning pretty loudly most of the night —"

"Oh, she knows," Charles said with an eye roll.

Allie looked at Mag quizzically. Charles took a pull from the vodka. He offered Mag and Allie some, but they took small sips, leaving most of it for him.

"It's m' strategy. Keeps people from botherin' me, 'cause I seem unpredictable."

"Keeps her in cots instead of on the floor like the rest of us," Charles snorted, disregarding the fact that Allie had let him have the cot the previous night.

"Really?" Allie asked with wonderment.

"Yep." Mag seemed proud of herself, and Allie was impressed by her simple ingenuity.

"So you're not crazy."

"Nuttier 'n a fruitcake," Charles mumbled.

Mag glared at him and then turned back to Allie. "I've had, um, problems since I was a teenager. Momma had me on lithium, Xanax, Prozac, and a few others I can't remember. She said they made me better, but I didn't like 'em — made me feel…" She rolled her eyes skyward, searching for the right word. "Weird. Like not myself, you know?"

Allie smiled and shrugged. She knew what feeling not like yourself was like, but she didn't think she knew how Mag felt. Not really. So she asked, "Where's your mom now?"

"Momma had a heart attack 'n died four years ago, bless her."

"I'm sorry." Allie rested her hand on Mag's.

"S'okay." Her eyes had welled up with tears. "She's gone to a better place, hopefully. I do miss her, even though she drove me crazy…HA! That's a funny one."

Allie smiled. Charles alternately studied the bottle in his lap and the surrounding trees, keeping his distance.

"Anyway, Mag went on, "After Momma was gone and not there to make me, I stopped taking all that medicine."

"Did you feel better then? More like yourself off of them?" Allie asked.

"At first I did. Now, I don't know. I just walked away from the house one day an' never went back. I couldn't take care of it after Momma was gone anyway."

"You have a house?" Allie was a little incredulous Mag

would be out on the streets if she had a warm bed nearby. Of course, Allie didn't have much room to judge.

"Had. Momma 'n I rented it. I helped with the rent money when I had a job, but with Momma gone, it was only a matter of time 'fore I got kicked out anyway."

"Don't you have any other family that could help you out?"

"Nah. They all thought Momma was just as crazy as me for not putting me in the mental hospital."

"Why? Just because you were, what, depressed?" Allie could see Mag had some problems but committing her seemed extreme.

"It was more 'n that. In high school, I was…difficult." Mag looked off into the distance, and Allie had the feeling she didn't want to talk about it anymore. She didn't press her to explain, so they sat in silence.

Mag dug a stub of a cigarette out of her pocket and lit it with a red, plastic Bic lighter. She returned the lighter to her dingy coat pocket and dragged heavily on the butt.

"What's your story, girl?" Charles suddenly piped up.

"Me?"

"Yeah, what happened to your thumb?" Mag asked.

"I cut it off," Allie answered, looking down at her left hand in her lap, trying to wiggle the stump under the bandage a little. She wasn't sure she even needed the gauze anymore.

"No shit! On purpose?" Charles exclaimed.

"No, of course not! I was chopping vegetables. It was…an

accident."

They were silent, waiting for her to elaborate, so she decided she might as well.

"I was chopping vegetables for a salad, and my left hand got tired. I was getting a blister, so I decided to use my right —"

"You're left-handed?" Charles interrupted, "Me too!"

"Shhh!" Mag said, eyes fixed on Allie.

Allie continued, "I'm pretty good with my right, but then I guess I wasn't paying attention. I got to staring out the window at the woods, and the knife slipped, I guess."

"Bullshit!" yelled Charles. "You cut yourself not payin' attention. But to cut a thumb clean off…nah, bullshit."

Allie could feel her insides tense, but then Mag said, "Don't pay any attention to him," and rolled her eyes. "Couldn't you have saved it? Can't they reattach 'em now?"

"I don't know," said Allie, trying to ignore Charles's brazen disbelief, "I wrapped a dish towel around my hand and picked up my phone to call 911, but it was dead. I just stood there in the kitchen, dripping blood and staring at my blank phone. I got really hot all of a sudden, like hot from the inside. I had to get out of there, get some air. So I left."

Both Charles and Mag looked confused. "Where'd you go?" asked Charles.

"There's greenbelt behind the house. I just needed some air; I needed to get away. I went to the clearing, then I kept going to the cave, then…" She didn't want to talk about the cave. "I didn't go back."

Charles and Mag were both gaping at her, and suddenly she felt small and selfish. She began to babble, "I…I just couldn't do it anymore — that house, that job, all the shit people expect you to do all the time. I felt…smothered. It was too much." She finished in a small and quiet voice.

"Too much?!" Charles roared. "You walk away from a perfectly good house, perfectly good life because you got some responsibilities?! Horseshit!"

Angry tears sprang to Allie's eyes. "Isn't that exactly what you did?"

"That's not the same at all. I didn't want to live on the goddamned street. I got kicked out. I lost everything! You just couldn't stand the heat!"

Mag spoke up then. "Maybe it is the same, Charles. Maybe a little bit, it is."

Charles got up with a sigh of indignation and stalked, drunken and wobbly, over a few feet from them to sit against a tree, finish his drink and sulk.

"Maybe he's right," Allie said to Mag, swallowing the lump in her throat. "I left Mitch, I left everything, and what did I have to complain about? Lots of people have miscarriages and don't go lopping appendages off."

"I'm sorry," said Mag. Her eyes were full of sympathy. "Is that why you left? You lost a baby?"

"No. Maybe. Partially. I mean, I was getting to be fine with it, but everyone kept looking at me, all full of pity. And some people were all, 'When are you going to try again?' and 'Everything happens for a reason.' It made me want to punch them in the face. But no, I smile and nod and do everything a good girl is supposed to do. I'm grateful for the casseroles; I'm gracious about all their stupid sympathy. What if I don't ever have a baby? What if I don't want a stupid, soul-sucking, nine-to-five job; what if I don't want to marry Mitch and have a house with 2.4 kids and a dog and a 401k? Can that just be okay? Can it?!"

She was shouting now, and Mag was leaning back, looking nervous.

"I'm sorry," Allie said, quieting herself. She didn't want to scare Mag. "I guess I've had that bottled up a long time." She looked back down at the hand in her lap. The bandage was dirty and torn. As she picked at it, she saw she didn't need it anymore. The pink skin underneath was healing nicely. She wiggled the stump. Then she sighed and balled up the dirty bandage, shoving it in the pocket of her dirtier jeans.

Charles came weaving back over to Allie and Mag. "'M sorry. I didn't know about your baby."

"It's okay. I mean, it was hard, but I'm okay with it now."

"It's just everything else you're not okay with?" Mag asked.

"Yeah, I guess. You guys probably think that's bullshit, though. I kind of do, too."

Charles grunted. Mag cocked her head to the side and shrugged. "Momma always said, 'Judge not lest ye be judged.'"

––––––––

Allie filled them in on what she'd done since she left her house and Mitch, which mostly amounted to wandering the woods and trying to feed herself. She left out the part about the rabbit. When she got to losing her pack, they seemed especially interested.

"That Rose woman is horrible mean," Charles said. "She's chased me away from the door more 'n once."

Mag's brow was knitted together in thought, and then suddenly, she piped up. "Wait!" she said excitedly. "I think I might know where your stuff is!"

CHAPTER 9

Day 4

Mitch was sitting on the couch with his bum leg propped up on the coffee table, waiting for Murphy. She'd agreed to come over for an in-person visit when he wouldn't discuss his new intel about Allie over the phone. She knocked on the door, and he shouted, "Come in!"

She opened the door and peeked in.

"Sorry," said Mitch pointing to the boot. "Lugging this thing around is tiresome. He was still fatigued from dragging it through the woods with Aiden and Tyler the day before.

"What's this stuff you can't discuss over the phone?" she asked, sitting down in the chair opposite him. "This isn't Watergate, you know."

"I know, it's just that it's complicated, and it's easier in person."

"Okay?" She spread her hands out in expectation. She seemed impatient.

Mitch filled her in on everything Aiden and Tyler had told him – about them being in the woods the night Allie disappeared and Gentry circling back toward the cave on his own. He left out the boys' names and didn't mention the gun. He was trying to maintain the confidentiality he'd promised them the best he could, but he needed Murphy's help. Considering he'd discovered from Lianna that Murphy was very much local, withholding names seemed prudent, as did their running around with Tyler's dad's firearm.

"What do you think happened after boy number three left the other two?" she asked cautiously.

"I don't know. I'm afraid…What if he assaulted her? I mean, according to the other two, he was pretty messed up, but Allie was hurt…"

"Don't go down that road just yet. I'm guessing you want to go back out to the cave."

"Right. Let's go."

Murphy drove, and they headed out to the back road that would get them close to the cave. It was mid-morning, and the sun was out. It was a beautiful day.

"You know I'm going to have to know these kids' names at some point, right?" Murphy said.

"Yeah, probably, but hopefully, that won't come from me. I promised."

Murphy pulled off the side of the road in the same spot they had last time, and they made their way via the orange stakes that still marked the path to the cave. Following them was easier in the light.

The cave looked the same to Mitch, minus all the cops. Murphy climbed in and gave Mitch a hand up. They began poking around in the dry leaves, but Mitch wasn't sure what they were looking for. He imagined the forensics people had been over it pretty thoroughly.

"Well?" Murphy stopped poking and looked at Mitch. "Nothing seems to have changed since last time."

"I guess there's really nothing here. 'Don't know what I expected to find," Mitch mumbled, feeling useless. He felt driven to find her. He told himself it was because he was worried about her, but a voice in the back of his head was asking, since she didn't seem to want to be found, if it was really more about Mitch and what *he* needed.

"Let's have a look around down there," Murphy said, gesturing outside.

They clamored out of the shallow cave, using the large rock at its base as a step stool, just as they had to climb in. Mitch felt dejected, coming down from the high he'd been on after Tyler and Aiden had given him new information. At the time, he thought it was revelatory, but now, he realized it was just minutia likely leading nowhere. He looked around at the trees, halfheartedly, as if in vain hope Allie might materialize out of them.

"Look," said Murphy. She was examining some broken tree branches around the left side of the cave. The ground there led gently downhill. Mitch walked over and saw there was a line of them — broken branches on four separate trees leading down the deer trail on which they now stood.

"Could've been an animal," Mitch offered.

"Maybe. But they're too high for deer." Murphy walked down the slope, miming grabbing the tree branches as she went.

Mitch followed her down the slope, his breath quickening, thoughts picking up speed. *Had Allie come this way? What did those broken branches mean? Was she losing consciousness, maybe losing blood from her thumb or maybe, something else, something to do with Gentry?*

"There's a creek down here, right?" Murphy asked.

"Yeah — ahem." Mitch cleared his throat, which was suddenly very dry. "'Might have some water in it now."

As they approached, they could indeed hear the gurgle of a small creek. Murphy came to a halt at the drop-off to the creek bed below. She lay on her belly and peered over the steep edge. Mitch joined her.

There was just enough water in the creek for it to flow, barely a trickle. It was shady, with big cypress trees growing tangled with undergrowth bushes, right up to the edge of the drop-off into the creek on either side. Bright green moss covered the rocks at the edges of the tiny flow of water. *Allie loved that moss,* Mitch remembered. She'd tried to bring some home. She planted it in a pot on the back porch. She'd watered it every day, but it had died just the same, not meant for the heat of their yard.

The drop into the creek bed was around 12 feet. In flood times, that trickle of water would turn into a torrent that rose every bit of the height of its banks. The exposed tree roots sticking out of the sides were evidence of high-water erosion.

"There," said Murphy, pointing straight down the steep bank on the same side on which they lay prone.

Mitch squinted into the shade, straight now, and saw what looked like a red sleeve. There was a wrist as well, but where the hand should have been was just a ragged stump.

———

Cops were crawling the place like ants scurrying to rebuild their hill after it's been trampled. Murphy had climbed down to confirm that what they'd seen was a body, and it was, indeed, deceased. Then, she'd called it in.

"Mitch, you're going to have to give me those names now."

Mitch sighed, hoping the kids wouldn't hate him for this. "Boy number three was Gentry," he said, starting with the one he cared for the least. "I don't know his last name —"

"Detective, can I see you for a second?" One of the forensics people called her over. He had his back to Mitch, so he could see Murphy's face as he spoke, but her expression didn't give anything away.

"What was that about?" Mitch asked when she returned.

"Seems one of our guys recognized the body. He's fairly certain it's Gentry Turner, Mayor Turner's son." She stared at Mitch hard for a second. "I'm going to need names."

"One was Aiden, the other was Tyler? or maybe Taylor?"

"Which is it, Mitch? Half the kids in the town are Tyler or Taylor."

"Not sure."

"Last names?"

"Didn't ask," Mitch responded, which, he reasoned, was technically true.

"Approximate ages?"

"Fourteen, fifteen, maybe? I'm not good at judging ages." Mitch wasn't sure how long he could play this evasive game with Murphy, but he was going to do his best to keep his promise as much as he could.

"Listen, I'm going to find these kids anyway, you know that, right? Be a decent person and help me get there a little faster."

"Sorry. I really don't remember any more than that. Listen, I'm really tired, and my leg is killing me. Can you take me home, please?"

Murphy sighed heavily and stalked off down the path back toward her car, not waiting for Mitch, who hobbled after her. By the time he got back to the road, she was already sitting in the car with the engine running. He dropped into the passenger seat with relief.

As she revved the engine and spun the car in a U-turn,

Murphy muttered something under her breath.

"What?" asked Mitch.

"I said," she repeated loudly, "You're a shitty liar."

———

After watching Murphy's car back down the driveway, Mitch picked up his phone and tried Aiden first. It went to voicemail, as did Tyler's. Then, he tried texting and got a response from Aiden right away.

"Head's up. It's a good day for a walk in the park," Mitch typed. It was incredibly cryptic, but he didn't want to risk saying anything specific. He hoped Aiden would catch his meaning.

Aiden responded, "Got it. Thanks." Then, "I'll invite Tyler."

Mitch answered, "Good idea."

They were smart kids, and Mitch thought they got it. His hope was that by the time Murphy figured out who they were, they'd at least be away from home and out of parental earshot. There would be a chance, at least their folks wouldn't find out, and Mitch could ease his conscience about bringing Murphy in on what he'd learned from them.

Mitch thought about Gentry. He didn't know what exactly had happened to him, but he'd overheard from one of the cops that he had an open gash on the back of his head. The hand had likely been chewed off by animals post-mortem.

Mitch was exhausted from climbing all over the woods with

his boot, but his brain was moving too fast to rest. He wanted to pace but settled for sitting on the couch with both feet on the coffee table, restlessly wiggling them back and forth.

Scenario #1: Gentry was fucked up and wandered off his intended target, the cave. He stumbled down the path, breaking the branches, then fell into the creek gashing his head and bleeding to death right there.

The problem with that was the creek bed was almost entirely dirt and very few rocks. Mitch hadn't seen anything hard or sharp enough to gash a head, though he admitted to himself he didn't know the physics of it. Maybe an impact with hard dirt would do it?

Scenario #2: Gentry met up with someone, possibly Allie, who hit him with a rock. Then, he stumbled away and fell into the creek.

This seemed plausible, though it was hard for him to imagine Allie attacking anyone. Of course, up until recently, he wouldn't have imagined her cutting off her thumb and running into the woods, either, so what did he know? Based on what Tyler and Aiden said about Gentry's aggressive personality – as much as Mitch hated to imagine it – if Allie did hit him, it was probably in self-defense. But Mitch had noticed when they pulled Gentry out of the creek, he was an exceptionally big dude. Evidently, he took after his ex-linebacker father. Mitch didn't think Allie would be able to reach his head where the gash was…if he were standing up. But the gash being in the back of his head…that didn't sound like defense against imminent attack.

Scenario #3: Aiden and Tyler did it. Maybe Gentry threatened to rat them out to their parents or was blackmailing them in some way…

Well, that just seemed sort of ridiculous. And the boys wouldn't have come to Mitch if that were the case. Anyway, Mitch got the feeling Tyler and Aiden were both pretty close to Gentry, despite his current nefarious doings.

Mitch knew he was grasping, just making stuff up based on very little real evidence. He knew he needed to call Jamie. He'd been avoiding it, not wanting to deal with the fallout, but it was past time. Jamie needed to know, and she might have something to offer. Maybe Allie had been in touch with her.

CHAPTER 10

Still day 17ish

"Was it a big backpack, like the kind hikers wear?" asked Mag.

"Yes! Did you see it?" Allie was cautiously optimistic. She knew the odds, or lack thereof, of finding her things.

"Yeah, I saw that kid with it, I think. Charles, you know the kid that hangs out on the strip, always stealing people's stuff? It was green?" Mag asked.

"Yes!" Now Allie was getting excited, in spite of herself.

"C'mon, then!" said Mag.

It was Allie's stuff, but Mag and Charles seemed just as excited to find it. Allie got the idea Mag just enjoyed being useful to someone, whereas Charles, she wasn't sure. Allie and Charles followed Mag, making their way out of the park and closer to the center of town.

Mag said, "I followed him once. I know where he dumps the stuff he doesn't want. I snag some of it sometimes."

They rounded a corner into an alleyway. Mag led them to a pile of broken furniture — a stained couch that was once a floral print, with broken wooden chairs, maybe from some long-defunct restaurant, piled all around it. There was trash everywhere. It looked like people had been dumping stuff there for months, maybe years. Allie wondered why the city didn't clean it up. Were there trash piles in every alleyway in this little burg? Mag scurried around behind the couch.

"Is any of this stuff yours?" she called, looking down at something unseen to Allie behind the mound of furniture detritus.

Allie ran around to where Mag was and found a mini-mountain of discarded goods — plastic cups, wallets with nothing in them, a couple of purses – one with a pink plastic hairbrush sticking out of it. And then she saw it: the navy blue bag of her water filter. She snatched it up, finding the filter still inside and intact.

"My water filter!" she exclaimed.

"What's that for?" asked Charles.

"To filter water so it's safe to drink," Allie answered.

"You filter your water?" asked Charles incredulously.

"Not in the city…" Then Allie was distracted by one of her water bottles she spied in the pile of junk. She eagerly grabbed it, clutching her newly rediscovered possessions to her chest tightly as she rooted for more.

Eventually, she unearthed her backpack, which someone had slashed open with vicious disregard for the zippers. She found several of her tent poles but no actual tent and no sleeping bag. She recovered her cook pot, too. She then gleefully piled her treasure into the damaged backpack. Despite the slash, it stayed in well enough. She'd find duct tape or something later to fix the hole.

"Thank you, Mag. Thank you!" She felt like she could kiss the woman.

Mag smiled broadly and pushed her shoulders back, standing up a little taller, "I helped, didn't I?" Pride was almost visibly radiating from her.

"We could probably pawn summa this stuff, you think?" Charles asked.

"No!" Allie said sharply, clutching the pack to her chest. "I mean, I need it."

"What are you gonna do with all that stuff, anyway?" he asked.

Allie looked down at the contents of the now-dilapidated backpack. He had a point. In the woods, this stuff was vital, but in the city, it wasn't much good. You couldn't start a fire in the park to cook on without drawing the authorities. Water came in bottles and fountains, and tent poles weren't good for much without a tent. But Allie was still loath to let go of any of it, now that she had re-claimed her only possessions in the world. She was starting to get hungry again, though.

"Let's hang onto it for now," she conceded. "I'll sell it if we need to, though."

Charles looked at her dubiously, possibly thinking no money and no booze put them at "need to" already, but Mag was still smiling to herself, not seeming to register the conversation around her, lost in her own reverie.

Allie hoisted the now light pack and started out of the alley. Charles followed. As they began to turn left onto the street, they realized Mag hadn't followed. She was standing back at the pile of chairs where they'd left her, staring off into space, still smiling.

"C'mon, Mag!" Charles shouted irritatedly.

Mag's head turned, and her eyes refocused on Allie and Charles out on the street. Allie thought she looked almost surprised to see them. She shook her head slightly and began walking toward them.

———

Mag knew of a soup kitchen open Thursday through Sunday, so the three of them headed toward it. They each got a bowl of stew, a roll, a small can of fruit cocktail and a bottle of water. They sat at one of the long picnic-style tables with a mishmash of other people — some old, some in their 20s, a couple of mothers with children and one entire family — and ate without pause.

The stew was pretty good, Allie thought. It sure as hell beat gamey rabbit and was a lot easier to procure. She kept her pack pinned between her legs and the bench. When she glanced at the faces around her, most of them looked tired, sick and stressed. A couple of children, who couldn't have been more than two and three years old, chased each other, giggling around the tables. Too young to pick up on the gravity of their situation, which wasn't necessarily a bad thing, Allie thought.

When they'd finished eating, Allie, Charles and Mag got up and left the building, as was required, to make room for more people.

"You going over to the shelter tonight?" Mag asked Charles when they were back outside on the street.

"I hate that place," he muttered. "Think I'll sleep in the park tonight. 'Won't be too cold, I think. Probably won't rain," he said, looking skyward.

Allie noticed a woman standing outside the soup kitchen door next to a huge cardboard box filled with blankets. She was offering them to people coming out of the building. Allie approached her, and the woman held a blanket out to her.

Allie took it and asked, "Can I have two more for my friends?" She gestured toward Charles and Mag.

"Yes, but they have to come get them themselves, " she said, but with a kind smile.

Allie motioned for them to come over, and they each got a

blanket too. Allie was looking forward to sleeping outside again. She'd not relished the idea of spending another night on the floor of the shelter, though she probably would have done it if that's where Charles and Mag were going.

———

Allie, Charles and Mag stayed in the park that night. It was a little chilly, but with the blankets, it was far superior to the shelter. Charles had found his favorite bench — a standard, metal sit-upon tucked behind a copse of trees, hidden from the rest of the park. He'd finished off his bottle and promptly passed out, snoring.

It had been a long day, and between the runs the rabbit meat gave her and a hungry night in the shelter, Allie hadn't slept well in a while. She fell asleep quickly, under her free, warm blanket on the ground, feeling the cool night air brush her face, the sound of crickets in the background. Her backpack made a decent pillow. Despite the hard-packed ground, she didn't wake once during the night.

Allie awoke in the morning, blinking into the light of a new day, taking a few seconds to remember where she was. She lay there, looking at the sky through the trees, blinking her eyes, yawning and stretching, her back stiff from sleeping on the ground. When she felt good and awake, she turned over and saw a blanket lump rising and falling slowly with each of Mag's sleeping breaths. Allie sat up and looked toward the bench. There was Charles's blanket, half hanging on the ground, but no Charles.

Allie got up and walked over to the bench, frowning, studying it as if Charles could be hiding between the slats. She scanned the surrounding area. "Charles?" she called softly so as not to wake Mag.

She began making small circles around their little camp area, looking to see if he'd wandered over and passed out by a tree somewhere, still calling softly. When she returned to her blanket, Mag was sitting up. "Is he gone?" she asked.

"Seems to be, but where would he go? Why would he leave in the middle of the night?"

The empty handle of vodka still lay on its side under the bench, the cap nowhere to be seen.

"Who knows," replied Mag. "He's a drunk, you know," she said matter-of-factly, without a hint of judgment in her voice. "Prob'ly got up havin' to pee or something, then wandered off in the wrong direction. Prob'ly he doesn't even know why."

"Should we wait for him?"

"Nah, no point. Prob'ly doesn't even remember he was here."

Allie was concerned about Charles, but she and Mag had themselves to worry about, too. "You hungry?" Allie asked.

"Gettin' that way. I know a place over on 4th where we can get something."

As they walked, blankets bundled under their arms (Allie had gathered Charles's as well), Allie marveled at how resourceful Mag was. She seemed to know every place in town for food and shelter. "How do you know about all these places to get food?"

"'Been about four years since I left the house. Some other people told me about. Some I just found."

"Mag, um.." Allie had a question that had been nagging her since the day before, but she felt uncomfortable asking it. "Do you like living this way? Outside, I mean, on the street?"

Mag threw back her head and cackled. "Yeah, I just looove sleeping cold in the park and worrying about my shit getting stolen almost every second. It's a blast not knowing where my next meal's gonna be!"

"Sorry, I didn't mean —" Allie was flustered. "I thought since you said you walked away from the house, didn't like people telling you what to do…" Allie couldn't finish her statement. She felt like a jackass.

"I *couldn't* do what I was supposed to do. That doesn't mean I didn't *want* to. Sure, the first several days I was out felt free, but this shit gets old real fast."

Allie had to admit that was true. Aside from being lonely, in a lot of ways, living in the woods was easier. It was coming into town that got her pack taken, and in the woods there were no police to harass you. But as much as she loved the forest, she had come back to civilization because she'd been sick, needed supplies, and she'd needed some companionship, too. Both places were harsh in their own right.

They walked for a while in silence until Allie just had to ask, "Do you ever think about, you know, trying to get a real place to live? Maybe find a job somewhere?"

Mag chuckled, and Allie's face colored, knowing it was at her own naiveté, even if she didn't quite get why.

"Now how'm I supposed to do that? I spend all my time tryin' to eat, stay warm, not get beat up by someone who wants my coat. Where does that leave room for job interviews?

"A while back, I did fill out an application at the grocery to stock shelves, but I didn't have nothin' to put down in the space where it said 'phone number' and 'address,' so how they gonna get in touch with me? I don't think they's too impressed with my appearance, either, based on the side-eye they gave me."

Allie began to see. Even if Mag could somehow manage to get a job, she had some sort of mental illness, based on what she said. How long could she keep it?

They came to a bakery, and Mag led Allie around back. Mag knocked softly on the back door and waited. Allie was just about to say she didn't think anyone had heard when the door opened.

"Hi, Mag! Who's your friend?"

"This is Allie."

"Hi, Allie"

While Mag spent a couple of words introducing her, Allie took in the person standing in the doorway – a girl of about 16. "Just a sec," she said and disappeared back into the store. When she returned, she handed Mag a large brown grocery sack with the top folded down. Then, she reached over to a counter inside and produced two steaming cups of coffee and handed them to Allie.

Allie's eyes went wide. *Coffee!*

"Thank you!" she said graciously.

"Don't worry about it," the girl said, smiling. "Y'all enjoy. I gotta get back before my uncle misses me. He don't like me givin' stuff away. Even though he throws extra away almost every day at the end." She rolled her eyes. The door closed, and Mag and Allie made away with their loot.

The two walked back the way they'd come, stashing the bag out of sight in Allie's torn backpack. They holed up on the edge of the woods, not far from where they'd slept. This was a good spot so as not to attract hungry would-be thieves. As generous as Allie normally was, she was starving again and not keen on sharing with anyone but Mag. And she was hoping to run into Charles.

The bag contained a full dozen doughnuts. Mag and Allie each eagerly consumed their six. The coffee was black, and normally Allie liked a little cream and sugar, but she hadn't had coffee since the internet diner, and it tasted divine.

"Mag?" Allie said through a mouthful of doughnut.

"Mmm?" Mag responded through her own mouthful.

"Thank you. I don't know what I would've done without you in this town. I would've starved."

Mag rolled her eyes but was clearly pleased. Allie wondered when the last time was anyone had thanked Mag for anything.

―――――

As they sat in the aftermath of their doughnut binge, still sipping wonderfully warm coffee in silence, Allie began to think. As hard as finding food in the woods was, it felt less stressful than surviving in the city, worrying about all of the unpredictable people. She was ready to get back to hiking. With any luck, she'd find just a few more supplies in town today and could strike out before dark. She looked at Mag, staring for just a few beats, feeling a twinge of regret. "I gotta get back to the woods."

Mag didn't protest or ask questions. She was probably accustomed to people drifting in and out of her life on whims, Allie thought. She just nodded and said, "I'll help you."

They spent the rest of the morning combing through dumpsters, alleyways and people's personal trash bins for the last few things Allie needed. Mag knew the most likely places, so Allie followed her lead. Once, a man chased them away from his trash cans, shaking his rake at them and yelling as if they were raccoons.

By around noon, Allie had a few various short lengths of rope, one faded bungee cord and a blue tarp that only had one hole in the corner. Mag even found her a faded, yellow and pink quilt as they perused the town junkyard. Once upon a time, someone had lovingly hand-stitched it, perhaps for a baby, Allie thought. Now, it was lying faded and oil-stained amongst the other forgotten detritus. She gratefully stuffed it into her backpack with the other treasures.

The last thing Allie needed was food. While Mag was resourceful when it came to meals, it was hard to get enough to save for later. They went through the dumpsters at the backs of the restaurants and Cars R Us, though, and came up with a few dented cans, a half-loaf of stale-ish bread, some generic hard candies and the biggest score - a large, partial block of cheese that only had one hard end.

Allie's pack weighed her down now. Canned goods and quilts were quite a bit heavier than backpacker-designed sleeping gear and dried foods. She'd used one of the ropes and the bungee cord to compensate for the rip, so her new loot wouldn't fall out.

Mag asked if she wanted one more hot meal before she left, and Allie easily agreed. Now that she had her stuff gathered, she wasn't quite ready to leave Mag, and at this point, she knew better than to turn down a free meal. They headed toward the soup kitchen, which was just opening for the evening.

They heard the place before they could see it. There was a commotion coming from the kitchen's door.

"I'm nottdrunk!" they heard someone yell.

Allie and Mag exchanged glances and approached cautiously.

"Sir, I can't let you in if you're —"

"Fuckyou, I gotta eat!"

It was Charles. Allie saw he was arguing with a younger guy at the door to the soup kitchen. The guy was standing in the doorway, blocking Charle's entrance. Charles was swaying back and forth in front of him. He pawed clumsily at the guardian of the door in a weak attempt to push past him, but the door guy adjusted his body in front of Charles and said, "I can't let you in, sir."

Charles pulled his right arm back in preparation to deck the guy, but he moved like he was underwater. It was like watching a cartoon windup for a punch. Old Bugs Bunny dialog came back to Allie: *Oh, wise guy, eh? Why I oughtta….* Only she didn't laugh.

The younger man easily ducked away from the slow-motion blow and then shoved Charles. He didn't push him very hard, but Charles tumbled backward onto the sidewalk on his back.

"Now go on!" door guy yelled. "I don't want to call the cops on you, but I will if you make me!"

Charles wobbled to his feet. "Fine! Soup tastes like dirty fuckin' socks anyway!" He began weaving down the street in Allie and Mag's direction.

When he got close, Allie stepped in front of him, gently taking his shoulders and trying to look him in the eye. His were cast at the sidewalk below. "Charles! Are you okay? Wait here, okay? I'll get you something to eat and bring it out."

"Getoff me!" He hollered, pushing away from her. He looked Allie in the face, still swaying, eyes unfocused and uncomprehending.

"Charles, it's me, Allie. Come on. We'll help you."

"Who?!" Charles looked at her with utter lack of recognition, then pushed past her and wove off down the street, stumbling against the curb and barely keeping to his feet before shuffling on.

As she watched him, feeling helpless, she said, "I should go after him."

Mag answered softly, "What for, honey? You gonna save him from himself?"

"I guess not," she said, then muttered, as an afterthought, "Maybe someone needs to save *me* from *my*self."

After their meal at the soup kitchen, Allie knew it was time to go if she wanted to put distance between her and the town before dark. And after the incident with Charles, she very much did. They were milling around up the street from the kitchen, Mag smoking a stub of a cigarette she'd found on the sidewalk. Allie could look between the buildings and see her woods. She sighed.

"I gotta get going, Mag." She was eager to be in the quiet of the forest again, but she'd grown attached to Mag in just the past couple of days. "Hey, want to come with me?' she asked, though she knew the answer.

Mag chuckled, as one would when indulging a child's fantasy, "No, but thanks. My place is here. I wouldn't know how to make it out there." She looked into the deep, shaded greenbelt, and a look of apprehension passed over her face.

Allie laughed in return. "Apparently, I don't either. I love the woods, but I keep ending up back in the city."

Impulsively, she reached out and enfolded Mag in a hug. Mag stiffened at first, then gently put her arms around Allie.

"Thank you for everything, Mag. I couldn't have made it without you. I'll miss you."

"Aw, you too. I liked helping. It was nice to feel useful for once."

"See you later," Allie called as she hoisted her tied-together pack and turned toward the woods.

"Bye, Allie," said Mag.

Allie lit off into the woods at a fast pace and only looked back once to see Mag's silhouette in the fading light. It saddened her that she would, in all likelihood, never see her again.

The woods here weren't too thick. The large trees had crowded out the sunlight, preventing much understory growth. Allie hiked quickly and easily to put as much distance between her and civilization as possible. She wished she'd been able to give Mag something in return for all her help. She'd thought about leaving her some of the canned goods they'd found, but truth be told, she couldn't spare it. And Mag had more access to provisions right now than she did.

CHAPTER 11

Day 7

Mitch leaned his head against the back of the couch, staring up at the ceiling as he listened to the phone ring. It was 8am in Minnesota, same as Lime; Jamie ought to be awake now, getting ready for work. Finally, there was a click and the muffled sound of fumbling with voices in the background. Jamie answered.

"Hey, Mitch! What's up? Haven't heard from y'all in a while. 'Started to think you were dead."

"Yeah! Uh, well…" He shrugged his shoulders awkwardly, even though Jamie couldn't see him, but she picked up on his demeanor anyway.

"What's wrong?" Jamie asked, her voice turning sharp.

"Nothing," he responded automatically, then realized it wasn't true. He sucked in breath, preparing for what was inevitably next.

"Why are *you* calling me?"

It was true, though Mitch loved Jamie and they got along great, he didn't normally instigate a phone call. Allie did that. "Jamie, Allie's missing." He leaned back against the couch and exhaled at the ceiling.

"What?! What do mean she's missing? Where'd she go?"

Mitch picked up his head and ran his fingers through his hair. He was no good at delivering bad news like this. He even hated telling clients when their offer on their dream house was outbid. He took a deep breath.

"She walked off into the woods about a week ago —"

"A WEEK ago! And you're just calling me now? Shit, Mitch. I'm on my way."

"Wait, wait! You don't need to come down here." He didn't relish the idea of a house guest at the moment, and what could Jamie do that wasn't already being done? "I'm working with a detective. We've got things under control."

"What do you mean 'under control?' Tell me what happened with my sister."

So he started from the beginning, the day he'd come home from work to find her gone. When he told her about finding Allie's thumb on the cutting board, she lost it.

"What the everliving FUCK?!"

In the background, he could hear Daniel, her husband. "Hon, language!" He was undoubtedly worried their two-year-old twins would pick up their mother's colorful epithets. Jamie's voice fell to a fierce whisper.

"I'm coming whether you want me to or not. I can help. More people, more eyes, more perspectives is better. Besides, I know her."

"You really don't need to come," Mitch protested, though he knew he'd already lost this one. "Having company right now would just complicate things. Besides, you have a family and a job that need you."

"I'll stay in a hotel. Look…I need to come. Whether you need me or not, I can't just sit here hundreds of miles away and wait. There's no way I can focus on work right now. I need to be there."

As much as he wanted Jamie to stay put, he got it. It was probably just like how he felt confined to the house while Allie was out there hell knows where. "Okay, let me know when your flight gets in. I'll pick you up."

"Thanks, Mitch. I'll text you. See you soon."

"Jamie?"

"Yeah?"

"You can stay here. If you want to."

"I don't —"

"I *want* you to."

"Thank you. Talk soon."

The line went dead, leaving Mitch to stare at the ceiling. As much as he'd like to pretend he was just fine by himself, it would

be nice to have family around. And Jamie was the closest thing
he had.

———

"What the hell happened to your foot?" Jamie asked. She'd
managed to get a flight out that same morning right after talking
to Mitch. She hadn't noticed the boot until they were getting out
of the car at the house. Mitch popped the trunk, and Jamie
pulled her small suitcase out of it.

"Long story. Let's go inside."

After Jamie stashed her things in the guest room — the one
that would've been the baby's — they situated themselves on the
couch with some coffee. Mitch asked, "How was the flight?"

"Fuck the flight. What happened?" Mitch had put her off
with small talk in the car, which hadn't been hard since Jamie
spent most of the ride furiously texting and emailing from her
phone for work. She did marketing for a small but growing in-
dustrial design company. They'd been hired to completely re-
think and overhaul a line of ambulances, and the product rollout
was imminent, she'd said, apologizing for ignoring him.

Mitch had always admired Jamie's directness and the fact
that, despite having toddlers, she still cussed like a college kid.
Mitch filled in the gaps he'd left on the phone, which included
everything that had happened after finding Allie's thumb.

"I've been sitting here," he concluded, "in this boot, trying to figure out what's going on in her head, you know? I worry that she's sick or badly hurt or…" He sighed and stared off at the wall, not really seeing it. "I thought I knew her, inside and out, after all these years together. I guess there's a side she never showed me. D'you know she was married before? To a Chris somebody?"

Jamie paused, eyeing Mitch, seeming to weigh him in her thoughts.

"Why didn't she tell me? It wouldn't have bothered me."

Jamie's eyebrows went up, "Really? Are you sure?"

"Of course!" Mitch answered a little defensively. Because suddenly, he wasn't so sure. He felt insecurity bubbling in his gut. *Why doesn't she want to marry* me?

Instead, he asked, "Why'd they break up? Did he do something to her?" He wondered if that was the reason she didn't want to talk about it, didn't want to open old wounds.

Jamie sighed. "Look, these really aren't my secrets to tell. It's not that I don't want to, but it's not my place."

"Jamie, please. I'm desperate here. Maybe it has something to do with why she left. Help me out."

She looked at him for a long time, and he could see the wheels turning. She was trying to decide something. "Mitch, I'm going to tell you some things, but that's because you already know the basic facts. It's driving me nuts how you're getting the details wrong. You've made some pretty big assumptions here."

"What do you mean?"

"Chris was Allie's wife. You assumed Chris is a man, but it was short for Christine, not that it really should matter. She's a woman."

"I got that! I just…I'm surprised, that's all." He was more than surprised, though. He was thoroughly confused and didn't know what to make of this. Was Allie gay? Had their whole relationship been a lie?

Jamie took a sip of her coffee and settled back into the couch, getting comfortable. "In high school, Allie only dated boys, as far as I know. Then, in college, she started dating girls sometimes, too. She really fell for Chris. They were together all. the. time.

She paused for another sip. "I liked Chris well enough, but it sorta drove me nuts. I never got to spend time with just Allie. They got married Allie's senior year of college; Chris was already out and working, and then they moved to Dallas when Allie got out of school. It lasted about two years. They seemed to be doing well, and they were even talking about having kids. Then, all of a sudden, Allie moved out.

"They got divorced, and Allie moved back to Austin to 'start over,' she said. When you two got together, she told the family not to mention Chris. She said she didn't see any sense in dragging you into her painful past; she didn't want to upset you. I didn't really get it, and I'm sure there's more to it than that, but she's my sister, so…" Jamie shrugged.

"I knew she dated someone named Chris in college, but she

didn't tell me anything else about him — her. Am I an asshole for assuming Chris was a guy?

Jamie laughed, "Oh, you're an asshole, all right, but not because of that."

"What do you mean?" Mitch feigned offense. This was a schtick he and Jamie had done before, and it made him smile in spite of himself.

"No, but seriously," Jamie continued, "No, it doesn't. I'm sure Allie wanted you to make that assumption. She doesn't like to be untruthful, but she's all about the lie of omission. She probably deliberately avoided pronouns. That's what she did with our parents at first.

"More coffee?" Mitch went to get up for the pot in the kitchen.

"Let me get it, gimpy," Jamie said. "Actually, I could go for a glass of wine. It's afternoon, isn't it? Got anything?"

"Just whiskey."

"That doesn't sit well with me ever since I had the twins — heartburn," she said, her hand rubbing her chest in grimacing anticipation.

"There's a bar around the corner, walking distance. It's pretty divey, but —"

"Perfect. Let's drive, though. You don't look like you need to be walking anywhere, even around the corner."

———

They sat at a sticky table in the corner of the small pub, a pilsner in a frosty mug in front of Mitch, a chardonnay in a slim wine glass for Jamie. The decor wasn't much, but they took pride in how they served their drinks. A forgettable playlist droned in the background. They ignored it along with the few other patrons playing pool and throwing darts at one in the afternoon on a weekday.

Jamie looked around. "Does anyone work around here? How is it everyone has time to hang at the bar in the middle of the workday?"

Mitch searched the faces of the other people in the bar and didn't see anyone he knew, which was rare. "A lot of people work from home and have flexible schedules."

Given the probable age of the couple at the bar, they were likely retired and doing whatever the hell they wanted. Mitch refocused the conversation. He wasn't done with Chris.

"Do you know where Chris is now?"

Jamie didn't answer. She just looked at him unblinkingly as if she were sizing him up. It made Mitch uncomfortable, prompting him to fill the silence with explanation.

"I'd like to meet him…her. Jeez, old habits die hard."

"Do you really think that's a good idea? How could that possibly help?"

"I don't know, but if I could just get in Allie's head, maybe it would help me find her. You never know. It might help."

"Good luck with that," she smirked at Mitch but then conceded, "I have an address. It's not too far from Dan and me in Minneapolis, actually."

"No shit, really? Hell of a coincidence."

"Not really. Right before the divorce, they were planning on moving there. Chris had a job opportunity, and Allie was looking forward to being close to Dan and me." She smiled wistfully. "But they split up, and Chris decided to take the job anyway.

"Here, I'll text you the address." As she fiddled with her phone, she said, "If you do go see her, know that Chris can be a little volatile."

"Yeah? I thought you said you liked her"

"I did. I do. She was actually really cool, but I don't think she and my sister were a good match. Chris kind of freaked out when Jamie left, even though it was Chris who did the breaking up. I'm not sure how she'd react to you showing up unannounced. Maybe it'd be no big deal, but..."

"Okay, thanks. I'll be careful."

Mitch and Jamie booked the same flight back to Minnesota two days later after Mitch sloughed off some of his responsibilities on junior realtors. Jamie realized that, truthfully, she couldn't do a lot to help in Lime, and her phone was constantly pinging with emails from work. Since Mitch was headed up to see Chris anyway, she figured she might as well fly home.

Jamie slept most of the flight, and Mitch tried to watch a movie, but he kept getting distracted by his thoughts. He imagined what Allie's life with Chris might have been like and wondered why she had left so seemingly abruptly. It was odd that even Jamie didn't know the details. He was anxious to meet Chris and find out.

They took a cab from the airport and arrived at Jamie and Dan's house on the outskirts of Minneapolis, where they'd moved from Austin three years ago for Jamie's job, near 11pm. Dan greeted them at the door.

"Hey, man. Good to see you," Dan said, giving Mitch a hug. Mitch found himself tensing in surprise at first, not realizing they were on hugging terms, but then relaxed. "Y'all look exhausted." He hugged Jamie, too. He hadn't lost his Texas twang. "I'm sorry to hear about Allie. I can't imagine…"

"I know," said Mitch. "Thank you." Mitch always felt comfortable around Dan. He was the kind of person who always seemed to know what to say and just how to say it.

Inside the house, they tiptoed and whispered so as not to wake the twins. Mitch took a shower and fell into the guest bed, drifting off to sleep almost immediately.

CHAPTER 12

Day??

Hate fucking rain, Allie thought. It had been raining for two days straight. She'd managed to stay mostly dry with the blue tarp, wrapping it around herself as she hiked or huddled close to the ground when she rested.

She used to like rain — loved sitting inside and watching it out the window, curling up with a book and a cup of coffee. When you lived outside, rain just sucked.

It was important to stay dry, both for her health and comfort, and she mostly had, but the biggest discomfort was that she was bored. In light of the downpour, she camped more than she hiked because it was easier to stay dry when she was still, and she didn't have anywhere to be anyway, but she couldn't make a fire.

She unfastened the ropes and bungee cords from her torn pack to rig the tarp over her in a makeshift tent, wrapping part of it underneath her to sit or lie on. She lay there, staring out at the rain, making up stories in her head. She'd lost the few sheets of paper she'd commandeered back at the internet café. She had no books, no cards, and only her brain for company.

She'd caught a mild cold while in the city with Charles and Mag. She was congested and had a cough — nothing terrible, but it added to her sense of gloom and despair. She didn't know where she was going. For the first time since she'd left, she felt truly aimless. She'd have to get back to civilization soon to get food, but then what?

She had always relished solitude when it came, but now she was lonely. She missed Mitch. She missed her mom and Jamie; they didn't see each other often, but she rarely went more than a few days without talking or texting with them. She missed Mag and Charles and having someone to talk to, period.

One morning, after she'd been away from the city for some days, Allie awoke. She sniffled and coughed a little. Her cold was still there but getting better. She laid on her back and stared at the blue tarp rigged over her head, tied to two trees just the right distance apart. Under the quilt and the layer of tarp she lay on was a soft cushion of fallen leaves. One advantage to this life: she could spend hours looking for the perfect spot to camp. What else did she have to do?

As she stared at the light of a new day filtering through the blueness of the tarp, she began to inhale and exhale in slow, deep breaths. It had finally stopped raining. Only the trees dripped on her homemade tent. She knew where she needed to go.

Allie packed up her gear, made even heavier because it was soaked with rainwater. She headed out, munching the last of her stale bread and cheese, and she hiked. She was going to need a bus ticket.

CHAPTER 13

Day 10

Mitch was standing on Chris's porch, ready to knock but hesitating. He had no idea what he was about to uncover. There was this whole part of Allie's life he knew very little about, a whole part of her he didn't know, and it made him uneasy to find out, to shatter the image he had of her.

He took a few deep breaths and tried to steel himself, but the door flung open before he could muster the courage to knock.

"Mitch?" She stared at him with an almost accusatory countenance.

"Oh! Hi, yes, I'm Mitch. Um, nice to meet you." He recovered quickly and extended his hand toward Chris, but she was already turning away from the door and walking down the hall.

"Come on in," she mumbled over her shoulder.

Feeling awkward, Mitch wiped his hands on his jeans and followed her to the living room. It was a small house with an amicable amount of clutter in it: a pile of mail on the desk in the corner, cat toys on the floor, a mug on the table. It reminded Mitch of Allie, and he wondered how many of the habits he thought of as uniquely hers came from Chris.

Suddenly, he wasn't sure what the point of this was. Chris hadn't even seen Allie in years. "Look, I just found out that y'all were married. She never told me, and it turns out there may be a lot of things she didn't tell me. I just thought if we talked, maybe you would know something that would help. Maybe not. I don't know. But I'm kind of at a loss, and you're the only lead I have."

That wasn't exactly true. He had Tyler and Aiden, but he was pretty sure they'd told him everything they had, and unless he figured out how to commune with the dead, Gentry wasn't going to be any help at all.

Mitch stared back at Chris for a few moments, waiting. Then, she sighed heavily, unfolded herself from her chair and went to the kitchen.

"Do you like tea?" she called.

Clattering noises came from the next room, and Chris returned with two steaming mugs, handing one to Mitch. He thanked her, blew on it and sipped. It was actually pretty good — spicy.

Chris put her mug down on the table between them. "I really didn't want to like you, but you seem pathetically desperate."

Mitch tried to hide his indignation at "pathetically" and asked, "Then why meet me?"

"Morbid curiosity, I guess." She shrugged and stared at him. "We were married for two years until she fucked it all up."

Mitch raised an eyebrow and waited.

"Allie wanted kids. I wasn't sure I was ready, if I'd ever be ready, but she wore me down. We were just starting to explore our options — adoption, a sperm donor or whatever. She was really excited about it."

Mitch tried to wait her out again, but he couldn't stand it, so he caved. "Then what?"

"Then, she got pregnant."

———

Mitch was completely confused, as if someone had just told him one plus one did not actually equal two. "What? But how ——"

"She fucked a guy, genius." Chris picked up her mug but didn't put it to her lips. She stared into it, swirling the tea gently as if trying to divine something from the leaves.

"I came home from work one day, and she was sitting on the floor of the bathroom crying. I thought she was sick. She had a plastic stick in her hand. I knelt down in front of her and asked her what was wrong. She was crying so hard, and I thought someone was dead or something. Then, she handed me the stick. I didn't even know what it was until she told me."

"So what happened? How did she…"

"Get knocked up? She was taking this art class at night. They'd all gone out for drinks after class one time, and she ended up back at his apartment." She let out a sharp, cynical breath. "I remember how late she'd gotten home that evening. I didn't have a fucking clue; I just thought she was making friends."

"So then what?"

Chris laughed sharply and rolled her eyes toward the ceiling. "She actually convinced me — I really can't believe it now — to keep the baby."

"What?!" he asked. *Did Allie have a kid?* His heartbeat quickened.

"But she miscarried," Chris continued.

"Oh."

"Honestly, I was relieved. I know that's not a great thing to say, but I'd finally agreed to keep the baby because it made sense on paper. It's what we'd been planning anyway. But that child would have been a perpetual reminder of what she did. I wasn't going to get over it.

"After she miscarried, we just couldn't get it to work anymore. We went to counseling, we talked, we fought, but I couldn't get over the fact that she'd disregarded our marriage for a one-fucking-night stand. I started getting migraines all the time.

"In the end, I told her I just couldn't do it. She moved out. I ended it, but I felt like she was the one who left first."

It began to make sense to Mitch why Allie seemed to see miscarriage coming. He felt like he was on a precipice, as if he had finally glimpsed a small slice of who Allie actually was. And he was realizing there was a lot more there that he couldn't see.

Finally, Chris filled the silence in which Mitch had been ruminating. "How long have y'all been married?"

"We're not, technically. " He sighed. "Allie never wanted to."

"Oh."

Mitch looked at Chris and saw that her hard demeanor had softened, and she was looking at him with a subtle but knowing sympathy. They just sat there, then, the silence now feeling more comfortable — *two sad sacks in a living room*, Mitch thought, pining for a woman neither of them apparently knew.

———

Mitch didn't linger at Jamie and Daniel's. When he got back to their place, he booked a flight home for later that day, inspired by Jamie's decisive action. He thanked Dan for letting him stay and promised to get in touch soon if he found out anything new about Allie.

Mitch wanted to rehash what he'd learned from Chris and see if Dan knew anything about Allie's first miscarriage. He and

Jamie were dating by then, Mitch thought. But Dan was feeding the twins lunch, or rather, Max was eating while Jenna methodically smashed each half-grape onto her placemat with her thumb.

"Man, Jamie's going to be sorry she missed you. 'Sure you can't stay for dinner?"

Mitch told Dan he really needed to get home, though he wasn't sure for what. There wasn't much more he could do to find Allie, and he was too distracted to work. He just needed to be there, nearer to Allie, or at least to where he'd last seen her, now that he'd followed up on the Chris lead.

"Say 'bye' to Uncle Mitch," Dan said to the twins.

"Bye-eeee!" called Jenna. Max didn't say anything but grinned devilishly at Mitch as he waved from the door and left. He smiled as he carried his overnight bag down the steps. The kids' unabashed joy made him feel a little lighter as he walked toward the waiting Uber.

On the flight back to Austin, Mitch had plenty of time to think. His mind wandered, pondering the twins and what it would be like to be a parent full-time. He knew it would be hard, but he looked forward to it. He wanted that chance someday. The thought of it not ever happening gave him a heavy, hollow feeling in the pit of his stomach, something that felt like remorse for something that hadn't happened yet.

He inevitably worked his way back around to Allie. He didn't know what to make of what he'd learned from Chris, except for the first time, he was wondering if there was someone else. Had Allie really left on a whim, as it seemed, or was she on the way to meet someone? The thought filled him with a weird mixture of anxiety, anger and dismay. He tried to shove those feelings away. After all, there was no evidence whatsoever (aside from her past with Chris) that Allie was cheating on him.

This won't go on forever, he reassured himself. Allie was bound to turn up somewhere eventually. She'd get in touch with Jamie at the very least, and Jamie would tell Mitch if she heard from her…right?

Mitch tried to sleep on the plane, but his brain wouldn't let him. He knew now he'd been overly confident in how well he knew Allie. By the time they landed, he was itching to get home and search the house.

———

As soon as he was off the plane, he texted Murphy and asked her to meet him at his house around eight. That gave him a couple of hours to search. He'd done little more than glance at the clutter in the house since Allie disappeared. It was time to be more thorough. He felt a little guilty going through her things, like he was violating her privacy, but his need to know won out over propriety.

He went through her nightstand first and found little — used Kleenexes, chapstick, old issues of *Psychology Today* and *Zoetrope*. There was nothing of consequence in her bathroom drawers either, so he moved to the living room. He began looking through Allie's piles of books, searching for a pattern in the titles or the subject matter — mostly fiction, ranging from classics to true crime to fantasy and sci-fi, with a few non-fiction histories mixed in.

He plopped down on the couch and tried to take a wider view, surveying the room. The coffee table was a mess of mugs and glasses he'd left there. Housekeeping hadn't been a priority as of late. Mixed in with the dirty cups was the latest issue of *Hill Country News*, still in its bag, a few pens, a yellow notebook.

The notebook. He snatched it up. He realized that he'd seen Allie writing in it from time to time, but he'd not really paid attention to it until now. He thumbed through the lined pages. It was full of Allie's writing, dates at the tops of some of the pages.

Mitch felt grandly stupid. Murphy, who didn't even know Allie, had intuitively known she would have a journal. He lived under the same fucking roof, and it had taken him this long to find it.

He hobbled to the kitchen to pour himself a drink. He set the glass on the kitchen table, sat down with the notebook and began to read.

As he read, his excitement slowly faded. He didn't know what he'd expected to find — some earth-shattering secret that her real name was Mark and she was in the witness protection program or something — but it was pretty mundane. She missed her sister, working at the newspaper was wearing on her, she was frustrated about not finding time to write. She wanted a dog, no maybe a cat, no maybe that would be too much work… There were things about their relationship, about Mitch wanting to get married, but nothing he didn't already know.

Mitch read carefully at first, looking for meaning in every scrawled word and piece of punctuation. Then, he started skimming. Finally, he slammed the notebook and sighed. It was useless — no mention of wanting to run away or hurting herself, no deep secrets, not even the ones he'd learned as of late, no secret affairs, thank god. Mitch rested his forehead on the glossy yellow surface of the notebook, breathing, thinking. *Allie, help me. Where did you go?*

A knock on the door startled him out of his trance. "Hello?" Murphy called from the door. He'd forgotten she was coming. He glanced at the clock and was surprised to find it was already a few minutes past eight.

Murphy dropped her bag by the table. She glanced at Mitch's whiskey. "Mind if I have one of those? It's been a long day."

She collected his glass from the table and went to the counter. It occurred to him that it should be odd, her making drinks in his house, but it felt comfortable all the same. He trusted her.

Murphy returned with the drinks and sat across from Mitch, looking at him expectantly.

Mitch recounted everything he'd learned in Minnesota and Chris and the miscarriage.

"Well…shit." Murphy stared at him. "It's just like a soap opera or something — infidelity, accidental pregnancy, hidden marriages."

"Is that your professional opinion?"

"It's my personal one. I'm off duty. Wouldn't be having a drink if I weren't. Mitch, this isn't an official case anymore. At this point, I'm just helping out a friend and using some of my professional resources."

Murphy went on to tell him how the DNA test had finally come back on the hairs found in the cave. She said they were Allie's, which Mich had expected. He'd almost forgotten about the hairs. They didn't seem so useful now. But then, Murphy said, "They were someone else's as well. We matched the others to Gentry."

Mitch swallowed a lump in his throat, thinking he was about done with surprises for the day. His head suddenly felt hot, burning from the inside.

"Most likely," Murphy was saying, "Gentry was in the cave at some point, maybe with Allie. And then he was dead."

"Jesus Christ." Mitch drained his drink and went to refill it.

When he sat back at the table, she continued. "Something

else. I talked to the boys, Aiden and Tyler. I finally caught up to them at the Sonic drive-up. It took a bit of convincing, but they were willing to talk as long as I didn't call their parents. Tyler seems terrified of his dad. Did you know Gentry's his brother?"

"Yeah," Mitch responded sheepishly.

"Listen," she said, "I know a lot about what goes on in this town, and not just from working it. I used to live over on Live Oak, so the odds of you being able to keep stuff from me for long are slim."

"Yeah, I heard you used to live here. Lianna Buckman told me when I went to get the note from her."

Murphy laughed. "I should've guessed. News travels fast."

"And gossip faster."

Murphy raised her glass to Mitch, and they clinked. "Cheers." They polished off the rounds, and Murphy made them another.

"Anyway," she continued, "I remember when Gentry graduated high school and then went pretty much nowhere. He hung around town, working at the Nutty Brown Café and then at the gas station next door when he got fired. That was before I made detective. We picked him up on the regular for public intoxication, disturbing the peace, general being a drunken asshole stuff."

"Sexual assault?" Mitch asked pointedly.

She paused and sighed. "Yeah, but I know what you're thinking. I can understand why you're worried, but Gentry was anything but stealthy. We picked him up once for groping a woman in a bar. When we got there, she'd already incapacitated him with a hard knee to the crotch. He was rolling around on the floor hollering."

"But what about if it weren't in a public space, like say, a cave?"

"I get your point. You're right; you never know. But try not to get upset about what may or may not have happened. It's not going to help us find her." She took a sip and continued her abbreviated history of Gentry.

He'd lost his job at the gas station, too. His parents, embarrassed, kicked Gentry out of the house; a deadbeat adult son hadn't looked good for the mayor. So he moved into a trailer outside of town. There were rumors he made his money selling weed and cooking and selling meth. His family had effectively disowned him, though he and his brother were still hanging out sometimes.

They paused, both in their own thoughts for a moment, then Murphy nodded at the notebook still lying in front of Mitch on the table. "You going to tell me about that?"

"Oh yeah. I found Allie's journal. You were right."

Murphy raised her eyebrows, but instead of saying *I told you so*, she asked, "Have you read it?"

"Yeah, a lot of it. There's not much there — nothing earth-shattering — just ramblings about work and her sister and stuff. There were things about us but nothing I didn't already know.

And nothing about why she'd been pretending to go to work for over a month."

Murphy looked at Mitch thoughtfully. "Can I read it?"

He shrugged. "Sure." He passed the notebook over the table and got up for more drinks while she began to read. Murphy covered her glass and shook her head. She was already engrossed in Allie's journal and obviously finding it more fascinating than Mitch had.

He sat there while she read, sipping his drink and fiddling with his phone. Then he got up to go to the bathroom and wash a few dishes that were in the sink. He was restless, wondering if Murphy saw something he didn't in those pages. Finally, she put it down with a slap, and Mitch returned to his chair expectantly.

"You really don't see it, do you?" Murphy said, her eyes boring holes in his.

"What?"

She shook her head as if trying to clear it. "You were looking for some smoking gun, some evidence she'd been hiding an evil alter ego, but what's going on with her is right here," she said, pointing down at the yellow book. "She's unhappy, Mitch, and she has been for a long time — not depths-of-depression, suicidal unhappy, but the slow subtle kind, the kind that wears on you for years."

"But she *seemed* happy," Mitch said quietly. He felt lost for a split second, and then his inner hackles rose. "How would you know, anyway? You never even met her!"

But Murphy was unperturbed by his rising voice. "I'm sure she did. Lots of people *seem* happy. She probably even fooled herself into thinking she was. But there's a theme here, the same use of language, words like 'unsatisfied' and 'lonely' and 'unfulfilled' over and over again. She's not screaming her unhappiness from the rooftops, but this journal spans a year-and-a-half, and she basically talks about the same thing the entire time. And it was going on even before that. Did you read this one?"

She paused to flip through the notebook toward the end where Mitch had given up. "Here." She turned it so he could see. "She talks about the time she got arrested, the one in her record I told you about. She remembers it, and she wasn't walking the wrong way by accident. She says she wanted to go home, only "home wasn't where home was supposed to be."

January 23

I read an article the other day about a guy who got hit walking down Highway 71 in the middle of the night. He was high as a kite; he's in intensive care and probably won't make it. It got me thinking about that time I got arrested back in college. I was drunk, yes, and I was wandering down a road — not a good idea, I'll admit. When they picked me up, and I said I just wanted to go home, they told me I was going the wrong way. Town was that way. But I wasn't. I knew where campus was, I knew where my dorm room was, but I didn't want to go there. And I didn't want to go to my parents' house. I was headed out — out to wherever I didn't know, but I wanted out — to opt out of life. No more school, no job, no house to take care of or bills to pay. I did it because I was drunk, but the thoughts behind it were stone-cold sober. Home wasn't where home was supposed to be.

Mitch put the notebook down. "I don't really know what this means," he confessed. His irritation at Murphy faded as quickly as it had arisen, as he had to admit, *he* didn't even know Allie. Who was he to talk?

"She didn't write it for anyone but herself, so it isn't clear, but can't you tell? She's been dissatisfied with regular life for at least fifteen years."

They sat in silence for a while. Mitch's shoulders slumped. He felt like he was sinking into his chair. He couldn't help but take it personally, as if he'd failed her in some way. He was feeling a little drunk. He wondered if Allie felt the same way with Chris, if everything she'd done — the one-night stand, getting pregnant, moving in with him — had been her way of trying to figure it out, trying to make herself happy in the workaday world. He shook his head to clear his thoughts. He didn't want to go down this rabbit hole right now. It was too hard.

He got up again, this time returning with the bottle. "So tell me about you, Murphy. What's your story? You used to live around here?"

"Yeah, my husband and I lived over on Live Oak in that weird old house. Is the scaffolding still there? I haven't been by in a long time. We had these grand ideas about totally renovating it."

"So you were married?"

"I met Brian when I was twenty-five, and I had just started

at the department. Man, I thought he was great," she said, remembering with a smile. "Spontaneous, adventurous. He actually got me to go bungee jumping. I was terrified." She laughed. "He was always the life of the party. I thought we made a good team. I was on top of our finances, into details and planning. He kept me from turning into a habit-encrusted hermit."

"So what happened?"

"We got engaged. Then I got pregnant. At our wedding, my mom kept telling me, 'You don't have to do this.' At the time, I didn't understand why. We made so much sense together on paper, and with a baby on the way…"

"You have a kid?" Mitch made a mental note to stop being surprised when people said the words "pregnant" or "baby."

She nodded. "Mariah. She's eight. She's with my dad right now."

"I had no idea you had a kid."

"Why would you?" Murphy asked with honest surprise. "Anyway, when Mariah was born, I kind of lost steam with the house. I remember I'd look at Brian in the living room sometimes and think, *What's wrong with me? Something is missing.*

"I tried to talk to him about it, but I did a shitty job of expressing myself. I felt like I was being dragged along. I went to work, picked up Mariah from Dad's and came home to whatever plans Brian had made for the evening. He ALWAYS had plans. He wanted us to drag her along to the movies, to dinner, to clubs with friends. I was the one who sat with her while she slept on my shoulder, both of us wishing we were at home. I can't believe I put up with that, to look back on it."

"Why did you?" Mitch asked.

Murphy paused to take a sip of her drink and shrugged. "I was younger then.

"One evening, I came home from work, and I could tell something was wrong. I thought someone died or something. I didn't have a fucking clue," she laughed ruefully.

"He said, 'It isn't working,'" and then blabbered on about how he just needed to get out, I was too hard to be around. And the whole time, I'm thinking, *I should be more upset about this.*

"He left that night. Mariah doesn't remember him, so it's not a big deal to her, at least not yet."

"Really? He hasn't been in touch with her at all?" Mitch couldn't imagine having a child of his own out in the world and not knowing them.

"Yep. My dad's retired, so he picks Mariah up from school. My mom died a few years back from an aneurysm."

"I'm sorry."

"Yeah, me too. I miss her." She stared into her drink. Then she looked back at Mitch and shook her head to clear her watery eyes. "I gotta get going. It's late." She stood and wobbled slightly. "Whoa, maybe I better have some water first."

While she filled a glass from the fridge, Mitch studied her. It was weird how closely they'd been working on finding Allie, on his own, very personal life, and he'd just now learned about hers.

He felt embarrassed he hadn't asked her about herself earlier. "Murphy, what's your first name?"

She laughed. "Murphy *is* my first name. My mom insisted on naming me after *Murphy Brown*."

"Really? That's so cool."

"When I was a kid, I didn't think so, but I've grown into it. Most cops use their last names, but I got tired of everyone mispronouncing mine."

"What is it?"

"Svoboda. It's Czech, or at least that's what my dad always says."

"That doesn't sound so hard."

"You should see it written down," she said and rolled her eyes. Anyway, I always felt more like a Murphy."

Mitch laughed. "Fair enough," he said. Murphy looked different to him now, and not just because he was a little in his cups. She was starting to seem less like a detective and more like a whole person. "Listen, if you're not good to drive, you can stay here."

"I might take you up on that."

"Let's go sit on the couch. I need to put my foot up." Mitch wasn't ready to call it a night yet. They adjourned to the living room, he with the remains of his drink and Murphy with a second glass of water. She turned to him on the couch as they sat.

"One thing I don't understand about Allie. How do you think she cut off her *left* thumb?"

Mitch's addled brain had a little trouble switching topics, but when it did, he was glad someone was finally as mystified by that as he was. "I don't know. She was prone to using her right hand sometimes. She said there were never left-handed scissors growing up, so she had to learn to use her right. But I never saw her do it with a knife. Even if she did it on purpose, which I can't imagine, why not do the right one?"

"Maybe she sort of did do it on purpose."

"What do you mean?"

"We see it sometimes when we respond to accidents, car wrecks mostly. You interview the person and just get a sense… they're being reckless with their own life, like maybe they half want to die. Tempting fate."

"You think Allie was suicidal?!"

"No, no, but maybe she was tempting fate all the same. Daring something to happen to shake things up."

"I don't know. Why not just leave, then? Cutting your dominant fucking thumb off doesn't make any sense."

"Yeah, in a way, it does make sense. And anyway, it doesn't have to."

"Huh? You're losing me."

She smiled. "I can tell."

Murphy was staring right at him, and for the first time, Mitch noticed her eyes were hazel. She'd helped him more than anyone else through all of this, and she was here on her own time. That meant something, didn't it? She was here, on his couch, by choice, not by duty. And she was looking at him, her eyes on his. They were both alone, he thought, and here they were, together.

Mitch slowly placed his drink on the table without breaking eye contact with her, which was sort of a trick, considering how drunk he was now feeling. He was also feeling something else, something like gratitude but more. Here was someone who actually wanted to be with him, someone who was interested in his happiness.

Murphy was still looking at him. *She feels it, too,* he thought.

He inhaled deeply and leaned toward her, taking in the sultry scent of whiskey on her breath, anticipating the softness of her lips. Then, Murphy's hands were on his chest.

"Whoah, tiger." She pressed him away from her.

"No?" He blinked, confused, "But I thought —"

Murphy chuckled. "You dudes always do. You gotta make it weird, don't you? I should go."

She stood and went searching for her bag in the kitchen. Mitch sat slumped on the couch, feeling drunk and embarrassed. "You can still stay here," he said. "It's okay. We have a guest bedroom."

"No. Dad is waiting, and Mariah will be expecting me in the morning."

"It's late, and it's raining again. You're not exactly sober. Call your dad, stay here. No ulterior motive, I promise." He was desperate to make up for trying to kiss her now, to prove he wasn't a total idiot.

Murphy paused from digging through her bag for her keys, rubbed her eyes and looked wearily back at him. "Okay…okay."

After she was set up in the guest room, Mitch crossed the hall to his own — the one that was feeling less and less like his and Allie's. He knew he was going to be hungover and feel like an asshole in the morning.

———

When Mitch woke up, it was well past ten o'clock. Murphy was gone, but she'd left a note:

Thanks for letting me stay. I enjoyed our conversation last night.

-M

He downed some water and ibuprofen for his headache and made a cup of coffee. He wandered out on the back porch with it and stared at the woods. He remembered, hazily, trying to kiss Murphy the night before. He groaned inwardly and felt his face grow hot with latent embarrassment. He would have to apologize.

It was a beautiful day — the kind Allie would love. Mitch wondered if she was enjoying it somewhere. He'd been seriously neglecting work, which was both a perk and the downside of being his own boss. The pile of mail was steadily growing on the kitchen counter, as he hadn't bothered to open any of it since Allie left. It was always just grocery store circulars and glossy ads for dentists, anyway.

He pondered what Murphy had said the night before about Allie's journal. He still didn't see what she did, or maybe he did, but he didn't understand why Allie couldn't schlep along like everyone else. Sure, work wasn't fun, and there were bills to pay, but there were good things, too, right? *There's us*, he thought. *Am I not enough for her?*

As he went over all that he knew in his head — Tyler and Aiden's stories, Murphy's take on the journal, Gentry and whatever happened in the cave — he couldn't make sense of it, couldn't put it all together. He didn't know where to go from here.

———

Two weeks had passed since Mitch read Allie's journal, and he felt no closer to finding her. He'd tried to get some work done, had shown a few houses, but he was having a hard time concentrating. He found himself resentful when clients would call to ask perfectly legitimate questions. He wanted to spend his time looking for Allie, though he had to admit to himself he didn't know where to go with it next.

Murphy, who honestly seemed to appreciate his apology when he made it, had stayed in touch. Mitch was relieved that the evening he'd tried to kiss her hadn't made things too awkward between them. He was still embarrassed he misinterpreted things in a moment of drunken neediness, but what he really needed was her friendship.

Murphy was the one who suggested he get back to work and take his mind off Allie for a while. "I'm not saying give up," she'd said when he protested, "just take a step back for a while. You might see things more clearly."

He was trying to take a step back, but he was failing spectacularly.

One afternoon, he spotted the pile of mail he'd been too distracted to sort through and decided to tackle it. Most of it was trash. Near the bottom of the pile, after sorting out a couple of bills and reserving the rest for the recycle bin, he found a hand-addressed letter. It was the same shaky writing from Allie's note to the Buckmans. There was no return address. He tore the flap open. The letter itself was typed.

Dear Mitch,

I'm sorry it's taken so long for me to get in touch with you. I know you must be confused and probably angry, too. It's hard to explain why I left. When the knife slipped and I cut my hand, something snapped. Something that had been brewing in me for a long time.

I want you to know that I'm okay. My hand healed fine, and I'm learning to get by without my thumb. I don't know why I can't just live life like everyone else, go to work, get by, grin and bear it, but I can't. I can't do life the way you want to.

I'm sorry for how I left. I do love you. I'm writing this because I thought you deserved to know what happened. I'm in Galveston right now, and it's just like I always imagined it would be, living near the beach. I bike to work every day. It feels free.

If you want to come out and visit, that would be okay. I miss you.

Love, Allie

There was an address with an apartment number written below her signature.

Mitch crumpled the letter in his hand and threw it with all the force he could muster. She was right about at least one thing; he was angry at her for putting him through this, for being so irresponsible.

He looked down at his foot still in the boot and used it to kick the kitchen cabinet, leaving a huge dent. "Fucking GREAT!"

As he stomped through the house, slamming things around, pretending to tidy up but really just venting his freshly awakened anger, a litany ran through his head:

Selfish, irresponsible, flighty, inconsiderate, impulsive…

He realized this anger was unproductive, but he didn't care. He slammed his fist into a painting of sailboats on the water — one Allie had always loved. The painting was done on wood and broke clean in half, allowing Mitch's fist to hit the stud in the wall behind it. "MotherFUCKER!"

Hand throbbing, he slammed the back door open and planted himself in a chair on the back porch, panting with effort and anger. As the anger ebbed away, his breathing slowed, and he began to study his now swollen knuckles. He felt tears well up in his eyes as his anger morphed into grief. Had he lost her? It felt like he had, and he didn't understand why. He put his head in his hands and let the tears come.

CHAPTER 14

Day 38

The wind whipped through Allie's hair as she pedaled along the coastal road on her beach cruiser. She'd always wanted one of these bikes. She finally had a reason to own one. The day was gray but warm, even though it was only March. Spring was edging in, and she could see small sprinklings of yellow wildflowers along the road here and there. She was headed home from the Countess Café, where she waited tables part-time.

She'd been in Galveston a little over two weeks. She was renting a small apartment not too far past the end of the seawall that kept the city from succumbing to the ocean as it had in 1901 when a hurricane had all but wiped the growing community off the map. Allie had been coming here for years with family or friends, and the legend of that storm lived on in more than one museum and book. That story, for Allie, was part of the allure of the seaside town; even with the seawall, Galveston was constantly rebuilding after hurricane damage, retaining its history yet reinventing itself.

Allie had wanted to live close to the main part of the city for convenience but not too close. When she'd first arrived, she managed to clean herself up enough to land the serving job. This was the off-season, and they weren't that busy, but two people had recently quit, so they were desperate. Lucky for Allie.

When she'd found a modest apartment, she'd gotten the landlord in touch with her new employer and was able to put off the first month's rent until she got her paycheck. Since people weren't exactly knocking down the door to rent the place, Allie lucked out again.

She couldn't help but think of Mag and Charles and marvel at how much she could attribute to random chance. When you don't have anything, she thought, getting your backpack stolen, landing a place to sleep, convincing someone to give you a job — much of it was random chance and the kindness of the occasional stranger. The diner just as easily could've said "no" since Allie didn't even have a phone number yet. The apartment manager certainly didn't have to take a chance on her; most wouldn't.

She missed her two friends from the street. They had both been so open, so honest about their plights. And Mag especially seemed like one of the kindest souls she'd ever met. She hoped they were both well-fed and safe.

As she rode, she planned her evening: *Leftover spaghetti in the fridge for dinner. Then I'll write some, maybe take a bath, or go for a walk on the beach if the weather cooperated. Maybe I'll get a pet, something low maintenance, like a cat.*

She was looking forward to having drinks with a couple of the wait staff who'd invited her out to their weekly gathering the next evening. It was nice to be with people again.

Soon her building came into view. The structure couldn't be more than a few years old, but it already had rust and mold tracing its edges. The salt and moisture of the Gulf were hard on human-made structures. Allie saw that someone was sitting on the steps, blocking the way to her place on the upper floor. As she drew closer, squinting at the figure, it stood up and turned toward her, its movements familiar.

She stopped the bike about ten feet from him, her shoulders suddenly tense, wary. "Mitch."

"Hi," he said, as if they'd just parted a few hours ago.

"Hi," she responded with uncertainty. She didn't know what to say. She had missed him on and off over the past weeks, but she felt taken aback to see him so suddenly.

"You look like shit," she said matter-of-factly.

"Thanks," he said wryly. He was thinner than she remembered, and his eyes were slightly bloodshot, like when he was hungover. He had the beginnings of a beard, though not a well-groomed one. She wondered if he'd been working at all.

He took a few steps toward her, and she noticed he was limping.

"Are you okay?"

"Yeah, I hurt my ankle right after…you left. I just got out of the boot a few days ago. It still hurts when I've been sitting for a while. Just a minor fracture. No big deal."

She knew she was supposed to ask him what had happened, how he'd broken his ankle, but she either didn't want to know or didn't care. She couldn't tell. Perhaps a little of both.

"Want to come up?" she asked as she hoisted her bike to carry it up the stairs.

"Let me get that," he volunteered.

"S'okay. I got it."

Allie unlocked the nondescript brown door to her apartment and leaned the bike up against the wall inside. She'd almost forgotten she'd sent him the letter when she'd first gotten here. She'd been feeling nostalgic; they'd always enjoyed the beach together. But now that he was here in the flesh, she felt…weird, awkward. Maybe she'd been lonely when she'd written to him, but since then, she'd settled into her new surroundings. Having Mitch suddenly appear now was like two different worlds colliding. She wasn't sure whether she was glad to see him or not.

She dropped her backpack on the floor next to her bike. She looked at him. He looked at her. He averted his eyes and swept his gaze over the sparsely furnished apartment. He didn't say anything.

Come in, she acquiesced, turning away from him and speaking over her shoulder. He followed her past the kitchen to the living room, where, backed up to the long window, there stood one sagging couch the previous tenant had left, plus a table lamp sitting on the floor.

He sat without comment, and Allie rummaged in the kitchen cabinets for water glasses. As she filled one coffee mug and one plastic cup, both from the café, with tap water, she said, "I've only been here a little over two weeks, so I haven't had a chance to get much furniture."

"Uh-huh."

She handed him the plastic cup, which he sipped and sat on the floor. She took the spot next to him on the couch and sat looking at her knees. Even though he hadn't said much, she felt like a chastised child caught running away from home. And that feeling stirred anger in her gut.

"Allie, what the fuck is going on here?" Mitch said suddenly. He wasn't looking at her, she noticed, but staring out at her shabby little space as if he were a decorator critiquing her taste for one of the renovation shows he liked so much.

"What do you mean?" She knew she was being obtuse, but she wanted him to say it – give voice to exactly what he objected to about what she was doing, what she had done. Exactly what beef he had about who she was.

"Are you living here now? How are you paying for this?" Mitch flung his arms out toward the apartment and turned to face her, staring, demanding an answer. Like a parent.

"I have a job, and I don't know." She said evenly and faced him with a cool stare.

"You don't know if you're living here? Because a place to live and a job sure make it seem like it. Were you even going to tell me?" His eyes were pleading now for a certainty she couldn't give.

"Look, I don't know. All I do know is this is where I want to be for now," she said, looking down at her hands. He followed her gaze.

"Christ, Allie, your thumb. I can't believe you —" He stopped himself. Then, he took a deep breath and reached into his pocket and fished something out. Her ring. The one that had been on her thumb when she'd lost it. She had barely thought of it. He held it out to her. She took it, held it in her palm and closed her hand around it.

"Thanks."

"I went and got it back from the police station before I came." She knew there must be a story there, too, but again she didn't ask.

"Allie," he said, "I love you." She appeared blurry through his watery eyes. "This is killing me. I can't work, I can't focus on anything else. Think of our life together, our plans, the family we want to have. Please come home."

Her heart ached for him. She didn't want him to be unhappy. And she missed him. They leaned towards each other, and she could smell his familiar scent — his deodorant, his soap, and the unmistakable pleasant fragrance that just seemed to be him. He cupped her face with both of his hands and kissed her. She could feel herself basking in the warmth and comfort of him. No one had touched her so tenderly since she'd left Lime. She still held the ring clutched gently in her right fist.

As they moved to the bedroom, Allie shushed the distant, warning voice inside her and allowed herself to enjoy him, their bodies moving in the assured way of people who know each other. She relished the sensual feel of his weight on top of her, the way he pushed into her in rhythm. Afterward, he went down on her. She didn't even have to tell him to.

CHAPTER 15

Day 39

Mitch awoke with the sun streaming through the window, reflecting in sparkles off the ocean in the distance. Out here, waking up to the light didn't bother him so much. He'd always loved the ocean. He glanced over with a smile on his face to see Allie asleep next to him, mouth open, snoring softly. It was good to have her back.

After he showered in the narrow stall in Allie's bathroom, ducking under the too-short shower head, Allie still wasn't up. He decided to make breakfast. He poked around the kitchen, which contained the bare minimum of cookware, and found bacon, eggs and bread for toast. As the aromas of cooking permeated the apartment, Allie wandered in, still looking sleepy, wearing a big tee shirt and sweatpants.

"What's up, sleepyhead?" he called cheerfully. He felt happier than he had in weeks. Perhaps months, even.

"Whatcha doin'?" she asked through a yawn.

"What's it look like? Making breakfast. I found some stuff."

Allie frowned. "I was saving that."

"For what?" He hadn't expected criticism for cooking her breakfast.

She'd invited her neighbors, Julian and Brad, over for brunch on Saturday, she explained. He was surprised, as Allie had never been particularly outgoing. Her inviting two guys she barely knew over for a meal seemed weird.

Mitch felt a pang of, could it be, jealousy?

"Um, sorry about using up your stuff, then," he mumbled.

She responded with a shrug and sat down at the folding card table in the kitchen, where Mitch served her a plate of food and sat down across from her.

"So," he began, trying to smooth over the coolness that had overtaken their conversation this morning, "where are you working?"

"Countess Café," she said between bites. "I'm thinking about getting a job at the bookstore too. I saw a wanted sign there yesterday. The restaurant's only part-time. It might cut into my writing too much, though."

Mitch could feel his spine and his shoulders clench. "You've been writing a lot?"

"Yes!" Allie's eyes lit up. "I'm up to 28,320 words, further than I've ever gotten before. There are no distractions here, and I can write for hours every night if I want to. I borrowed an old laptop from Juleesa at work. The 'x' is broken, but I don't need it all that often anyway. It's not as hard typing without a thumb as I thought it would be; it turns out I didn't even use it that often."

He knew he should ask what the story was about. That's what people ask when someone says, "I'm writing a book." It was probably the kind of question he should've been asking her all along, and he was dimly aware he didn't even know what she liked to write about. But it wasn't what he wanted to know.

He'd thought that after her letter, after last night, she was reaching out to him, that she wanted to come home. But now, this morning, the eggs sat like lead in his belly. He was no longer sure.

"Allie?" She looked up and met his eyes. "When are you coming home?"

She wiped her mouth with the paper towel next to her plate and looked at him thoughtfully. "What if I *am* home? Mitch, I never felt like I quite fit in Lime in that house. But you know that."

"No, I don't. How the hell would I know that?"

"Because I *told* you. I was always saying, 'Sometimes I'd like to just run off in the woods.'"

"But that's just talk," he said desperately, "That's something you say when you're annoyed or whatever. Not something you actually DO."

"I told you," she insisted, "I didn't like my job, told you I hated all the sickening sympathy people gave me with their sad eyes after the miscarriage." her voice was rising to match his.

"Yeah, but everyone hates their jobs. And hates people. Sometimes."

"And HOW was I supposed to make you realize I was serious? Write it in blood on the bathroom wall?"

"No, you did the rational thing and cut your goddamned thumb off. You *did* do it on purpose, didn't you? Murphy was right."

"Who the hell is Murphy?"

"Speaking of miscarriages," he spat, feeling the rage boil up inside of him, "I hear that wasn't your first one. I heard you were *fucking* married before."

Allie's face went pale. They were both standing now, though Mitch couldn't remember when either of them had pushed back from the table.

"I didn't lie to you," she said evenly.

"Didn't lie but didn't tell me the truth, either. WHAT'S THE FUCKING DIFFERENCE!"

He was seething, fists clenched at his sides, teeth grinding. How could she be so goddamned calm when she was bringing their world down. "So what, are you going to just stay here, be a mediocre waitress, dick around with the boys next door and pretend you're writing a book?"

It was her turn to clench her fists. "See, now you're getting all hostile and insulting. This is why it's so hard to talk to you. I *like* it here. I'm tired of being judged, Mitch, tired of other people pushing their expectations onto me."

"Who does that?"

"Everyone. You, my mother, society, everyone. It is in everything that you do. It's in the job you accepted in that bullshit little town before even consulting me on it —"

"You didn't have a job! You could move!" he shouted incredulously.

"Not when you accepted it! I was still working for *The Chronicle* when you accepted."

He paused for a moment, trying to remember if that were true, and he couldn't. *Godamnit, she was jobless when I decided to get the place in Lime. Wasn't she?* Mitch shook his head; he was getting distracted.

"Allie, you can't live this way! This place is a dump! You're a smart person; you're just going to waste your life waiting tables?! How are you going to pay bills? What if you get sick? What about the future?" he yelled desperately. Couldn't she see this was unsustainable?

"Maybe I'll be a best-selling author in the future. Maybe I won't. Maybe I'll be content living out my days here, working part-time and writing on the side forever. Or maybe I'll move on to a new place when the mood strikes me. I don't know.

"But what I do know is this: I don't want to plan out the rest of my life right now. And I don't want to drown in the shit of modern life, being constantly connected, constantly judged, having a houseful of crap we don't need. I don't want to feel suffocated anymore. I want to be free."

Tears were running down her cheeks, but she still met his eye with a hard stare. "You need to leave."

"But there were all of these things you didn't TELL me. You're like this whole other fucking person I didn't know! Why did you write me that fucking letter! You're so fucking confusing!" He stepped toward her and reached out to grasp her shoulders but thought better of it and put his arms back down. He was close enough to smell scrambled eggs on her breath.

"I missed you, Mitch." she said, shrugging her shoulders, "At the time. I thought maybe you'd get it now. Or maybe I just hoped you would." She sniffled, tears beginning to dry on her cheeks.

"But I drove all the way down here! We slept together! Doesn't that mean anything to you?"

"Not really, no. You can't just come out here and fix everything with your dick." She crossed her arms and stared at him stonily. "Get out. I don't want you here."

Now he did grasp her shoulders as if he could convey reason into her through his arms and hands. "Allie, please —"

"Let go!" she shouted and shoved him, and he came back at her, arm raised.

———

He heard it more than felt it: his open hand coming into contact with her cheek. She stumbled backward. Then, with her thumbless left hand holding her reddening cheek, she looked up at him in disbelief. Mitch looked uncomprehendingly at his palm, still tingling from the slap.

Time hung, suspended for a moment. Mitch became, suddenly, acutely aware of the sound of a lawnmower in the distance and the cries of seagulls overhead nearby.

The shock writ large on Allie's face began to smolder and morphed into not just anger but hatred right before his eyes. "Get the fuck out. Get out now."

Mitch couldn't believe himself. He was feeling so desperate for her to listen, for her to see, and somehow it seemed his hand had flown without his permission, a reptilian response.

"Oh my god, I'm so sorry, Allie. I—" As he took a step toward her, she took a step back. "Let me get you some ice," he said, heading for the freezer.

"Mitch," she said. And as he turned back toward her, he saw she had a cell phone in her hand. "Get the fuck out, or I will call the police." She was scared of him now, he realized, and it was an agony blooming inside of him that he could scarcely contain. He had done something that caused her not only to mistrust him but to fear him.

She would call the cops; Allie didn't bluff. He grabbed his keys off the counter and walked out, running down the stairs and toward his car as if he could outrun what he'd just done. Outrun himself.

———

He drove up the road toward Sea Wall fast, disregarding the speed limit, the ocean roaring distantly off to his right. His heart was hammering in his chest, and his breath was rapid and shallow. It was like a nightmare, one of his very own, in fact. He'd dreamt before of hitting Allie, always horrified afterward and relieved to wake up. But this had really happened. The scene was replaying in his head on repeat.

She wouldn't listen. She shut down. She wouldn't talk to me. We slept together last night, and then she wouldn't come home. So frustrated, so angry, so confused…

He saw the part where he slapped her from above, an aerial view. Try as he might, he could not actually recall hitting her from within his own body. Something had risen up in him, something that wanted to *make her see* how irrational she was being.

Somewhere from far away, the rational part of his mind was telling him to slow down, that he was going way too fast for this piddly two-lane road full of potholes, but his foot, lead on the accelerator, wouldn't listen.

Her words replayed in his head, *…fix everything with your dick.* He hadn't thought that, really, had he? He had thought that it meant something, though, that when they'd slept together, it had been a reunion. That it meant she was coming home. *Maybe I'm the one who doesn't want to see.*

He saw the rusty red Honda Accord pull out of the gas station and knew it was too late to stop. The speed limit was 35, and he was doing at least 60. He slammed on the brakes and swerved left, missing the other car but losing control of his own. The world spun, and then there was nothing.

CHAPTER 16

Allie gritted her teeth as she stared out the window, thinking, stewing. What made her angriest, she thought, was that she'd been afraid of him. She'd seen the wild look in his eyes the instant before his hand few, and for a brief moment, she thought he may have lost his sanity.

It had been a couple of hours since he'd left. Allie had called in sick to the café. She'd been sitting on the couch, looking out the window and thinking, periodically holding an ice pack to her swollen cheek. He had slapped her so hard her ears had rung, and despite three Advil, she now had a throbbing headache.

She finally decided to call her sister. She hadn't spoken with her since she'd left the house in Lime, but it was time. She really needed someone to talk to. She punched her sister's number into her new cell phone, and Jamie picked up after several rings.

"Jamie, it's me, Allie."

"Oh my god, Allie. Where are you? Are you all right? Where

have you been?" Jamie's voice rose in volume and pitch with each word.

"It's okay, Jamie, I'm fine. I'm in Galveston."

"Why haven't you called? Mitch is worried to death! I was worried. Are you sure you're okay?" Jamie rapid-fired questions at Allie, and it was making her head spin, though she could hardly blame her sister for sounding panicky.

"Yeah —" Allie began, but her voice began to crack. "Um, do you have time to talk?" She wanted to apologize. She knew of all people, she should've called Jamie to let her know she was okay. She felt bad for making her worry, but as usual, Jamie didn't dwell on guilt.

"Sure, give me a sec." Allie heard shuffling and the shutting of a car door. "Okay, I'm in the car. It's my lunch break. What's going on with you?"

Allie knew her sister probably wanted her to start at the beginning, from that day that seemed so long ago now, when she trekked, bleeding, into the greenbelt, but she needed to talk about what just happened with Mitch, and she knew her sister would indulge her.

"Mitch was just here, and…" Allie told her sister the story, starting with finding him on the steps of her new apartment. She had to stop to get a hold of herself here and there. The tears didn't seem to want to stay down, but Jamie waited in comfortable silence for Allie to restart each time. She told her sister all of it — the sex, the breakfast, the argument, and how he'd slapped her at the end, and she'd thrown him out.

"Fucking asshole," Jamie spat. "I'll kill him. I can't fucking believe it."

"I'm just so angry at him," Allie continued. "But I…It's also understandable, you know, how confused he is. I know I haven't been making much sense lately. And he thought, I guess, since we slept together…I don't know, maybe I should've been more understanding."

"Look, Allie, you've kinda gone off your rocker lately, and confusion *is* understandable, but slapping you is not okay. Having sex with him may have been misleading, but misunderstandings don't warrant violence. You're trying to blame yourself for getting hit. That's bullshit, and you know it."

Allie sighed. Jamie was right. He had absolutely no right, and she hoped she never fucking saw him again. Separately from that, though, she still couldn't blame him for being confused.

"Jamie, I know everyone probably thinks I've lost my mind, but I really feel more like I've found it. Something was…off, missing. There I was, living with Mitch in that house, and I began to realize I never really questioned my goals in life — go to college, get a nine-to-five job, get married, have a family. I mean, it's what everyone in our family did, so I guess I just went with it.

"I wanted the chance to explore some other things, and Mitch keeps wanting to know what my plans are, but that's just it. I'm discovering I *like* not having plans, at least for now."

"Okay, but I don't see how cutting your thumb off plays into this."

"I didn't really mean to cut off my thumb; it just seemed like," Allie trailed off, searching to put words to her feelings. "Well, all of a sudden, my life was different. I didn't have a thumb. If that can change just like that, maybe I can too."

Jamie sighed, "I can't completely relate, but I get where you're coming from. I mean, it's not as if, growing up, we saw a lot of unconventional examples of how to be an adult. I thought you really wanted kids, though."

"I'm not saying I don't. It's just hard to know what I want when everyone, myself included, just always assumed that's what I would do. I want the chance to find out for myself."

"Makes sense. When I got pregnant with the twins, everyone assumed I would be the one to stay home with them. I remember, at the baby shower, all the aunts were like, 'When's your last day of work?' without even thinking I might not quit.

"I kept putting off giving notice, and it wasn't until a few weeks before they were born that Daniel and I had a heart-to-heart. He wanted to stay home with them, and I really wanted to keep working. People still look at me weird when I say he's a stay-at-home dad. They're all, 'Doesn't he miss working?' I guarantee they wouldn't be asking me the same thing."

"Exactly. I mean, I still love Mitch, and I have missed him. That's why this is all so confusing, why I wrote him that letter —

"

"You wrote him a letter?" Jamie's voice took on an edge of incredulity.

"When I saw him sitting there on the steps, I was surprised. I wrote him on a whim weeks ago. He's got these expectations. They're perfectly normal — that I live in a house with him, make friends, have kids, get a job — but what if I'm not normal? He can't entertain the idea that someone could be happy without owning a house or a lot of stuff or having a savings account to fall back on. He thinks it's irresponsible. He thinks I'm running away, but I think really I was running toward something."

"Allie, just because it's 'normal' doesn't mean it's what's best. Hell, a lot of people are unhappy living the conventional life. They just don't have the guts to leave the security of it like you did."

"Huh. I never thought of it that way. I always thought of it as a weakness, but maybe I'm a pioneer."

"Well, let's not get crazy and break out the bonnets and wagons, but seriously, I'm kinda in awe of you. You've got balls. I mean ovaries. Can ovaries be balls, too? Because 'You've got ovaries' just doesn't have the same ring to it."

"It sounds like 'You've got mail,'" Allie giggled.

"Sending you balls of ovaries in the mail."

They both laughed themselves to tears, and Allie thought, *This is what sisters are for*.

————

After the call with Jamie, Allie felt tired but better. Just as she was settling into a much-needed hot bath, her phone buzzed on the countertop. It was Jamie again, so she picked it up.

"Allie, I just got a call from the hospital in Galveston. They didn't have your number. Mitch has been in an accident."

————

Allie knocked on her neighbor's door, nervously bouncing on the balls of her feet. Julian answered, shirtless and wearing sweatpants.

"Hi, um," she began, then blurted "Could you give me a ride to the hospital? A friend's been in an accident."

Mitch wasn't her friend. He was both more than that and less than that at the moment, but it was the best she could do.

"Umm, yeah, sure." He ran his fingers through his hair and began scanning the room behind him. "Lemme get my keys. Everything okay?" he asked as he rummaged through a bowl on a hallway table.

"I really don't know. He was in a car accident. I don't have details yet."

"Oh. Sorry to hear that. Ready?"

"Do you want to put something else on?" she asked.

"Like what?" He seemed genuinely confused.

"Like a shirt, maybe some shoes?" she asked with raised eyebrows.

Julian disappeared into a bedroom and returned, pulling a t-shirt over his head. He paused in the entryway to retrieve a pair of flip-flops thrown carelessly against the wall.

———

"I really appreciate you taking me. Thanks," said Allie once she was belted into the passenger side of Julian's truck, whose small backseat appeared to hold the trash from every fast food meal he'd eaten in the past year. It smelled like old fries.

"Sure, no problem. I don't have to work til tonight. I'm the door guy over at Club Said."

"Like a bouncer?"

"Kinda, but people there are pretty tame — not much need for bouncin'."

They were silent for a while. Allie looked out the window at the surf beyond the highway. It was a grey day, and v-shaped flocks of pelicans traversed the sky, occasionally diving for fish. She wondered what she was going to say to Mitch. Would he be conscious? She was antsy to make sure he was all right but also dreading a confrontation with him.

"So who's this friend you're going to see?" Julian asked.

"Oh, just this guy. I've known him a long time," Allie wasn't sure how much she wanted to share. How she currently felt about Mitch was the very definition of complicated.

"Like romantically, or…I'm sorry. You don't have to answer that. I'm just always curious about people."

No, it's okay. Yes, romantically. He always wanted to get married. Then, a few weeks ago…" She hesitated for a second and then, bolstered by Jamie's idea that it had been something of an act of courage, thought, *aw fuck it.* "I cut my thumb off and escaped into the woods." She held up her left hand and wiggled her remaining fingers at him as evidence.

"Really? That is fucking awesome! I mean, who does that? Man, I bet you have some stories."

Allie was taken aback by his vehemently positive response, but it set her to grinning all the same. She thought for a moment, "Yeah, I guess I do.

"A while back, I ate some rabbit that didn't agree with me, so I ran into this diner, and my pack got stolen while I was in the bathroom."

Allie told the story in all of the detail she could remember — how Rose had shouted at her, how panicked she was when she couldn't find her backpack. She talked about Charles and Mag and how they'd helped her find the remnants of her stuff. She was enjoying herself. It was a really good story, she realized, in addition to being part of her fumbling and flawed bid for freedom.

By the time they pulled into the parking lot, Allie had almost forgotten why she was there. She'd gotten lost in telling her stories to Julian, who was clearly enjoying them. He laughed at parts Allie hadn't realized were funny.

She got out of the car and closed the door, leaning back in through the open window. "Thanks for the ride. I really appreciate it. I owe you gas money or dinner or something."

"Nah, but let's get together for beers sometime. I'd like to hear some more stories."

"How about next time you tell me *your* story," she said, suddenly conscious that she'd done all the talking.

Julian laughed. "I'm not that interesting. Hey! How are you going to get home?"

"Don't worry; I'll figure something out."

"Okay. Bye, Allie." And with that, he puttered out of the parking lot back onto the road.

Allie watched his truck for a few moments with a bit of wonderment. He was…different. Then, she turned to go inside.

———

Allie'd been directed to ICU by the guy at the front desk, and she knew that didn't bode well. She was apprehensive as she tried to follow his directions, checking signs, passing through magnetic door after magnetic door. She'd briefly escaped the gravity of Mitch's accident in stories in Julian's truck, but now it was all beginning to feel too real again. The hospital was a labyrinth, but she finally found ICU.

"Hi, I'm here to see Mitch McConnelly. Can you tell me what room he's in?" she asked anxiously at the desk. Now that she was about to see him, she was apprehensive again.

"Are you a family member?" asked the nurse.

"I'm his wife," Allie said. She was afraid they wouldn't let her see him otherwise.

As Allie followed the nurse, she could feel her pulse beating in her ears. There was a flutter in her throat, and she couldn't seem to take a deep breath. Finally, he stopped at a door and knocked gently. There was no answer. He peeked inside, then told Allie Mitch was sleeping, but she could still go in. He admonished her not to wake him and added, "He's on some serious pain meds."

The nurse turned to leave, but Allie stopped him. "Wait. What happened? Is he going to be okay?"

He looked surprised, and Allie felt the need to explain. "My sister just called me, and I came right over." She hoped he wouldn't ask why Mitch has her sister's number and not hers, and he didn't.

"He was in a car accident. Apparently, he was going pretty fast down Seawall and lost control. No one else was involved. His right leg is broken in multiple places. He's got broken ribs and a severe concussion. His pelvis is shattered. He has a punctured lung, but we've got that under control now." He paused for a moment.

She could feel the nurse assessing her, maybe deciding what

approach to take. She tried to push down the panic that was rising from her gut, threatening to make her hyperventilate. She swallowed the lump in her throat and tried to look collected, calm, concerned. *A shattered pelvis? Fuck!*

"He's going to be okay, but there's a lot of rehab in his future. It's good he has you. I was starting to worry when no one came for him earlier."

"I was 45 minutes away..." Her throat constricted; her thoughts were spinning. She hesitated, floundering for what to say, wondering what even mattered in a moment like this. "We're not living together right now." She was starting to feel guilty for some reason, and tears welled up in her eyes. She willed them not to spill down her cheeks.

"I understand. It's okay; don't feel bad about it. You came as soon as you could. You're here now. That's what matters." He reached out and patted her arm; it reminded her of the awkward way her mom always handled tragedy, but though the motion was the same, this seemed genuine. Allie was grateful for the comfort.

She was equally grateful when the nurse excused himself, saying he'd be at the nurses' station if she needed anything. He smiled and headed off down the hall.

Allie faced the cracked door. The last time she'd seen Mitch was hours ago, though it seemed like longer. Her nerves felt like frayed wires, sparking with erratic electricity. She took a deep breath and pushed open the door.

Her breath caught in her throat when she saw him lying there, motionless, under the stark white sheet. She had taken in the litany of broken bones and damaged organs, but she wasn't expecting him to look like this. His eyes were both blackened, and his face looked swollen. She could see an IV pumping fluids into one arm. His right leg was over the blanket so that she could see the cast that went all the way up to his crotch, where it wrapped around like a diaper.

Allie was glad Mitch couldn't see how rattled she was by his appearance. She willed herself to breathe again. She approached gingerly, although she doubted in his current state, any amount of noise would have awakened him. She could hear him breathing softly, with a slight rattle. She gently rested her thumbless left hand on his. He twitched slightly but didn't wake up. Now the tears that had arisen in the hallway spilled down her cheeks.

Allie had been determined never to see him again just a couple of hours ago. Now, she felt deep pangs of love and sympathy for this broken, unconscious man. Mitch, who had been so excited when she'd moved in with him, he'd reminded her of a puppy, running from room to room, showing her features of the house, where all her stuff could go. Mitch, who had just slapped her across the face.

She bit her lip and sucked in breath to keep from audibly sobbing with...*what? Love, rage, regret?* She was suddenly exhausted, the adrenaline of the past few hours, the emotions that threatened to consume her from the inside out. She dropped into the recliner next to the bed and fell into an uneasy sleep as her body sought a reprieve from Allie's cacophony of feelings.

———

Allie opened her eyes and then blinked. She was staring at a white ceiling devoid of any defining characteristics. It took a moment to remember where she was. She sat up in the recliner, rolling her head around to get at the crick that had settled into the right side of her neck. Mitch was awake, looking at her. There was a tray of food by his bed and a sense of dread in Allie's stomach.

"Hi," he said, his voice scratchy, as if he'd only just awakened himself.

Allie steadily met his eyes with her gaze but couldn't figure out what to say.

"Allie," he started, "I know saying 'I'm sorry' isn't enough, but I am. I am so sorry. I can't believe —" his voice broke.

"Shh," she said soothingly, "You need to rest." She firmly laid a hand on his shoulder, hoping it seemed reassuring – more reassured than she actually felt.

"I've *been* resting. And I've been thinking. If you can ever forgive me, I'll do whatever you want. We can live here. I'll get a job. People buy houses on the beach, right? Whatever you want, I promise."

"Shh," she said because he was starting to get worked up, and she didn't know what else to say. Allie didn't want to talk about this, didn't think they should be talking about this, given his current condition, but she also knew him. She knew he wouldn't let it go. She didn't want to lie to him.

"Mitch, I can't tell you we're going to get through this together. I can't lie to you. I don't want you to think it's all because you hit me," she began.

"But if I could just get better," he pleaded, "When I get out of here, we can stay, I can…I can try to understand."

"But you don't understand. We don't want the same things. Not anymore, if we ever did. You assumed I wanted what you wanted, and I'm sorry it took me this long to figure out I didn't."

"But—"

She interrupted him. She was on a roll, and she had to get it all out before he derailed her. "You wouldn't be happy here. You'd be subverting your own wishes for mine, and that would breed resentment in both of us. And yeah, I'd probably always be pissed at you, on some level, for hitting me. And you'd always feel guilty about it."

"I could be happy here," he said quietly, already seeming to concede he was losing this argument.

She didn't want to say it. She knew it would hurt, but he needed to know the truth, no matter how excruciating. "*I* wouldn't be happy with you here."

"How can you say that?" he asked softly. "After all the years we've been together?"

Allie looked at him. "She'd felt pity for him before — for his physical wounds, for the confusion he had about who she was and what she'd done. She'd felt guilty for causing so much anguish. But as he asked that one question, she realized it wasn't all her.

"Mitch, it's *because* of all those years together. I can't be the family you want. I thought I could, but I don't have it in me." She saw it now, with clarity. Her anguish at his decrepit condition and her roiling sea of violent emotions took a back seat to her utter certainty that she didn't want to be with him. And then, she needed out.

She turned and dashed out of the room, escaping before she could see his reaction. A series of elevators and wrong turns later, she came out of the hospital and collapsed onto a bus bench, breathing loud, raspy shallow breaths, her head hanging between her knees.

She would not be his nursemaid. She would not feel obligated. She didn't know who would do it, but he was a grown adult. Injured as he was, he would figure it out. That wasn't her job anymore. Allie looked out at the road in front of her, the grey sky overhead. Out here, she could breathe easier.

———

The bus schedule was so faded she couldn't read it, so she

decided to walk along the highway toward her apartment. She'd make it home eventually or catch a ride. She was in no hurry. She'd been walking for about 15 minutes and was beginning to realize just how far away home was, thinking maybe she should've made more effort with the bus schedule when a car slowed and pulled over next to her. Juleesa, from the café, leaned over from the driver's seat and called to her.

"What are you doing way out here? I thought you were sick." Her tone was more concerned than accusatory.

Allie opened the door and fell into the passenger seat. She'd only known Juleesa a short time, but she was one of those people who felt like a best friend almost instantly. Allie fell into the passenger seat, leaned her head against the headrest and sighed. "Sick in the head, maybe."

Juleesa pulled back onto the road and asked, "What's going on?"

Allie trusted Juleesa, but she was too worn out to tell the whole convoluted story. "It's been a fucked up day. A friend of mine was in a car wreck and…a lot of other stuff. I'll tell you sometime. I'm just too tired right now."

"Sure," Juleesa responded and left it at that. They drove in silence until she dropped Allie off. After thanking her for the ride, Allie trudged up the stairs to her apartment. She let herself in, went straight to bed fully clothed, and fell asleep instantly.

Allie awoke the next morning to the sunlight streaming through the bedroom window. She lay there, blinking, remembering all that had happened the day before — Mitch in her apartment, the hospital. She'd slept a full twelve hours, and despite her troubles, she felt refreshed. She got up and padded into the kitchen, made a pot of coffee and sat blowing on her cup at the kitchen table, thinking. As she did, she spied a piece of paper on the floor in front of the door. Someone had slipped it through the crack at the bottom where the weather stripping was missing. She retrieved it and read:

Allie,

How about dinner instead of brunch? At my place? I'll be home around 3. Just let me know.

-Julian

She had completely forgotten about brunch with Julian and Brad. Hell, she'd forgotten what day it was. She was relieved at the idea of dinner at their place since her planned eggs and bacon were gone. She decided to call the café to see if she could pick up an extra shift to make up for yesterday since brunch plans were off. Juleesa picked up.

"As a matter of fact," she said, "Brennan would probably love to go home. He looks hungover as hell."

Allie showered, glad to have something to do to take her mind off her worries. Before she left, she taped a note to Julian's door saying dinner would be great and she'd be home by eight.

———

By the time her shift ended, the café was all but deserted, and Allie was getting antsy. She wiped all the tables, rearranged the straws and utensils and checked the bathroom for toilet paper. She was looking forward to dinner. She hadn't made many friends here yet, and she was lonely for good conversation.

She picked up a six-pack of Modelo on the way home, changed clothes and headed over for dinner. Julian answered the door, this time fully clothed in jeans and a t-shirt.

"Hey!" he greeted her warmly. "Come on in."

She followed him to the kitchen where he began stirring something on the stove in a skillet. "It smells great in here," she said, and then, recognizing the delicious, spicy aroma, "Curry?"

"It's one of the four things I can cook."

"Where's Brad?"

"He's not here. He has a girlfriend who lives on Seawall. They spend most of their time at her place."

"I brought beer." She raised the six-pack. He hadn't offered to take it or put it in the refrigerator.

"Great! There're mugs in the cabinet. Pour us a couple."

Allie sat at the small table in the kitchen, which was almost identical to hers, sipping her beer as Julian cooked, feeling content without conversation in the warm embrace of cooking smells.

As they sat down across from each other with their curry over rice, Allie inhaled deeply and took a bite. The warm, unique flavor of the spice spread over her palate. "This is really good," she said earnestly.

After dinner, they stacked the dishes in the sink, poured themselves another beer and went out to the balcony to sit. Julian propped his feet up on the railing. Allie could just hear the surf of the ocean over the traffic if she strained her ears.

"So what's your story?" she asked him.

They sat there for a couple of hours, exchanging funny tales from their childhoods and their travels. Sometimes they were silent, listening to the lap of the waves. It was comfortable, Allie thought, way more comfortable than she'd expected to be with someone she'd known such a short time.

She'd had a nice evening. She felt relaxed. Though, she noticed Julian never really did tell her how he ended up in Galveston. It didn't seem all that important anymore, either.

Only when Allie was crawling into her bed that night did she realize…

He didn't hug me goodbye or try to kiss me. He didn't put his arm around me. He didn't even offer to walk me home.

He hadn't insisted on giving her a ride home from the hospital either. She smiled and fell asleep.

CHAPTER 17

Day 39

His whole self hurt. He could barely distinguish the pain in his body from his injuries from the pain in his heart. Mitch lay in his hospital bed staring at the doorway through which Allie had just left as if perhaps staring long enough would bring her back. He'd come down here assuming it would all work out between them. He'd been willing to compromise; why hadn't she? It was tempting, he thought, to blame her for everything, right down to his car accident, but even now, he knew that was bullshit.

The car, the pain, Allie…he couldn't process it all through the haze of grief and fentanyl. So he closed his eyes, let his mind go blank, and fell into a drug-induced sleep while tears leaked out from under his lids.

CHAPTER 18

Day 46

It had been a week since Allie had seen Mitch in the hospital. She'd thought about going back, felt like she ought to, but she couldn't get herself to do it. She was afraid she'd lose her resolve to relinquish responsibility for him. There was a part of her who wanted to take care of him, but she knew that if she did, she'd never leave, and she'd resent him.

Allie and Julian started spending a lot of time together. She'd met Brad briefly when he dropped by the apartment to pick some clothes up, but other than that, he was always gone. One evening, when she and Julian were both working a similar shift, they agreed to meet at the Burger Joint after work.

It was late when Allie chained her bike up in the parking lot — almost 1 am — but the streets were well-lit and populated with people. Julian pulled his truck in right behind her and they went in together, ordered at the counter, grabbed beers from the cooler and found a booth in the corner.

"So, how was work, dear?" Julian asked, in singsong parody, as he relaxed into his side of the booth.

Allie rolled her eyes, "Same shit. You?"

"Sam ol'. Oh, there was actually a fight tonight!"

"Really? You seem awfully excited about that."

Julian looked sheepish. "I know, it's just not much goes on there. The time drags, the music is shitty." He trailed off and sipped his beer.

"Anyway…?" she prompted.

Julian shrugged. "Just some drunk dumbass, you know."

Allie, "No, I don't know. I wasn't there."

"He was bothering this woman. It really wasn't that big of a deal. What about you?"

When they finished their greasy meal, Allie threw her bike in the back of Julian's truck, and they headed back to the apartments. As they climbed the stairs, Allie asked, "You want to come over for a bit?"

"Sure."

Inside, Allie pulled out a bottle of white wine. "Ooh, fancy," Julian said, "wine!"

"Calm down. It was six bucks." She unscrewed the cap and poured it into two juice glasses, then they sat on the couch. Allie opened the sliding door to the balcony. You could hear the surf better from her apartment than from Julian's, especially at this late hour when the traffic had abated. As she crossed the small patch of floor between the balcony and the couch where Julian sat, she realized she wanted something besides conversation from him. She had been wondering what it would be like to kiss Julian, to feel his naked body against hers. It had been before-bed masturbation fuel for several nights.

She sat down and took a sip of her wine. For once, the silence between them didn't feel comfortably lazy. It felt electric, like he knew what she was thinking. She couldn't think of anything else to say, so she just came out with it:

"Why haven't you tried to kiss me yet?"

"Why haven't *you* tried to kiss *me*?" he retorted with a grin.

Allie laughed softly. "Patriarchy dies hard. Fair enough."

She put her glass down and leaned into him slowly. His lips were parted, and she could feel his warm breath.

When their lips finally touched, it was the best kiss Allie could ever remember. Julian and Allie slept together that night in Allie's bed, both literally and figuratively. They had sex, made love, fucked; Allie wasn't sure what to call it, but it didn't matter. Here, with Julian, it felt…different. Listening to his soft breathing, Allie drifted into a deep sleep.

———

"Hey, baby." She awoke to him petting her lightly with his hand, alarm

bells going off in her head. Only this time, she couldn't move. She was paralyzed and terrified as he caressed her arm, then her breast then traveled downward under the waistband of her pants.

Allie struggled against an invisible assailant. She forced her way through her paralysis and bolted upright, waking with a gasp. She was sweaty and clammy in the sheet twisted around her waist. She blinked her eyes and her chest heaved as she registered her own bedroom around her.

Ever since that night in the cave, the dream came to her when she was least suspecting it. It varied a little, but it was always the same — she couldn't move, couldn't fight him off this time, no matter how hard she tried. Sometimes it was like moving through syrup.

She hadn't known who he was or what had happened to him that night after she pushed him. She'd stared at his body lying on the rocks below the cave entrance, willing herself to stay awake, afraid he'd get up and come back. Lying on her stomach, she could barely see him sprawled on his back below through the rain in the moonlight. She'd stared, breath heaving in and out of her chest pinned under her own weight, her hair catching drips from the top of the cave rim, in turn dripping the water onto the forest floor below.

Impossible as it seemed, she'd fallen asleep there without realizing it, keeping vigil over her attacker. When she'd awakened in the morning, he was gone. She was equally relieved he wasn't dead and afraid he'd come back.

Sitting up in bed, she took deep breaths, trying to shake off the dream. She glanced at Julian snoring softly next to her and smiled a little. The solid reality of him lying there helped her recover from the nightmare.

She shuffled into the kitchen for a glass of water. When she glanced out the sliding glass doors to the patio, she could just make out the beginnings of dawn off to the left. It was early still. As the vividness of the dream faded, she thought about Julian. She liked the ease of being with him. Several nights ago, she'd been tired after work and wanted to go home, write a little, and go to bed. When she turned down Julian's invitation to dinner, she worried she'd hurt his feelings, but he seemed completely fine with it. He didn't sulk or ignore her later in retribution. It was refreshing.

Jamie had once told her that was all a relationship was — a good friend you have sex with. She'd not known what to make of it at the time, but now she was pretty sure Jamie was wrong.

Thinking of Jamie reminded her of the conversation they'd had on the phone a couple of days ago. Jamie was apparently keeping up with Mitch, for which Allie was grateful. She said he'd been released from the hospital and was now at home. Allie still felt guilty for not taking care of him, but Jamie said some detective was helping him out. Apparently, they'd become friends. Allie wondered if they were more than friends. The idea actually made her feel better, like maybe Mitch would be okay.

She returned to bed, snuggling into the covers next to Julian's warm body and fell back to sleep.

———

It took a few days for Allie to realize he was gone. She'd knocked on his door after work the other day but assumed he was out or at work when no one answered. When days went by, and there was no sign of him, she dropped into Club Said one evening after work and talked to the door guy.

"Julian?" he asked with a frown. "I don't know him, but I just started here yesterday. Sherri's at the bar. Go on in and ask her."

Allie sighed and went in. She was tired from being on her feet all day. She felt run down, like she might be getting sick. She found Sherri at the bar, going through paperwork. It was Tuesday, so the place was practically deserted. The generic techno music was deafening and indeed, as Julian had said, shitty. She shouted at Sherri over it to be heard.

"Julian?" Sherri shouted back. "He quit last week. 'Said he was leaving town."

Allie went cold inside. Sherri had to be mistaken. He wouldn't leave without even telling her, would he? "Did he say where he was going?"

"Nope. Just collected his last check and left."

"Okay, thanks."

"What?!" Sherri yelled, cupping her hand to her ear.

"I said THANKS!" Allie hollered, adding a thumbs up for clarification.

She left the bar feeling deflated. She couldn't believe he'd leave like that. Maybe it was an emergency? But still, what kind of emergency made you leave town without saying goodbye, without even a note?

Allie biked home, so fatigued she almost fell asleep while riding. She'd been working a lot lately, trying to put together at least a little savings. Perhaps she was overdoing it. When she finally dragged her bike up the steps and parked it inside her apartment, all she could think about was bed. She fell into it and, despite her upset and confusion about Julian, fell into a dreamless sleep.

———

Over the next couple of weeks, Allie didn't do much but go to work and sleep. She was depressed; she missed Julian. There had still been no word from him, and she didn't have any way to get in touch with him. It was like he'd vanished.

She tried to sit down and write, but she always ended up yawning, staring off into space and then taking a nap instead. She hadn't managed to make any other real friends besides Julian. Juleesa was great, but she had little kids. Between the café and them, she didn't have a lot of free time. Allie never got around to telling her what happened that day Juleesa had picked her up on the road, and Juleesa hadn't asked.

Riding her bike to and from town — something she'd enjoyed at first — now seemed like an exhausting pain in the ass. Mostly what she missed about Julian was talking to him or just sitting on the balcony with him, sipping beers in comfortable silence. *This is what you asked for*, she chided herself, *no strings attached*.

Saturday morning, Allie was in no mood to go out, but she was out of coffee, so she pulled on some sweatpants and a t-shirt and headed out the door, dreading the bike ride ahead of her. As she locked her door, Julian's door to her left opened. Her heart rose up momentarily, but it wasn't Julian who emerged. She hadn't exchanged more than a handful of words with Brad, and that was back when she'd first moved in.

"Hey! Allie, right?"

"Yeah. Hey, have you by any chance heard from Julian?"

He shook his head. "Nope. I…Jess and me broke up, so I'm back here." He looked embarrassed.

"I"m sorry," Allie said. She felt her shoulders tense up into her ears as the awkward seconds of silence ticked by. " Well, I gotta go get some coffee. See you later."

"I've got coffee," he said, perking up from his dejected posture a bit. "Come on in while I find it."

Allie followed Brad into the apartment. It was a wreck — clothes piled and strewn on the living room floor, dirty dishes piled high in the sink and on every available surface. As he dug through the freezer, searching for coffee amidst frozen pizza and corn dog boxes, he continued talking. "So you and Julian, huh? He didn't say anything to you? That's kinda messed up."

She didn't want to have this conversation. She barely knew Brad. "Yeah. No. I mean, we weren't really serious."

Brad finally found the can of coffee grounds and turned to face her. "Still, though. You don't have to be engaged to need a 'goodbye' before he leaves town."

It was exactly what Allie had been thinking all these weeks.

"Hey, you want to stay, and I'll make us both a cup?" he asked, looking hopeful. He could probably use the company after his breakup, Allie thought. Maybe she could use the company too.

"Sure, okay."

He smiled and began brewing the coffee. Allie sat down in the same chair where she'd eaten curry with Julian. Brad handed her a cup and sat down across from her. He doused his own cup with creamer and sugar. They sat in awkward silence while he stirred, and she stared into the brown liquid in her cup. "What happened with you and Jess?" Allie asked, mostly just to make conversation.

Brad slumped back into his chair. "We got in a big fight. I know it was probably for the best; we never really got along. But I can't help but miss her. Or parts of her, anyway."

"I know what you mean," Allie replied, thinking about Mitch. Her stomach began to churn. Coffee on an empty stomach was probably a bad idea.

Brad looked up at Allie across the table and asked, "Are you okay? You look really pale."

"I'm feeling a little sick to my stomach. What's in this coffee? I better —" She bolted up from the table and just made it to the toilet in time to throw up.

———

Brad had insisted on walking her back to her place, even though it was only a few doors down. She reassured him over and over that she would be all right and that she would call him if she needed anything. She felt like she had the flu. She pushed the door closed on his anxious face and was relieved to be alone. She had no intention of calling him.

She got a cool wash rag for her forehead and laid down on the bed, breathing in through her nose, out through her mouth, trying to soothe her stomach into not throwing up again. For the first time in years, she wanted her mom. Her mother had been busy her entire childhood, given her advertising career, but she had always made time when Allie was sick, bringing her chicken noodle soup and crackers or Gatorade.

Allie lay on the bed for several hours, trying to sleep but failing. She began to feel a little better, maybe even hungry. She made toast and tentatively munched it, dry, standing over the sink. Yes, she definitely felt better.

She milled around her apartment for a while, cleaning things up here and there. She sat down to read a dog-eared paperback she'd found abandoned on a table at the café among the crumbs of the last patron's breakfast. She'd been halfway through it for weeks but couldn't concentrate. She decided she felt okay to ride into town and see if Juleesa was at the café. She could sit at the counter and visit with her, as pathetic as it seemed to hang out at work for entertainment on her day off.

She brushed her teeth to get the acrid taste of vomit out of her mouth, splashed water on her face and changed clothes. She felt refreshed. She walked out the door and was just turning the key in the lock when Brad emerged from his place again. Allie sighed.

"Hey! You feeling better? Where are you going?" He was a needy puppy, desperate to tag along.

"Yeah, I'm a little better. I was headed into work."

"Oh yeah? You work at the café, right? I could use a good meal. Mind if I come with?"

"I don't have a car," she blurted. "Just my bike."

"We can take my truck!"

"Thanks, but I enjoy the bike ride, the fresh air and all," she said, just as desperate to shake him as he was to insert himself.

"Sweet. I have a bike. I'll join you."

Christ, can't this guy take a hint? "Um, you know what? I'm ac-tually not feeling so well again all of a sudden. I think I'll stay here, call in sick. Thanks, though."

She had her door unlocked and was back inside with it shut before he could respond. She caught a glimpse of his bewildered expression just as she escaped. Exasperated, Allie plopped herself down on the couch.

I just want to be alone. That's what I should've said. Why couldn't she ever think of those things in the moment? But that wasn't the truth, either. She'd been going into town for company. She just didn't want *his* company.

"I gotta get out of here," she said out loud to herself. She pulled her phone out of her pocket and called Jamie.

CHAPTER 19

Day 130

It had been three months since the accident. The boot from Mitch's broken ankle, way back before all of this, still sat in the corner of his living room. He left it there because it made him laugh, however cynically. Having to drag that thing around was nothing compared to what he'd been through since Galveston.

His casts were off, and he had a wheelchair, a walker and crutches — all of which he used, depending on his pain and energy level and where he wanted to go. He went to physical therapy three times a week. He'd had surgery to repair his shattered pelvis; there were permanent screws in there now. His main task as of late was learning how to walk properly again and trying to get mobility back into his hip joints.

Murphy helped immensely. She drove him to therapy and

checked in on him periodically. Mitch was on short-term disability, so for now, he could at least pay the bills. There wasn't much left over afterward, though.

Therapy took a lot out of him as did even a simple trip to the store for a few groceries. He took a lot of naps. And Allie was never far from his thoughts.

He knew she'd been staying with Jamie, doing what, he had no idea. He'd spoken with Jamie on the phone a few times, but she'd been tight-lipped about any details concerning her sister. She always steered the conversation toward Mitch's recovery.

He didn't have much to keep him busy at home. Before Allie had left, he'd spent his time with her, sometimes with her family and with friends from work. Coworkers had stopped by with casseroles and balloons and get-well cards the first week he was home, but now they were all back to their own lives.

He'd been poking around the job sites online, trying to find something he could do from home — something to keep him from going crazy with boredom. He was doing just that one Friday evening when he heard Murphy call up the stairs to him.

"Mitch, you home?"

"No, I went swing dancing."

"Well, then I guess I'll drink this all by myself."

"Hold on. I'm coming down."

It took considerable effort, but Mitch crutched down the stairs and fell onto the couch. Murphy was in the kitchen.

Mitch could hear her dropping ice into glasses. She returned to the living room with two glasses of whiskey and water over ice. "So how are you?" she asked. That was one of the things Mitch liked about her. When Murphy asked how he was, she really wanted to know.

"As good as it gets, I guess," Mitch said, "gesturing toward his damaged limbs. "What's the occasion?" Murphy seemed particularly upbeat this evening.

"Friday!" she said. "Plus, I just closed a case, and I'm feeling good."

"Good for you," Mitch grumbled, realizing he was not above petty jealousy. He missed feeling productive.

"Oh, you mean, 'Congratulations, my friend! Tell me about it!"

Mitch sighed. "Sorry. I'm just frustrated. And depressed a little, I guess. I've been trying to find some work, mostly to keep from going nuts, but I can't seem to."

"Really? The job market is great right now, and it's not like you're unqualified."

"Yea, I know. It's not that. I guess my heart's not really in it, you know? But cheer me up; tell me about your case."

It was a relief to let Murphy's story absorb him and escape from his own problems for a while. After that, the conversation meandered naturally into other topics. They told stories from their own pasts and talked about family drama. Mitch was on his second drink and already feeling pretty loopy. He'd cut back after his surgery, not wanting to mix alcohol with pain meds, so his tolerance was lower.

He found himself telling Murphy about his family — something he rarely talked about. His mom had died of breast cancer when he was sixteen, and the aftermath and how his dad had gone so sharply downhill wasn't something he liked to dwell on. But something had come uncorked in him, something that had wanted to come spilling out ever since Allie left.

He told her how he hadn't actually spent much time with his mom in the end. As horrible as it sounded, as a teenager with a newly minted driver's license, he'd had friends, his job at the food truck, and a girl he was interested in. And when he looked back on it, he realized he hadn't really believed his mom would die, would really be gone, no matter what the doctors said. He couldn't fathom it was possible. When he had gone to the hospital, it was hard to see her that way — weak, tired, sickly — and he and his dad powerless to do anything to help her. The guilt still ate at him. As he told Murphy about it, a thick lump formed in his throat.

"You were a kid," Murphy said softly. "That's a lot for a sixteen-year-old to deal with."

"You know, as fucked up as it sounds," he said, staring into his glass, "when she died, I actually felt a little bit relieved. It was hard watching her suffer. God, it's so complicated. I didn't believe she could actually die, but I was glad when she did. And I missed her. I missed the well version of her."

"How did your dad take it?"

"Terribly." Mitch told her how his dad, who'd rarely had more than a beer or two in a sitting, started drinking heavily. He'd still managed to go to work and keep his job, but he was mentally absent. And with no siblings to mourn his mother with him, Mitch was left to do it alone.

It had gone on like that, Mitch staying gone from the house as much as possible, his dad and him avoiding each other because being together seemed to make the pain of losing his mom all the greater for the next two years until Mitch left for college.

"I hadn't been at school two weeks when I got a call from my aunt. He'd killed himself. Blew his brains out all over the wall of our fucking living room." Mitch's eyes began to water, and he shifted his gaze toward the kitchen.

"I'm sorry," Murphy said quietly.

Then, abruptly, Mitch asked, "Want another drink?" And sprang from the couch best he could in his condition, quickly limping off toward the kitchen with both of their glasses.

When he returned, setting both full glasses on the table with a clinking of ice, he asked, "So what's your story?"

"My story?"

"Yeah. I told you all my gory details. What about you?"

She gave a brief laugh and said, "It's late. Thanks for the drink, but I need to go. We can get into my shit another time."

Mitch visibly deflated. "Yeah, sure. Okay."

He liked Murphy a lot. He found himself thinking of her often. He'd see articles online he knew she'd be interested in or a tv show she'd think was funny. She'd been the one to bring him groceries when he first got home and couldn't get to the store. She drove him to therapy every week. Mitch had only known her a handful of months, but they'd spent so much time together and in such emotionally wrought circumstances it seemed like he'd known her for years.

He reached out and took her hand. She smiled and looked down at his hand over hers, resting on her leg. She squeezed the fingers that lay underneath her palm.

"Thank you," Mitch said, meeting her eyes earnestly, "for taking care of me, for doing all the things you've done over the past months. I didn't have anyone else, and …just, thank you. It means a lot to me. I —" He hesitated but then decided to just be out with it.

"I really like you. A lot."

"I like you, too, Mitch." She looked up at him with a pained expression. "But I don't want you to get the wrong idea."

"Which is?" he asked softly.

"Don't play like you don't know. I like you a lot, but you're my friend. I don't want you to think I mean it romantically or sexually. That's just not what this is for me."

"Why not? What is it about me that's so unappealing?"

A cynical bark of a laugh escaped her throat, and Mitch felt surprised and wounded.

"Look, I know you don't get it," she explained, obviously trying to control her annoyance, "but this is always the way it is.

Consider for a moment that it has nothing to do with you. Why does there have to be something wrong with you, from my perspective, for me not to want to sleep with you?"

"Is it because of Allie? Or your daughter? I'd understand if you didn't want to get involved right now," Mitch said, trying to be reasonable.

Murphy sighed. "Mitch, it's just that I've had this conversation so many times before."

"Well, I haven't. Humor me?" He shrugged his shoulders in bewilderment.

"I could tell you it was because of Allie or because I want to focus on raising my daughter, but that wouldn't be the truth, not the whole of it anyway. The truth is, I like you a lot, but I haven't been attracted to any guy in a romantic sense for a very long time."

There was a pause, and Mitch felt the need to fill it with something, so he tentatively said the first thing that came to mind. "Are you gay?"

"Are you fucking kidding me?" Murphy slapped her hands onto her thighs and glared at him. She looked as if she were about to spring off the couch and stomp out the door. "Just because I'm not attracted to you doesn't mean I'm a lesbian."

Mitch's face reddened with embarrassment. "I know, I know. Sorry. It just slipped out."

They sat there, staring into their glasses for a few beats until Murphy broke the awkwardness. "Not that there's anything wrong with that."

"With what? Oh, OH! Yeah." He forced a little chuckle.

"Look," Murphy said, "I'm not sure what it is. I just haven't felt like having that kind of relationship with anyone in recent years. I don't know if it's hormonal or what, but I don't miss it. I enjoy being around friends. I value our friendship immensely. I just don't feel the desire to entangle myself with anyone further."

"You don't miss it?" he asked rhetorically. "That's hard to imagine."

"For you, I'm sure it is," she said, smiling. "I've had a lot of male friends over the years. I *like* guys, but I've lost a lot of them when they couldn't get past my not wanting to sleep with them."

Mitch just looked at her, blinking expectantly, waiting for her to go on.

"Look, If you can't be my friend without wanting it to be something else, tell me, but I don't want you secretly expecting more. Please, whatever you do, be honest with me about it because I'm not going to change my mind about this."

Her eyes had a pleading look. Mitch looked at her and tried to imagine what it would be like to make friends and often have them expect more than you could give. "I'm sorry, Murphy. That must suck to lose friends like that."

Then, she looked at him curiously. "Mitch, have you ever had platonic female friends?"

"Well...Jamie."

"That doesn't count; she's Allie's sister."

Mitch just sighed and looked at her. This conversation was giving him a headache. Or maybe it was the whiskey.

"So," Murphy said with a smile. "Friends?"

By the time she left and Mitch dragged his crippled ass upstairs, it was eleven o'clock. He'd switched to drinking water, and his earlier buzz had worn off. He didn't feel sleepy, but his body was exhausted just from getting around the house. He lay in the bed that more and more these days felt like just his and stared at the ceiling.

He understood where Murphy was coming from, and he knew the value and rarity of a truly good friend, but there was still another little boy part of him that whined,

Why doesn't she like me? What's wrong with me? I'm an asshole. What if I never have sex again? What if I die alone?

"Oh, shut up," he said out loud, disgusted. He rolled on his side, pulled the pillow over his head and tossed and turned for a good long while before falling asleep.

CHAPTER 20

Day 130

Allie lay on her back on the guest bed, watching the sun spilling through the window, making swaying patterns on the bed through the tree branches outside. She'd gotten up, showered, dressed, made the bed…then collapsed back down onto it, unable to make herself get back up and start the day. Where would she go from here? She couldn't stay in this holding pattern at Jamie's house forever, but she felt paralyzed against taking whatever the next step was.

"Can I come in?" Jamie's muffled voice came through the door alongside a soft knock. She walked in with two steaming mugs in her hands. She put them down on the nightstand and plopped down on the bed next to her sister. Allie's body bobbled on the bed. She had shifted her gaze to the ceiling, not bothering to sit up.

"So is this what you've got planned today?" Jamie asked. "A busy morning of ceiling staring and navel-gazing?"

"You tired of my freeloading already?"

"I love having you around, and you've been a big help with the twins; I know Daniel appreciates it. But what are you *doing*, exactly? As much as I enjoy your company, you're going to have to figure this shit out sooner or later."

"What shit exactly?"

"That shit exactly," Jamie retorted, pointing to Allie's belly rising and falling with her breaths.

"What do you mean?" Allie asked, still focused on the ceiling, blinking blankly at it.

"Don't be obtuse. You're about three months along. I'm not an idiot. Talk to me."

Allie sighed and finally turned her head to look at Jamie. "I don't think you're an idiot. I just haven't been ready to talk about it."

Allie sat up, and Jamie handed her a mug. She blew on it, sipped and grimaced. "Since when did you switch to tea? Who do you think I am?"

"I think," said Jamie, "you're a pregnant woman who could stand to watch her caffeine intake."

Allie held the mug in both hands. She focused her moroseness on the weak, brown liquid within. At least it was warm. "I don't know what to do. Every time I start to think about it, I get overwhelmed."

"Do you want to keep it?" Jamie asked in a low voice.

"Of course!" Allie's tea sloshed in her mug, threatening to spill onto her lap, but it stayed contained.

"Calm down. I just want to be sure you're considering all of your options."

"I'm not having an abortion." Allie's voice rose and then softened. "I mean, I did think about it, but after the miscarriages and how much of a mess I was, I just… couldn't. When I think about being a parent, I want to; I'm ready. It's complicated." Allie sighed.

Jamie stared at Allie evenly, as if she were weighing what to say next. "Look, Allie. I am behind you, one hundred percent, no matter what you decide, but I do want you to think this through. What about adoption?"

Allie laughed sarcastically, "God, Mom would kill me if she found out. For her, that'd be worse than an abortion."

"Let's leave Mom out of this for now. This is your decision, and she'll have to live with whatever you decide, and that's IF you decide to tell her."

Allie's eyes, full of tears now, met Jamie's. "The idea of giving her up, I can't bear it. But also, raising her by myself…"

"Her?" Jamie asked with a smile.

Allie blushed a little. "I've just been thinking of it as a 'her' for some reason."

"First of all," Jamie said, "you wouldn't be raising her alone.

You've got support. You've got me, and you've got Mom. I know she's a pain, but she'd love to have a little grandbaby to care for."

"Not that she did a lot of caregiving when we were little," Allie said.

"True, but she's gotten softer in her old age," Jamie said. "But Allie…who's her father?"

Allie burst into tears and buried her face in her hands. "That's the thing," she sobbed. "I'm not really sure."

Jamie enfolded her sister in her arms and held her, letting her cry. Allie's shoulders heaved; she sobbed loudly, completely, gasping. Then, her breath gradually slowed and deepened. Her sister released her and then turned to the practical.

"What we're going to do first is get you some clothes," Jamie said. "You can't go around with your jeans unbuttoned all the time for the next six months. C'mon. I still have some stuff from when I was pregnant with the twins."

Allie followed Jamie to her closet where Jamie lent her a pair of maternity jeans, some yoga pants and a few flowy tops and t-shirts. When Allie was sufficiently outfitted, Jamie said, "It's already 11 o'clock; let's go to lunch! My treat. Lemme just pop downstairs and make sure it's okay with Daniel."

While Jamie was downstairs, Allie milled in the upstairs hallway, perusing the family photos. There were a few of Allie and Jamie together and their mother and father as well as some of Daniel's family, but despite their short amount of time on the planet, most of them were of the twins: as infants, swaddled in the arms of various family members, their first birthday party, playing at the park, the first time they went swimming. *They sure do take up a lot of space in a short amount of time*, Allie thought.

Allie heard the adult voices downstairs begin to rise. She tried not to eavesdrop, but she could hear Jamie loud and clear: "So I'm supposed to just let my sister mope around the house all day? She's got problems right now; she needs me. You don't *need* to go off and play golf for five fucking hours."

"Jamie, please. Language! I do actually need to play golf if you want me to keep from going insane in this house. You get out of it five days a week. I am here ALL THE TIME."

"But—"

"I know your sister's here. She's been here for three months. I love her, but I can't be expected to treat her like a house guest on a constant basis. I have a life, too! At least I used to."

Jamie's voice was quieter now. "You're right. I know you need some time to yourself. But she needs me right now, and I want to be there for her."

"How about I go play nine holes? That way, when I get back, it won't be too late, and y'all can go out." Allie marveled at how calm, how rational Dan sounded when a moment ago, he seemed like he was edging toward explosion.

"Sure." Jamie didn't sound thrilled with the compromise, but she was calmer.

Shortly after Allie heard Dan's car back down the driveway, she headed tentatively down the stairs and met Jamie on her way up with Max on her hip. "Bad news."

"Yeah, I heard."

"Sorry. I didn't realize we were that loud. The kids have a playdate in about thirty minutes. It'll only last an hour or two, depending on how long it takes them all to hit pre-nap meltdown. Wanna come?"

"As wonderful as you make it sound, I think I'll stay here and rest."

"Okay. We'll go to dinner then, yeah?"

Allie nodded and smiled at her sister.

Jamie took Allie to an Italian place where the lighting was low and the booths were cozy. Over lasagna, calamari and a carafe of chianti, Allie told Jamie about Mitch's visit to her apartment in Galveston and her short relationship with the amazing disappearing Julian.

"So mathematically," Jamie said, "It could be either one of them."

"Yes," responded Allie, color rising in her cheeks.

"And it didn't occur to any of the three of you at any point to use a condom?"

Allie full-on blushed. "I know it sounds dumb, but after losing the other ones and being so heartbroken, I just didn't think about it."

Her sister raised a quizzical eyebrow. "Because you got pregnant on accident twice before, you didn't think it could happen again? Help me out here."

"I don't know. I...just so much was going on in my head, and...I don't have an excuse. All I know is I didn't think about it, and I guess neither one of them did either." Allie slumped into the booth, embarrassed by her own defensiveness, feeling childish and sulky.

"They probably assumed you were on the pill. They tend to do that, you know. So, the million-dollar question is, when are you going to tell either or both of them? 'Cause you're going to have to tell at least one to figure out who the father is."

"Well, that's the thing," Allie said quietly. "I've been thinking, what if I didn't find out?"

"How is THAT going to work?"

"I don't know. I haven't thought out the details. I mean, why does it really matter who her father is? I could raise her on my own," Allie said.

"You could," Jamie conceded. "And you know we'd help out every way we can, but Allie, do you think that's really fair? To any of them? If either of them were horrible people, I'd say, 'Fuck 'em,' but they're not. I mean, they've both got issues, but who doesn't? Don't you think she would want to know her father?"

Allie was silent, staring into her plate, pushing the remains of congealed noodles and sauce around it. "He slapped me," she mumbled into her plate.

Jamie stiffened. "I know. He obviously lost his shit, and I sure as hell don't think you should forgive him." Jamie ran her hand through her hair and began rapidly twirling the ends with nervous energy. "I don't know, Allie. I'm pissed as hell at him. But I've also known him for a long time. If he is the father, you can talk to him about it. If he truly realizes what a horrible mistake he made, and if he's willing to make amends, I don't know, see a counselor or something…Do you really think he'd be a danger to his daughter?"

"No!" Allie said quickly. It hadn't even occurred to her he'd hurt a child, and she actually did not think he'd ever hit her again. She was not afraid of him. But could she forgive him? For being so dogged in imposing his idea of "right" on her, he lost control of himself and intentionally hurt her.

"What if it's Julian?" Jamie asked.

Allie sighed. "I like him a lot. He's a good guy. I think. But he just skipped town without so much as a "see ya," so I'm not sure he's dad material. But I only knew him for a matter of weeks, so what the hell do I know?"

On the way home in the car, night had fallen, and Allie was staring out the passenger window, lost in thought, when Jamie spoke up. "You don't have to marry him, you know. Whoever the father is, you don't have to be *with* him to have him be a father to the baby."

"Yeah," Allie said, "True."

———

For the next several months, Allie milled around Jamie and Daniel's house. She helped out whenever she could — watched the twins, cleaned up, did her best to make herself useful. Everything was going perfectly with the pregnancy, with one unexpected surprise.

When she and Jamie had gone to Allie's 24-week appointment, she'd been nervous. The anatomical ultrasound would show the baby in detail. It was the same appointment she'd found out she lost the last one.

As she lay on the table, cold gel on her belly while the technician rolled the wand around looking for a heartbeat, Allie held her breath. Jamie was squeezing her hand; she knew how stressful this was for Allie, even if the technician didn't.

"Ah, there!"

Allie dared to breathe. Then after a few heavy seconds, the technician, beaming with pride, said, "There's the heartbeat!" as if he'd somehow created it.

"Oh!" Jamie said softly. And for a minute, she and Allie just stared, watching and listening to the rhythmic thump of new life. Tears filled both of their eyes.

"See right there?" the tech continued. "Those are testicles, and that right there is a penis. It's a boy. He's giving us a nice, unobstructed view."

"Figures," Jamie snorted. But Allie was captivated by the black-and-white image on the screen. There was a little person inside her, a human being who was going to come out, by all accounts, healthy and whole in a few months. The fact that it wasn't the girl she'd predicted mattered so little, she barely noticed it. She couldn't hold her emotions in any longer. The tears spilled over the rims of her eyes and coursed down her face.

On the ride home, Allie and Jamie talked nonstop.

"It still could be a 'she.'" Jamie said thoughtfully. You don't know what gender it will identify with. Odds are, though, it'll be a boy with balls and a sense of entitlement all rolled into one."

"Shut up," said Allie laughing. "You don't really think they're born with that, do you? The sense of entitlement, I mean."

"No, but when I'm mad at them about it, I find it hard to give them the benefit of the doubt."

"Daniel isn't like that, though, is he?"

"Not for the most part. His friends poke fun at him about being a stay-at-home dad. It's just 'harmless teasing,'" Jamie said, raising her hands briefly from the steering wheel to provide air quotes, "but I can tell it bothers him. He loves being there for the twins, but he's not immune to other people's judgment. None of us are.

"Sometimes when he's been out with the guys, he'll go around for a few days trying to do things extra macho, like he's trying to prove a point."

"Like what? Kill spiders extra hard?"

Jamie snorted. "Actually, yeah," and both sisters laughed so hard tears began to flow again.

"I'm sorry," said Allie, "I don't mean to laugh at him. I know it's hard being someone besides who you're 'supposed' to be.

"You oughtta know," Jamie said, glancing down at her sister's left hand. Anyway, sometimes you laugh because you're tired of crying about it."

————

It had been three weeks since the ultrasound, and Allie was running out of time. She wished she could find out who the father was before deciding what to do, but barring hit-and-run DNA acquisition, that wasn't an option.

Allie went for a walk to think. The air was brisk and cool, and the sun was shining. She could feel in her hips that her walk was becoming more of a waddle. Jamie's old maternity clothes were now quite filled out on her body. Physically, she felt good, healthy.

She thought about those few short weeks with Julian and smiled. She had enjoyed the sex, but she'd enjoyed his company as well. She missed him the way she would a close friend. *Would he be a good father? Would he even want to be?* She didn't know him well enough to guess.

Mitch. She had so many complicated feelings about him. She resented him for taking so little interest in her opinions and life choices. She resented the whole white-picket-fence existence he strived for. With his parents gone, she knew Mitch longed for a family; she was sympathetic. She was fortunate to have her parents, her sister. But she didn't want to be steamrolled into his plans.

Allie smiled. She reminisced about when she'd moved in with Mitch, the two of them jostling her couch into the house, chipping the doorframe, and laughing as they dropped it and plopped themselves down on the cushions right there in the doorway.

She remembered when she'd miscarried, he had been right there with her, a companion who, comfortingly, reflected her own misery. The shock had been coupled with a deep, aching hurt in her gut and heart, but having him there eased the pain some.

She knew Mitch would be a good father. And they had a deep history together. Even if they weren't a couple, Allie could envision them working together to raise a child.

As Allie trudged up a small mound of white rocks to cross the train tracks, she suddenly stopped and looked up toward the tree branches crisscrossing the blue sky beyond. She realized she had begun thinking about which one would be the best parent, not which one was biologically the father.

"Huh," she said out loud to the trees.

CHAPTER 21

Day 220

It had been over six months since the accident, and Mitch was finally getting back to some semblance of what he thought of as normal. He was completely done with the wheelchair and only used the cane when tired. He was showing houses again and even going to happy hour here and there with friends from the office…Well, acquaintances who were good for a few drinks and bullshit conversation. But sometimes, that's all he wanted at the end of the day.

Sometimes he met Murphy somewhere, usually on the weekends. They'd see a movie or go to dinner. He still occasionally wondered, if they made such good friends, why it couldn't be more than that. But mostly, he'd let it go. He'd realized he wasn't in love with Murphy; with Allie having left and the accident and everything, he'd just been needy, much as he hated to admit it.

He went on a couple of dates with someone he'd met at a happy hour. She was the friend of the sister of a guy he worked with — Samantha. They had a good time; it was fine. They kissed in the car at the end of the second date, which was nice. But they didn't go out again.

He'd heard from Tyler and Aiden several times, mostly via short text when he thought to check up on them. They came by the house once, too. They'd sat on the edge of the back porch and talked about Gentry.

"My parents are having a tough time with Gentry's death," Aiden had said with his head down. "Mom keeps saying they shoulda let him come home. I found my dad crying in the living room late the other night, but he played it off like it was just allergies. I don't get it. They didn't even talk to him anymore."

"He was still family," Mitch said, thinking of his father. "They still loved him."

"I miss him," Tyler chimed in. "Not so much the way he was at the end, but how he was when we were younger, you know? When he used to play baseball with us in the backyard."

"Yeah," said Aiden despondently.

"It's complicated with family," Mitch said.

They'd eventually ruled Gentry's death an accident, with no evidence to the contrary. Based on Aiden and Tyler's report that he was extremely high and probably not just on the pot they'd smoked with him in the woods, it was assumed he fell and hit his head, then stumbled down to the creek, falling to the bed below.

Friday evening, Mitch was on his way back from a baseball game. He'd gone with Murphy and some of her friends. They'd had a couple of beers and ballpark chili dogs. He had a little indigestion, but it had been a fun evening. Murphy dropped him off on the sidewalk in front of his house, and as he walked up the path with barely a limp, he smiled. It was good to enjoy something as simple as a baseball game again, to do it with friends.

He put his key in the front door lock, hearing Murphy drive away as he did, but the key turned too easily. It was already unlocked. He froze; he knew he had locked that door. He was a little obsessed with door locking, always accidentally locking Allie out when she was outside in the yard. When she'd lived there.

He scanned the porch and the front yard. Nothing seemed amiss — no cars parked near the house — a peaceful evening, just barely gone dark, with a hint of light still at the horizon and the crickets tuning up.

He slowly pushed open the front door, listening, ready, his heart beginning to pump faster.

Allie was standing by the couch, still wearing her coat.

"Jesus!" he said, exhaling, "You about gave me a heart attack. I thought someone broke in!"

"Nope, just me," she said with a small, nervous smile. "I used the key in the rock."

He'd forgotten about the spare key Allie had put in the fake rock hidden deep in the bushes by the front door. He had never used it and had barely registered it when she'd told him she'd put it there.

She stood there, staring at him as he hesitated, still just inside the door. He was having a hard time processing that she was really there. It was like the dreams he'd had of her being just beyond his reach, there and not there, dreams he'd stopped having lately. But here she was, solid, in the living room, wrapped in a coat that was too warm for the weather and way too big for her.

For so long, Mitch had thought about her almost every minute of the day. He had longed for her to come home. He'd fantasized about her showing up just like this. He'd wrap his arms around her, and they would both apologize and start to mend their relationship.

The past several months, though, he'd finally begun to let go of the idea of her returning and things going back to the way they used to be. He thought about her less and less. But now, here she was, and images from their last meeting came flooding back to him as if they'd happened hours ago. She'd slept with him, made him believe, and then told him she wouldn't come home and he couldn't stay. And now here she was, standing in the fucking living room.

"Get the fuck out." he heard himself say.

"Mitch, wait—" The pleading look in her eye made him furious.

"No. You can't just show up here like this. You kicked me out last time; now it's my turn." He looked her in the eye and expected her to beg to stay or leave, tearfully, regretfully, but instead, he saw a hardening in her eyes.

"I kicked you out because you fucking slapped me. Or did you conveniently forget that part?" she spat.

He had beaten himself up about it for months after Galveston. But, in that moment, in his surprise and anger at seeing Allie, he actually had forgotten that part. At her reminder, he deflated. He dragged himself across the room to fall onto the couch. As he did, Allie adjusted her stance so she was just across from him, out of arm's reach. He grimaced.

"I'm sorry, Allie. God, I'm so sorry. I can't believe..." His head was in his hands. He was still angry at her, but that fell into the background of the remorse for what he'd done. She had behaved erratically, but that was no excuse for how he'd responded. "I've never done anything like that before! I've never even wanted to." He said, shaking his head.

"I know." Allie gave him a tight-lipped smile. "I've known you a long time, Mitch, and I know that's not who you are, but maybe you need to look closer at how you allowed yourself to get to that point, even just once."

Those words had the ring of a practiced speech, maybe something she and Jamie had discussed, but that didn't make them any less true. And here was the part he really didn't like to think about: If he'd done it once without even realizing what he was doing, what would it take to set him off again?

Mitch looked up at Allie over the coffee table, standing with her arms crossed. "You're right; I do need to think about that. I'm not good at that kind of thing, but I do."

She took a deep breath. "I came back here for a reason. I, well, I had this whole thing I was going to say, but now I've forgotten it."

Mitch looked at her expectantly. He had no idea what she was going to say. Did she want to stay? Did she want to pick up some of her things? Did he even *want* her to stay?

"Mitch, I'm pregnant."

Mitch sat on the couch gaping while Allie slowly removed her voluminous coat and placed it on the back of the chair in front of her. His eyes drifted to her belly, round and full. She clasped her hands together under it, cradling the new life inside. His eyes wandered back to her face; she was smiling but looked like she might cry at any moment. As her words and her image in front of him settled into his brain, he felt a rising excitement.

"Oh my god, Allie! You're like…"

"28 weeks."

"And everything's…"

"Just fine." Her smile broadened.

Mitch couldn't help himself. He leaped off the couch and walked around the chair with his hands out. "Can I?"

"Sure. He's your baby too."

Mitch fell to his knees and gingerly placed his hands on her belly. He felt something roll under his right palm. "Whoah!"

Allie laughed. "Yeah, he's been rolling side to side like that a lot lately."

"So, it's a boy?"

"So says the ultrasound."

Mitch stood and put his arms around her, thinking she might pull away, thinking he wouldn't blame her, but she returned the embrace. They stood entwined together for the first time in months, basking in the glow of impending life. Finally, they pulled apart.

"Sit down," he offered. "Do you want some water or something to eat?"

"Just water, thanks."

Allie sat on the couch while he retrieved two glasses of water from the kitchen. When he returned, she commented awkwardly, "So you're healing up nicely?" She eyed the crutches leaning forgotten in the corner of the living room.

"Yeah. I'm not going to lie; it was tough. A lot of physical therapy. I've never appreciated the simple ability to walk more than I do now. Getting around in a wheelchair or on crutches is a real pain in the ass."

"I'm glad you're feeling better. I'm sorry..," she paused, setting her water glass on the table, and looked into his eyes. "Part of me wanted to be there to help you, but—"

"Allie, don't worry about it. I was an ass. No one blames you." He felt eager to reassure her, to keep her here now that, suddenly, it seemed he might get what he'd yearned for. There was going to be a baby. He could hardly believe it.

"I know no one blames me, and…look," she sighed, brushing aside his comment. "After you slapped me, I was angry at you and even a little scared of you."

Mitch looked down into the water glass he held in his lap. That part hurt, most of all because it was valid.

Allie continued, "But that's not the reason I didn't stay with you in the hospital. It was *why* you slapped me."

He looked at her searchingly.

"Mitch, I'm the first person to admit that what I did was crazy." She looked down at the stump where her left thumb used to be. "But I've done a lot of thinking about why I did it. It wasn't on purpose, but it wasn't completely on accident, either."

"Allie, you don't have to tell me this." He wasn't sure he wanted to hear it.

"I know, but I need to tell you. And I need you to hear me,

okay?"

He nodded.

"On some level, I needed a way out. It's not that I don't love you; it's just that I felt trapped. I didn't know how to talk to you about it. I tried, but I guess I didn't do a very good job."

Mitch sighed. "I didn't do a great job of listening, either."

"I felt confined to this life, this little town, and I felt like I couldn't know myself here — too many distractions."

"Was I a distraction?" He asked quietly, leaning forward, his hands clasped tensely in his lap.

She nodded, "Yeah, I think so. And in Galveston, I realized that you didn't want to accept that things may turn out differently than you planned. You were so attached to us as a little nuclear family, you lost your shit when you realized you couldn't talk me back into it."

Mitch nodded. There was some truth to that. "But the baby —" He was starting to feel a little panicky. What if she took him away? What if she didn't want Mitch in their life? He'd only known about the kid for ten minutes, but he was already in love, and the thought of losing him was unbearable.

"Mitch, I came back to tell you because I hope you'll want to raise him with me."

"Yes! Yes, of course!" he responded, letting out a breath he hadn't realized he was holding. His shoulders relaxed.

"But I don't want you to get the wrong idea. I'm not coming back to you. I'm getting a place in town…"

"But you can stay here. This is our house."

"This is *your* house. It always was. I just moved in. No, I need my own space, but I'll be close. You can come to all the doctor's appointments, and when he's born, we can raise him together — two parents, just not in the same house."

Mitch frowned. "I don't know…" Then he looked at her, and he could see. "I don't have a choice, do I?"

"You can choose to raise your son with me, and I hope you will, or you can choose not to, but you can't make my choices for me. You can't make me move back in with you."

"But he'll grow up in a broken home!" He said with anguish.

"Broken home? What is this, 1950? He'll grow up with two parents who love and care for him, two parents who know how to work together and have his best interest at heart. We just happen to live in different houses. It'll be normal for him. Nothing's broken."

Mitch looked down at her beautiful, swollen belly and imagined the little person who would come out of there in a few months. He knew he didn't have a choice at all. He already loved him fiercely.

CHAPTER 22

Day 265

Allie sat in her little living room and smiled. It was small but sunny and cozy. She had a warm mug of ginger tea clasped in both hands. Herbal tea had grown on her over the past months. She propped her feet on the rickety coffee table and wiggled her toes inside her socks.

She'd found the duplex about 20 minutes from Mitch's place before she'd gone to see him. Afterward, she'd signed a year-long lease. As much as she loved the beach, her place in Galveston had never felt like home — more of a temporary stopover.

She hadn't told Mitch the specifics of her moving. She knew he'd want to help, and she wasn't ready for him to be that involved in her life. Jamie had come down and helped her pick out some second-hand furniture and paint the living room a sunny yellow color. The brightness livened up the room and distracted from the dings and dents here and there in the walls.

There were built-in bookshelves along one wall, and Allie had already made a trip to Half Price Books to populate them with a few of her favorites. With two bedrooms upstairs, the house was just big enough — a place to sleep, eat, write and a room for the baby when he arrived. Perfect. It felt cozy and homey to Allie already.

Mitch had tried to give her some money before they parted ways after that first meeting, but Allie had refused. She'd borrowed some from Jamie instead for the deposit on the duplex and the furniture. Her next task was to get a job.

Waiting tables sounded wholly unappealing at this point in her pregnancy. She considered inquiring at her old job, but the idea made her shudder. It would be too much like going back to her old life, and despite being back in Lime to be close to Mitch and raise the baby, she wanted this life to be new.

She'd seen a "Help Wanted" sign at a little boutique in town while furniture shopping with Jamie. She'd peeked inside, and the shop seemed cozy in a cluttered sort of way — intricate, abstract, modern quilts thrown over rocking chairs and little end tables; a section of old books in the back; ancient-looking, formal China that might be worth a fortune or might be junk; jewelry, handmade by local folks, adorning the counter by the register. Allie and Jamie hadn't bought anything, but the woman behind the counter (Allie was pretty sure she was the owner,) had been friendly; she'd asked about Allie's due date. Allie had pocketed a card for the shop, Knot Uncommon, so she fished it out of her purse and dialed the number.

———

They sat on the edge of the creek, Allie's bare feet dangling in the pleasantly cool water. It wasn't too far from her cave — the one she'd slept in with a throbbing, newly-thumbless hand all those months ago. It seemed like years. She and Mitch had come here after the appointment with the ob/gyn because Allie wanted to talk. She wanted to tell him about her job, so he'd quit offering to lend her money and maybe discuss how they were about to be parents and what that would look like.

"So you said you got a job?" Mitch prompted.

"Yes. It's that little store, Knot Uncommon." She shrugged her shoulders self-consciously. She could feel him looking at her as she watched the water below. "Shirley, the owner, is nice. I've only been there a week, but I like it so far."

"You know you don't have to work right now. I've got enough to support us both."

"I know, but I like working. And it still leaves me plenty of time to write."

"What are you writing these days?"

"A bit of fiction, a bit of memoir."

"Memoir, huh? You've got a lot of material there."

"Yep," she responded cryptically.

They were silent for a while, but Allie could feel tension crackling in the air between them. He had something on his mind. "Allie, there's something I want to ask you. What happened that night in the cave? I don't know if you know this, but they found a guy, Gentry Collins, down in the creek near that cave not too long after you were there."

"You knew I spent the night in the cave? I didn't think you'd remember that place."

"I didn't," Mitch said ruefully, pressing his lips together. "The cops found it during their search, found some of your hair in there."

Allie swallowed the lump in her throat and focused on her dangling feet. She hadn't expected to have to discuss that night in the cave with Mitch, but if this guy, Gentry, had been found, she supposed it was inevitable it would come back to her. She didn't speak, so Mitch continued.

"He died of a blunt-force wound to the back of the head. And I just wondered…What?"

Allie could feel the color draining from her face as she stared at him with dawning horror. Until that very moment, she could assume the man she pushed out of the cave had regained consciousness and limped home. After all, he'd been gone when she'd awoken. "He's dead?" She looked back across the creek, eyes unfocused, and told him.

"It was in the cave. I was wet and bleeding, and my hand hurt really badly, but I was trying to sleep. I was exhausted.

Then, he was just there. I don't know how he got there. I didn't hear him, maybe because of the storm, but I felt something. I opened my eyes, and he was right there, crouching next to me. He —" her voice cracked.

"Allie, shhh. It's okay." Mitch put his hand on her thigh in a gesture meant to be comforting. When she shuttered, he moved it back to his own leg.

"He got on top of me, and he was trying to pin my arms down and get his hand down my pants at the same time, but something was wrong with him. He was drunk or high or something. I could feel his stupid cock pressing into my leg. And I just, all of a sudden, I wasn't scared. I was mad.

"I wedged my knees between us and kicked with both legs, and he stumbled back off of me. Then I…I pushed him. He fell backward out of the cave, and when I looked over the side, he was lying on the ground.

"It was still raining hard, and I watched him. I was afraid he was dead and also afraid he wasn't dead. I can't believe it, but I actually fell asleep right there at the mouth of the cave, watching him. When I woke up, he was gone."

There was a pregnant pause, and then Mitch said, "I guess he got up, wandered off, and fell in the creek."

Mitch recounted how he met Tyler and Aiden, who had told him about Tyler's brother and how he and Murphy had discovered Gentry.

They were silent for a while again, and Allie could see Mitch taking furtive glances at her, as she kept her eyes trained on her feet. Finally, she spoke, her voice shaking. "I – I killed him. I can't believe – I just wanted him off me. Oh, god."

Allie buried her face in her hands. She was too stunned to cry. She felt frozen. This time, when Mitch touched her to put his arm around her back, she let him. They stayed that way for what seemed like hours to Allie, though the light hadn't changed, so it must have only been a few minutes.

"I'm not sorry he's dead," she whispered into her hands. "I *am* sorry for his family; I didn't want to kill him, I just wanted him off of me. But I'm not sorry I killed him. Am I a horrible person?" She looked up at Mitch and saw sympathy in his soft eyes.

"Not at all. It's the one thing you've said in the past year that I actually understand."

This feeling – the conflicting anger, guilt and grief roiling through her head about Gentry, and Mitch staring at her – it was just too much. She scrambled to change the subject. "So, who's this Murphy?

Mitch seemed relieved to move on as well. "Jealous?" he asked with a smirk.

"Not in the least," Allie replied, rolling her eyes. "Just curious."

"She was the detective assigned to your case. She helped me even after they decided you'd left on your own and shut down the official investigation. She came by a lot when I was recovering — took me to therapy, brought me groceries and stuff."

"You like her?"

"Of course. We're friends."

"No, I mean you LIKE like her, don't you?" Allie teased.

"I —" Mitch, blushing furiously, hid his face in his hands. "I tried to kiss her once," he admitted, peeking at Allie between his fingers.

"And?"

"She didn't want that kind of thing from me."

"Oh, she didn't like you like THAT?" Allie was still smirking, milking the grammar school humor for all it was worth. It felt good to joke around with Mitch again.

"Stop it. It was…misguided. She's right. We're much better as friends."

Allie smiled. She could feel that all-knowing expression cross her face. The one that always annoyed Mitch.

"What?"

"Very mature of you, Mitchell."

"Whatever. You don't want me, Murphy doesn't want me. I'm doomed to die alone."

"You're just cursed with a penchant for complex women."

He laughed, throwing his head back "Yeah, definitely cursed."

———

It was Monday. It had been three days since their conversation at the creek, and Allie hadn't thought much about Gentry. She worked at the boutique all weekend and was too tired in the evening to do much more than take a bath and fall asleep.

Shirley had given Allie a bike that had been collecting cobwebs in her garage. It was a lot like the beach cruiser she'd left behind in Galveston but older. At 30 weeks pregnant, it was getting hard to ride, and she always had to pee the entire time, but she didn't have much other option. Mitch had offered to drive her to work, then he'd exasperatedly offered to buy her a car, but she was having none of it. Allie didn't want to feel like she owed him anything; she needed to do this herself.

Today was her day off, and she was looking forward to relaxing — maybe doing a little reading or writing. After breakfast, she wandered around her new home with a mug of tea in her hands. The second bedroom was already set up as a nursery. The house was still a bit sparse, but all the necessary items were there. It was the first place Allie'd lived in her adult life that felt like hers. It didn't feel like a temporary stopover, waiting for something better, and she didn't share it with anyone else.

Allie thought about Gentry now. She felt like she should feel worse about it or at least conflicted. She'd grown so used to feeling guilty about even the tiny things, she was surprised to find no guilt was there.

She sat down at her little writing desk in her bedroom and

tried to pick up the thread of the story she was working on, but after crafting and deleting the same paragraphs several times, she gave up and went downstairs.

She thought about taking a walk, but one look outside revealed a thunderstorm rumbling not far off. She had no desire to get caught out in that again. She perused the few books adorning her living room shelves and selected an old favorite, *The Gunslinger*. The weather outside seemed perfect for it, but as she sat with her legs up on the couch, she couldn't get into the story. Finally, she closed the book with a sigh and stared across the room.

Then, she dug her phone out of the couch where it was often lodged and called Jamie.

"Hey, sis!" Jamie said. "Hold on a sec…Okay, I'm in my office now. What's up?"

"Oh, nothing really. I was just thinking, it would be cool if you could come out, and stay with me before the baby's born — sort of a last hurrah? We could go on walks, you could paint my toenails 'cause I can't reach them anymore. It would be fun."

Jamie sighed wistfully. "Yeah, that does sound like fun. I would love a break, but I only have a week of vacation left this year, and you're going to want me there *after* the baby's here. Trust me on this one."

"Yeah, sure; that makes sense."

"What's the matter?"

"I don't know. I guess I'm just kinda bored and maybe a little lonely. Also scared. I'm going to be somebody's mom. It's weird. I'm not sure I even know how to do that."

"I know what you mean. I felt that way, too, but you just sort of bungle through it. Everyone does."

"What if I screw it up, Jamie? I mean, I want to be there for this kid more than Mom was there for us, but what if I go too far and smother him? Or what if I can't give him enough attention because I have to work all the time? What if he has to go to daycare and hates it?"

Jamie laughed. "You are getting WAY ahead of yourself. Trust me, it'll work out. You can't plan this stuff out ahead of time. And believe me, you'll screw it up sometimes, but kids are forgiving little creatures. You'll be a good mom, Allie. I know it."

"Well, I'm not so sure." Allie felt tears forming in her eyes and a lump rising in her throat.

"Allie, are you okay?"

"Yeah, sorry," Allie said, wiping her eyes. "Stupid hormones."

"Everyone is scared when their lives are about to be upended by a baby. You have us for support."

"But you're all the way in Minnesota!" Allie wailed.

"I know. What about Mitch, though? You can lean on him, Allie. He's in this with you. What are you scared of with him?"

"I….I'm afraid to let him back in."

"He's not a vampire. If you invite him into your house, he's not going to set up shop and eat your neighbors. You can always kick him out if you change your mind."

"I know. I'm not scared of him. I'm scared of me. It would be so easy to fall back into those old patterns. They would feel comfortable, you know? But then what about after the baby's born? What about in six months or a year or five? What happens when I start to feel trapped again? I don't think I have the energy to pull myself out a second time."

"Shit, Allie. You are complicated. I mean, in a good way. Look, it doesn't have to be all or none. Be clear with Mitch that you have no intention of moving back in with him, but let him into your life. You're going to have to work with him to raise your son, so you may as well start practicing now."

Allie sighed.

" I've got a meeting, gotta go. But call me tonight if you want to talk more."

After she and Jamie hung up, Allie wandered around her house aimlessly. The storm had begun in earnest. Sheets of rain assaulted the windows and thunder rumbled every few seconds.

Mitch used to reserve Mondays for paperwork, so he might be home now. She thought about what Jamie had said. She was going to have to get over this if they were going to parent together. But she was lonely, which made it seem like a bad idea to call Mitch. She picked up the phone, hesitated, and then thought, *fuck it*.

CHAPTER 23

Day 268

Mitch was sitting at his desk in the living room when the phone rang. He'd been trying to slog through some rental agreement paperwork and was all too eager for a distraction. It was Allie.

"Hey, what's up?" he greeted her.

"Nothing much. I was just wondering, I thought maybe you could come over. We could talk about Cash and stuff…"

"Arc you okay?"

"Yeah, why?"

"This is the first time you've called since you've been back, and now you're inviting me over?"

"Forget it," she said hurriedly. "I just, never mind. I know you're busy."

"I'm not busy. And stop calling our baby 'Cash.' It's a terrible name."

Allie giggled. "Would you mind picking me up some milk on the way over? I've been craving it all morning, and I'm out."

"Sure thing."

Mitch grabbed his keys and skipped out the door.

———

Thirty minutes later, he knocked on her door, cold, half-gallon of milk in hand. She answered almost immediately.

"Hey! Thanks for the milk." She took it and motioned for him to come in. Mitch followed her to the kitchen where she retrieved a glass from the cabinet and poured herself a tall glass, then gulped half of it down immediately. "Want anything?" she asked. "I got, um, well, milk and water or tea? That's about it."

"I'm fine," he said. "No worries."

An awkward silence blanketed them and the house around them. Allie began doing that thing where she looked everywhere but him, and Mitch shifted his weight from foot to foot. He wondered if this was such a good idea. Then Allie suddenly asked, "Want to see Cash's room?"

"Sure," Mitch said with relief. "And stop calling him that!"

Allie trundled upstairs with her second glass of milk in hand, and Mitch followed. "So this is it," she said, gesturing to a small room on the right, as they reached the top of the stairs.

"It's nice," he said as he peered through the doorway. The room was yellow, like the rest of the house. It had a crib, a changing table and a chest of drawers. There was a mobile over the crib.

"Yeah, well it's not much. I want to add some things to the walls, but it will be fine for Cash." She smirked at him. She was doing it on purpose.

Mitch rolled his eyes, and Allie's expression morphed into a genuine smile. He felt his heartbeat quicken ever so slightly.

"So," Allie said, "the grand tour. You've seen pretty much the whole downstairs, aside from the closet. Here's the upstairs bathroom." She gestured to a room to the left of the baby's room, and here's my bedroom."

Mitch followed her inside and sat next to her on the bed. "It's nice," he said.

"Yeah," she replied and shrugged. "It's small, but I like it."

"It's very you. The big windows, the sunny yellow color, the books ev-ry-where."

Allie laughed. "That always drove you nuts."

"Not so much," Mitch answered softly. It used to annoy him — books on every available surface, some splayed open, pages down, where she'd left off. Now it didn't seem like such a big deal.

Mitch turned his head to look at Allie. She was sitting close to him on the bed, her eyes on his. His heart began to race in earnest, and he felt a familiar twitch. They'd known each other too long not to know what this was, not to know they were both thinking the same thing. He leaned closer to her, and she closed the rest of the gap between them, her lips sinking softly into his.

Their arms around each other, as they eased back onto the bed facing each other, Mitch thought she felt wonderfully, achingly familiar. As he eased his hands slowly under her shirt and felt the warmth of her back, she pulled her lips from his and said, "I really, really want you right now."

"I want you, too," he whispered. "I've missed you."

"But I don't want you to think this is something it's not," she said.

"It's okay," he said, but she persisted.

"I can't live with you. I can't marry you. I don't want to pick out furniture together, but I've been so horny these past few weeks —"

"Okay, then," he said soothingly. "Just love me."

She smiled, pressed her lips to his again and then paused again. She put her lips close to his ear and whispered, "Go down on me?"

———

Over the next couple of months, Allie and Mitch spent more time together. He finally talked her out of naming the baby "Cash," but they still couldn't agree on a name. She liked Charlie, and Mitch liked Ethan, which she hated.

Things felt more relaxed between them than it had since the beginning of their relationship, Mitch thought. So much so that he was loath to question it, lest he ruin it.

They went to the prenatal appointments together and often went out to lunch afterward. Allie quit trying to pay all the time and let him pick up the bill, which made him happy. She always thanked him.

Sometimes they got together just to hang out. They'd talk about their fears and hopes for their son and what it would like to be parents. They'd play cards or catch a movie. Allie seemed to prefer to hang out at her place now, rather than his…the place that used to be theirs.

They had sex one other time, and Mitch even stayed the night at Allie's place, but in the morning, she'd said she had some errands to run and shooed him out the door before 8:30.

They were enjoying each other, Mitch noticed — no tension, no unsaid disapproval, no fighting. He started to think maybe he could do this — this unconventional approach to family Allie seemed to be after. He still fantasized about her moving back in, though. He'd catch himself mentally noting little things she said or did, looking for signs she might reconsider.

CHAPTER 24

Day 330

"Hey, sis! How's it going?" Jamie answered the phone, an energetic lilt to her voice, sounding surprisingly awake for 7am.

"Uh…fine," Allie responded shakily. "I think I'm in labor."

"It's probably just Braxton-Hicks contractions. I got a lot of those with the twins."

"I don't think so. I read the book, and this doesn't seem like those." Allie had awoken around 4am with cramps thinking exactly what Jamie had, but she'd be unable to go back to sleep. She'd been pacing the floor and counting the minutes for the past few hours, the cramps becoming deeper, more intense, like nothing she'd ever felt before. "They've been going on since three this morning, and they're getting stronger."

"How far apart are they?" Jamie's tone had turned businesslike.

"I don't know. They're all over the place — first 10 minutes, then four."

"Four minutes?! Shit, Allie. You need to get to the hospital!"

"But, but," Allie stammered, panic creeping into her voice, "It's not time yet. He's not due for three more days —"

"Allie, babies don't know about due dates! He's coming now."

Allie had been hoping her sister would tell her she was not in fact in labor yet. She'd been sure Jamie would reassure her, and she'd go take a nice hot bath, maybe get back in bed. Now, she didn't know what to do.

"Umm, okay, I'll call a cab, and —"

"No, call Mitch, stupid! I'll be there as soon as I can."

CHAPTER 25

He crept as silently as possible out of Allie's dark bedroom avoiding the squeaky place in the floor. He turned the knob slowly and winced as it let out a jarring creak.

Behind him, he heard fussy baby squeaks he knew would turn into an all-out wail in a few seconds. Mitch sighed and turned back to the cradle where Jamie was fidgeting himself awake…again. He picked him up, put him to his shoulder and once again began pacing back and forth across the floor. It was the only way the baby would go to sleep. The rocking chair with its alluring, soft, green cushions sat mocking him in the corner.

"Little dude, I love you but right now you are killing me," Mitch whispered to the baby, trying a hunch then an arch to alleviate his aching back.

Mitch had argued with Allie about naming their son after her sister, because it seemed weird, not to mention confusing at family gatherings. But he'd talked her into "James" on the birth certificate, which was the name of his favorite grandfather.

Six weeks ago, Allie and Mitch were two people navigating only their own lives — jobs, friends and their own, amorphous relationship. Now they were more like soldiers in the trenches. Life seemed to be on hold indefinitely. They spent their time feeding Jamie, changing diapers and putting the kid to sleep. They talked about pacifiers, poop, breast pumps, developmental milestones and the prevailing wisdom on car seat placement. And nothing else.

Allie hadn't wanted Mitch to move in, nor had she wanted to stay at Mitch's place, so they'd planned to shuttle Jamie back and forth between their two houses every few days, taking turns caring for him, but that's not how it turned out.

That first night, Mitch had been the one to put Jamie to bed, and he was so tired, he was afraid he'd fall asleep on the drive home. So he'd passed out on the couch in Allie's living room. After that, though they hadn't talked about it, it just seemed easier for both parents to be in the same place. When Allie's sister had gone back home after that first week, separating and driving the baby back and forth seemed like an unthinkable hassle.

Suddenly, as Mitch paced the floor, resigned to another thirty minutes before he could sit down, Jamie let out a huge belch, and his whole body relaxed. A few more minutes and Mitch had him back in the cradle. This time, he managed to escape the dark bedroom undetected. He plodded downstairs with heavy feet and went straight to the kitchen for a drink. Then, he plopped down on the couch next to Allie with a sigh. She had her nose in a book with an improbably serene-looking baby's face on the front cover.

"He's asleep?" she asked, closing her book, her finger marking her place.

"Yeah, finally. My back is killing me. I wish he'd let us sit down."

"I know. What's up with that? The little tyrant." Allie's phone vibrated on the couch next to her. She glanced at it and reached over, silencing it. Then, she turned her gaze to Mitch. He knew that look – serious, thoughtful. *Shit.* He didn't need to hear it, but she said it anyway.

"I need to talk to you about something."

Mitch could feel his shoulders start to tense ever-so-slightly.

"You know that morning at my place in Galveston when you slapped me —"

"Jesus, Allie. Do we have to do this now? I'm exhausted. I just want to sit here, watch TV and not think about shit."

"I know. I don't really want to talk about it either, but we need to. And when is it ever a good time? We're always either with the baby or too tired."

Mitch didn't like it at all, but he had to concede she had a point. "Okay, fine," he said, his jaw clenched.

"Do you remember when I told you that you needed to think about why you did that? Back when I first came back? *Have* you thought about it?"

"Yeah."

"And?"

"And what?"

"Come on, Mitch. Stop being so obtuse. Help me out here!"

"Okay, fine. Yes, I have thought about it. But then I try not to because it makes me feel really shitty. It wasn't like I even made the decision to do it. It just happened, like my body acted on its own. And I hate that, that…loss of control."

"What were you thinking right before you slapped me?"

Mitch winced every time she said that. He took a big gulp of his whiskey and water. "I was mad at you."

He was staring down into his drink, but he could feel Allie looking at him, her questions drilling into him, even when she wasn't speaking. He watched his knuckles turn white as his grip on the glass tightened.

And when, in barely over a whisper, she asked, "For what?" he realized he was grinding his teeth. Mitch loosened his jaw and inhaled to respond.

"For being so…unreasonable! It was like you were this person that I knew or thought I knew and suddenly you were someone else. I just wanted you to come home and work it out, to be you again!"

"That's the thing," she said quietly. "All of that was, is, me." Her phone buzzed, and she again dismissed it.

"But you just fucking ran off! You didn't leave a note, there was all that blood. Allie, I was a mess. I didn't know what to think, I was so worried about you. How could you be that self-ish? Did you ever stop to think about how what you did affected everyone else? The people who love you — me?"

"I ALWAYS thought of you and your feelings," she said tersely, her voice no longer anything like a whisper.

"Until you didn't," he shot back.

"Yeah, until I was so sick of living caged in the life you picked out for us, I panicked and left." Mitch saw the challenge, the anger flash in her eyes.

"But I had no idea! You didn't tell me! How is that fair?"

"I did tell you. All the time. You just didn't fucking listen." She broke eye contact and, exasperatedly threw herself against the back of the couch, eyes rolled ceiling-ward.

Mitch sat, looking at her, perched on the edge of the couch, muscles coiled tightly. He felt the vibrations of Allie's phone through the cushions. "Who the fuck keeps calling you?!"

They sat in charged silence for a few moments, neither of them moving. Mitch felt the tension ramping up in his body. He drained the rest of his drink and slammed the glass down on the coffee table.

"You know what, Allie? You want me out of your life, fine. No problem. He stood up, strode across the small living area and left, slamming the front door so hard behind him, the whole house rattled.

He was almost to the car when he realized he'd left his keys on the kitchen table. He didn't want to go back in, so he just stood there, fists clenched at his sides, willing himself not to lose it completely. He tried to slow his breathing with minimal success. He turned and dragged himself back toward the front door, unsure as to whether he was retrieving his keys or going back in to stay.

When he walked back in, Allie wasn't there. Mitch stood still and looked toward the stairs. He could see the bedroom door ajar, the dim glow of the night light peeking out. He heard the faint sound of hiccups — Jamie, at the end of a crying spell. Mitch realized he'd awakened him when he'd slammed the door. Crap.

Mitch stood as though frozen in place, indecisive. Then, strode into the kitchen for his keys, but when he headed back through the living room, it was too late for a clean getaway. Allie was coming down the stairs. She stopped on the second to last one, fixing her eyes on him.

"So, you're just going to leave?" she said stonily.

"I can't be here right now with you. I can't deal with this."

"Oh, yeah? Well, what if I can't be here with *you*? What if *I* can't deal with this? We have a kid, Mitch. You can't just leave whenever you feel like it."

"Allie…" he said through clenched teeth, his eyes feeling burning. Mitch turned his back to her and left.

He sat in his car for a long time. Worked up as he was, he didn't trust himself to drive. As the fury subsided and his thoughts slowed, his eyes drifted upward to the bedroom window where Jamie now slept. He couldn't see anything, but he could imagine him, his round little head, his tiny fists balled up as he slept. His little rosebud lips parted in total relaxation. Mitch envied him that. His heart ached. There was a literal throbbing in his chest. Whatever happened with Allie, Mitch knew he couldn't leave Jamie, his son. Not now, not ever. He got out of the car and went back inside.

———

The next few weeks with Allie had a businesslike feel. He went back to work, but he went directly to her place most evenings. Sometimes she'd leave while he was there, and sometimes she'd shut herself in the nursery, that Jamie still wasn't sleeping in, with her laptop. They were civil to each other but not much else.

Mitch had taken Jamie to his house a few nights. He'd had a room set up for him before Jamie was even born, but the kid wouldn't really settle into a good, deep sleep there. He woke up a lot more, and he didn't like taking a bottle at night, so under duress, Mitch and Allie had resorted to the awkward sharing of Allie's house.

Sometimes, when Mitch would trudge over there, usually around four in the afternoon, he'd drive extra slow, dreading the inevitable encounter with Allie, however brief. Then, he'd think of Jamie's face and how he was beginning to take interest in the world around him, focusing on Mitch's face sometimes intently. Mitch even saw the hint of a smile now and then, which made him much more enthusiastic about entertaining his son. The thought of Jamie would get him over his reticence toward Allie.

Mitch knew the situation was untenable in the long term. He and Allie couldn't go on like this forever, but he was too tired from work and taking care of the kid — and too enamored with him — to care. They'd just have to bungle through and adapt somehow. Jamie would grow, things would change, and they'd figure it out along the way. It would be better when Jamie could stay with him, he thought.

As Mitch expected, things did change. But he was blindsided anyway.

CHAPTER 26

Allie sat in the back room of the boutique, feet up on a box, munching an apple and some cheese. She'd given birth twelve weeks ago, but her body still felt messed up — looser all over. She'd been cleared to exercise by her OB at six weeks postpartum, and she had laughed in his face when he'd suggested she start jogging.

She thought about Mitch. When he was in the house, she could feel the negative tension between them even when she was shut in the unused nursery and he was downstairs. She tried to ignore it because it made her want to cry every single time. *Fucking hormones*, she thought, *fucking life*.

Her phone, resting on the box she was using as a footstool, suddenly vibrated, sending little shockwaves she could feel in her feet through the cardboard. She stretched to pick it up and saw it was the same unfamiliar number that had been badgering her for days. Irritated, she grabbed the phone and answered, ready to vent some of her frustrations at an inconsiderate salesperson.

"Hey, Allie. It's Julian."

———

Allie burst out of the back room of the boutique, keys in hand. "Shirley…"

"Are you okay, love?" Shirley's startled look at the way Allie slammed through the backdoor gave way to a genuine look of concern.

"I — I'm not feeling well."

"Well, go home and rest, then. I can handle it here. Let me call Mitch to come get you."

"No! I mean, no thank you. I can ride my bike, really." Allie tried smiling a little to show she was okay. She sure didn't *feel* okay. She was out the door and pedaling fast before she could hear Shirley's response.

When Allie got home, she found Mitch on the floor on his stomach, eye-to-eye with Jamie, who was on his belly on his play mat — a brightly colored blanket with toys attached to it that had been a gift from his namesake aunt. The two of them looked like animals in the zoo staring at each other through their enclosures.

"Hey!" said Mitch, getting to his feet. "Are you all right? Shirley called and said you weren't feeling well and were coming home, but that was like 45 minutes ago. I was about to send out a search party."

Allie could see the concern in his eyes, covered by the weak joke. "I'm fine, just really tired." She'd taken a circuitous route home, needing time to think. She scooped Jamie up off the floor, and he smiled at her with a big, gummy, open-mouth grin. "How's my little one, huh?"

And then, without breaking eye contact with Jamie, to Mitch, "You can go ahead and go."

"Are you sure? If you're not feeling well, I can stay and watch him. You can take a nap."

"No, I'm just a little tired, but we'll be okay. Promise," she said, forcing a smile.

After Mitch left, Allie gratefully climbed the stairs to her bedroom, Jamie on her hip. They nestled into the bed together, and she put him to her breast. She closed her eyes and let her mind relax. She had some things to figure out, but not...just... now.

———

She had missed four calls from Julian by the time she put Jamie to bed. Allie sat on the couch, laptop open, not writing but researching. She wrote down a phone number and closed her laptop, rubbing her eyes and yawning. She glanced at her phone — now five missed calls from Julian and a text:

Please call me back. We need to talk. I know you're angry, but I have more information I need to give you. Please.

She couldn't bring herself to call him tonight. It was late. She dragged herself upstairs and crept quietly into her bedroom. She stopped to look at Jamie lying in the cradle on his back, one little, loose fist by his head. She smiled down at him, his blissful baby unawareness carrying her troubles away for a few seconds. After brushing her teeth, she was asleep almost immediately.

CHAPTER 27

"Sure, I can watch him," Mitch said. He was sitting at his desk, bare feet propped up, talking to Allie on speaker as he scrolled through his email, mostly deleting junk without opening it. "It's a slow day."

That was not technically true. Mitch had a showing scheduled and a mountain of paperwork to get through, but the idea of spending the whole day with Jamie was too tempting to pass up. It was beautiful weather, and Mitch was already mentally making plans for a walk to the park with his son.

"Okay," Allie said, "because I just have a few errands to run, and it shouldn't take all that long, maybe a few hours."

"Allie, you work too hard. Take some time for yourself. I'm thrilled to spend the day with the little dude. Go get a massage or something." He started to offer her some money, thinking she might not feel she could afford such a luxury on her meager salary but then didn't. She wouldn't take it, and it would just irritate her like it did every time.

"Okay," Allie said, uncertainly. "Well, then I'll just text when I'm on my way back?"

Mitch drove over to Allie's thinking he'd see if Murphy could take a long lunch, maybe make that trip to the park with them. When Mitch arrived, Allie was bustling around the living room with Jamie on her hip. He couldn't tell exactly what she was trying to do. She just kept moving things around with her free hand — a small stack of books from the floor to the table, some papers from the coffee table to the shelf.

"Hey, what's up, little guy? Wanna come see me?" Mitch held his arms out to Jamie, and he grinned his toothless baby grin at him. Mitch took that as the go-ahead and gathered Jamie out of Allie's arms into his own. "How's it going, dude?"

"He was up four times last night," Allie answered, "Twice he wanted to eat, once he had a poopy diaper, and the last time, he just wanted to play…at 3am!"

"A night owl, huh?" Mitch said, smiling at Jamie.

Allie scowled at Mitch. His jocular mood seemed to be offending her. She looked tired and more than a little frazzled.

"You got spit up on you," Mitch said, gesturing at Allie's left shoulder.

"Crap," she said and stripped off her t-shirt right there in the living room and tossed it in the general direction of the washing machine in its corner closet. She began digging through a basket of presumably clean laundry until she found another shirt to pull over her head.

"So, he just ate," Allie said, now in instructional mode, "but he'll probably be hungry again around noon. There's more formula in the fridge —"

"Formula? I thought you wanted to stick with breast milk until he was six months old?"

"I changed my mind, Mitch. Things change. Is that okay with you?"

"Of course. I just —"

"You just what?" Allie had her hands on her hips now and was glaring at Mitch. He noticed her fresh tee shirt was tight across her breasts.

"Do you need to pump before you go?" he asked.

"No, I don't." She took a deep breath and sighed. Her whole body slumped. "Look, I'm sorry for snapping. I'm just tired."

"It's okay. I've got little man. You go. Relax."

"Okay." Allie crossed the room and kissed Jamie on the head. "I love you, kiddo. See you later." Jamie grabbed a fistful of her hair, and as she peeled his fingers away one by one, she looked at Mitch.

"What?" he asked. Her expression was inscrutable.

Allie shook her head. "Nothing. I just...thank you." She put her arms around Mitch, enfolding him and Jamie together in a hug. It was the first time she'd touched Mitch in months. It startled him, but for a second, he felt the cohesive warmth of family. His family. And then it was gone.

Mitch and Jamie watched and waved as Allie backed down the driveway in Mitch's car. Jamie waved with Mitch's help. As she drove away, Mitch wondered what was going on in that head of hers.

He went back inside and put Jamie down under his play gym so he could flail at the multicolored butterflies that hung from it. He called Murphy, who sounded more than eager to play hooky at the park. He changed Jamie's diaper, packed up what seemed to be enough for a two-week cross-continental journey, strapped Jamie into the stroller and headed out.

When Mitch and Jamie pulled up at the park, Murphy was already waiting by her car in the parking lot, furiously typing on her phone.

"Hey, what's up?" Mitch called.

"Nothing. Just a sec…Okay, sorry about that. I've been gone ten minutes, and they already have a crisis they can't solve on their own. I'm mentoring a few newbies, and they can't even decide to make coffee without consulting me." Murphy sighed and stuffed her phone into her pocket. "How's this little guy?" she asked, brightening as she squatted down to greet Jamie in his stroller.

"He's good," Mitch responded for his son. "Let's go sit over there. He likes to watch the kids on the swings." They set themselves up on a bench, and Mitch pulled Jamie out of the stroller, facing him out so he could see the playground.

"How's the new dad bit going?" Murphy asked. Since Jamie

had come along, Mitch and Murphy hadn't had much chance to visit. And, ever since Allie had come back, Mitch had been a little reticent to spend too much time with Murphy. He didn't want Allie to get the wrong idea about them. Not that it seemed to bother her.

"Pretty great. I can't get enough of this little guy. I miss him on the nights I'm not with him. But according to Allie, he didn't sleep so well last night, so I can't say I'm sorry I missed that."

"How is Allie?" Murphy asked, emphasizing "is," and leaving the space after her question filled with anticipation of an honest and thorough response.

"She's… good? I don't know." He sighed heavily as he leaned back on the bench looking up towards the cloudless sky. "She seems stressed out or worried or something. She looked at me all weird just now before she left. She actually hugged me."

"So are y'all getting along again, then?"

"I have no idea."

"She's probably just stressed out — new baby, not getting enough sleep. It's not easy."

"Yeah, maybe. She stopped breastfeeding. 'Switched him to formula."

"Oh? Well, breastfeeding can be hard. Especially if you're working. I remember sitting in my car on my lunch break and pump every single day. I felt like a cow."

"That's what Allie says, too! She feels like a cow. But she was so committed to it, it just surprised me."

"Mitch, I know becoming a parent was a huge change for you, but the transition is even harder for Allie."

"And why is that?" Mitch asked. He didn't understand why everyone always talked about how hard it was on the mom. He happily cared for Jamie just as much as she did.

Murphy gave him a hard look. "Allie pushed a whole human being out of her body four months ago. Her hormones are all out of whack, her body feels different, everything's all loose and floppy, and she's sleep-deprived on top of everything."

"But the doctor said, in six weeks —"

Murphy cut him off with a laugh. "Six weeks is nothing. Jamie was in there squishing her organs for nine months. It's going to take at least that long for Allie to feel anywhere close to normal again."

Mitch felt a little dumb. Faced with the biological facts, he had to admit, he could not imagine what it felt like to grow another human being inside your own body for the better part of a year.

"Don't be too hard on yourself. You're a good dad; you're doing your part. And you couldn't have very well birthed Jamie for her. There's a ton of books out there on how to take care of the baby but a lot fewer on what a mess a woman's body feels like after giving birth. I remember, I had eleven episiotomy stitches, and I was afraid to poop —"

"Okay, okay, TMI!"

"Hey, it's reality, my friend. You're lucky you have the luxury of ignoring it."

"I don't — ah, crap." Mitch held Jamie aloft, a dark stain running out of his onesie onto Mitch's lap.

Murphy laughed. "Literally."

Mitch gingerly held Jamie out to Murphy. "Can you hold him? I'm going to go wet this in the water fountain," he said, plucking the burp cloth off his shoulder.

Murphy held the baby, suspended out in front of her, as Mitch hurried to the fountain. When he returned, a woman, probably in her sixties, had stopped to talk to Murphy.

"I was just saying," the woman said, turning her gaze from Murphy to Mitch, "they always save the poopiest ones for Mom, don't they?" She winked in Murphy's direction.

Mitch ignored her and began wiping the spot on his jeans.

"I see she got a little on you too, Dad!" the woman continued.

Mitch gritted his teeth. Then, Murphy stepped in. She handed Jamie back to Mitch and said, "Actually, I'm not his mother, just a friend." She smiled at the woman who was now furrowing her brow. Instead of the apology Mitch expected, the woman turned her attention to Jamie and said in a gratingly saccharine baby talk voice. "Where's your mommy, little one? Little girls need their mommies, don't they?" Then she turned her attention back to Murphy.

"So are you the stepmother? I know people have all sorts of crazy family situations these days. It's not like it used to be. Call me old-fashioned, but I still think it's best when kids are raised by a mom and a dad. It gets confusing with all of these half brothers and step aunts and what have you," she finished, coughing a little and straightening herself.

Murphy met the woman's eyes with her own, even gaze and said matter-of-factly, "old-fashioned."

The woman looked confused, taken aback, and Mitch burst out laughing.

"You asked for it," he said, still chuckling as she scowled at him.

As the woman hurried off, looking affronted, Mitch called after her, "He's a boy!"

He laid the changing pad out on the bench and knelt to change Jamie's diaper. After their laughter had subsided, asked, "Why did she think he was a girl?"

"Because all babies look the same, and people are idiots. Does it really matter?"

"No, I guess not." Then, as he commenced cleaning Jamie up, he said, "I just see it coming. I'm going to have this conversation with people for the rest of my life."

"About Jamie's gender identity?" Murphy asked.

"No, not that. Allie and I aren't together, and I'm going to have to explain that every fucking — sorry, little man — time. When we meet people in the park, when he starts school…"

"Yeah, I'm sure it will get old, but it won't be so bad as he gets older, though. Lots of kids' parents aren't together.

"I just want it to be simple, you know? Allie and me, together, in the same house, raising him. I mean, we don't *have* to get married, but it would be easier if we were under the same roof."

"Mitch, nothing about a relationship is easy or simple, even if you do live in the same house. It's just a different kind of hard. There are lots of unhappily married people who make each other and their kids miserable. Is that what you want?"

"No." Mitch sighed as he finished fastening the clean diaper around Jamie.

"Eventually, Jamie will know that a lot of people's parents live together, and he might have some awkward conversations with other people, but that's going to happen about something regardless. And he won't have the trauma of y'all splitting up; living apart will be his normal. Having two parents who actually cooperate to raise him — that's gold. Not everyone gets that."

"But what if Allie and I don't always get along? Things are pretty good right now, but I'm afraid Jamie will feel it if we start arguing again."

Murphy actually laughed at him, and Mitch glared at her. He was serious. "I'm sorry for laughing," she said, "but did you hear what you just said? I mean, *everyone's* parents fight sometimes. Didn't yours?"

Then Mitch laughed, "Yeah, I guess they did. I mean, I romanticize my parents' relationship sometimes I think. I know they were very much in love with each other until the day mom died, but yeah, they fought sometimes. Sometimes they'd go a week or more without speaking to each other."

"See?"

And he did.

CHAPTER 28

Allie sat in the office, her legs bouncing nervously. *Reactive.* That's what the woman, Jen, who sat on the other side of the desk, had said. Thanks to the internet, Allie already knew what that meant. She was positive.

"So I've got HIV," Allie said, her voice sounding hollow and far away to her. She thought, *I should be worried or upset right now.* But all she felt was impatient.

"Not necessarily," replied Jen with a kind and soft tone.

"But when I looked it up online —"

Allie paused as Jen put her fingers to the bridge of her nose and closed her eyes. "I know. I wish people wouldn't do that," she muttered and then returned her focus to Allie. "There's a lot of misinformation on the internet, and the testing process is more complicated than most people realize.

"Your test was reactive, which means you *may* be positive for HIV. We'll have to send off to an offsite lab for more conclusive results."

"How long will that take?" Allie asked, distressed at the thought of having to wait even longer. She'd thought she'd know today that the uncertainty at least would be behind her.

"A week," said Jen.

"Shit." Allie exhaled and looked down at her lap.

"I know it's hard not knowing, but there are some things you can be doing in the meantime. You said you were exposed about a year ago, correct?"

"Thirteen months, yes."

"And you haven't experienced any symptoms, right?"

"Well, I got kind of sick after I was…exposed, which I read could be a sign of the virus, but I was also pregnant, so I thought it was just morning sickness."

Jen responded in a businesslike manner. "And what was the approximate date of conception?"

"Around June? Maybe the first part of June?"

"And were you tested for HIV at the time? It's routinely of-fered —"

"No, I didn't see a doctor until I was 16 weeks along, and I didn't have any idea." Allie's eyes welled up, and she found her-self unable to hold back. Her feelings were catching up to her. She started to cry, wiping the tears away furiously, willing herself to stop bawling in this stranger's office.

"Hey," said Jen, her softer tone returning. "It's okay. You can cry. This is a big deal. Let it out."

———

Allie had to give a blood sample to be sent off; then she left the clinic. With the freedom that Mitch's car provided, she drove aimlessly, circling the outskirts of Lime, thinking, trying to calm herself down enough to go home. She thought about calling her sister, but she didn't have the energy to go through the whole story again. Maybe she wasn't even positive, and all of this worry was for nothing. Irritating as it was, she'd just have to wait.

After she'd gotten ahold of herself in Jen's office, she told her everything. It was a relief to pour everything out to a stranger — someone removed from the whole fucked up situation. Allie hadn't known what to expect at the clinic, but she had been afraid of being judged and had intended to tell them as little as possible, but Jen had been so kind and understanding. Allie had even told her she wasn't sure whether Julian or Mitch was Jamie's biological father. Jen had reassured her that, either way, it was still plausible Jamie hadn't contracted the virus, but they'd need to test him as soon as possible, which led Allie to a dilemma: Could she get Jamie tested without Mitch knowing? She sighed. She was a terrible liar and probably couldn't pull it off even if she wanted to. She was sick of carrying this secret around, and much as it horrified her to think of Mitch's reaction, keeping up the charade sounded even more exhausting.

It was around four o'clock when she finally felt calm enough to go home. She pulled Mitch's car into her driveway past a truck parked at the curb. She sat in the car gathering herself for a few moments, trying to decide how to tell Mitch that Julian, whom he'd never met, may well be Jamie's father and that all four of them might be HIV positive. There was no good way. She was tired and considering putting it off until tomorrow, but she felt she might lose her nerve if she didn't tell him now. *Just get it over with*, she thought.

She crossed the lawn and opened the front door quietly. It was unlocked. Jamie often took a short evening nap, and she didn't want to wake him. As she crossed the threshold, she looked toward the living room. Mitch was sitting on the couch, and someone else was next to him.

CHAPTER 29

Mitch had been sitting next to this guy who introduced himself as "Julian" for three long, awkward minutes. He'd said he knew Allie when she was in Galveston. Mitch was just about to either offer him a drink or suggest he go home and leave his number for Allie when Allie walked through the door.

"Julian! I thought you were in Portland. What are you… How did you find…?"

Mitch looked from Julian to Allie. The guy had an apologetic look, but Allie was gritting her teeth, her eyes wide in..anger? Fear? Mitch wasn't sure.

"I need to talk to you," Julian said, and then he launched into a story that sent Mitch's head spinning. He was talking about an ex-lover, how he'd left him, and how he and the ex were both HIV positive. Julian mostly talked at Allie, who was frozen in the hallway, staring at both guys on the couch, but he'd occasionally nervously glance at Mitch.

Mitch couldn't figure out why he was telling them all this until it dawned on him that Julian and Allie had probably slept together. His gut clenched, and his chest constricted with jealousy, and he repressed the urge to punch Julian in the side of his face.

"And so," Julian was saying, pleading, "Allie, I just had to see you when you said on the phone there was a baby because I didn't know…" There was the waver of impending tears in his voice, but Julian took a deep breath and appeared to collect himself. Mitch wondered what Jamie had to do with anything.

Allie's face looked stricken and pale. "I shouldn't have told you about Jamie," she whispered. "I panicked. I blurted it out; I was so upset…" she trailed off.

Mitch looked at her, trying to read the anguish in her face. What the hell was going on? Why did he feel like he'd missed the middle part of a movie, and why was that making him feel so incredibly anxious?"

Julian continued as if Allie hadn't spoken, "…I thought that the baby might have it, too, and well, if I'm the father, I don't want to run away from this. I mean, I shouldn't. It's my responsibility," he said, sounding more like he was trying to convince himself than Allie.

The air felt thick and heavy, as if it had suddenly turned to syrup. Mitch could feel it pressing down on him. He was dimly aware that Julian had stopped talking and Allie was still standing rigid, statuesque, in the hallway.

———

When Mitch came back to himself, Allie was sitting across from him on the couch instead of Julian. She was wringing her hands in her lap and looking at him with fear and trepidation.

Mitch's brain began to assemble what Julian had said. He didn't want to know, and yet he had to. He closed his eyes, "Allie," he whispered, "What. the. fuck?"

"I'm sorry, Mitch. I…we… I slept with Julian. In Galveston. Right around the same time you and I were…together there…"

She was still talking, but Mitch wasn't listening. He was starting to panic. *What if Allie's HIV positive and I am and, oh Christ, Jamie is, and what if I AM NOT HIS FATHER? Oh my god…*

CHAPTER 30

Allie paced back and forth across the living room, biting at her thumbnail, trying to slow her racing thoughts enough to figure out what to do.

Mitch barely seemed to register what she'd said at the end. He hadn't answered her, only stood silently facing the door for a few moments before leaving. He didn't slam the door or peel out of the driveway in his car. An onlooker might think he was running to the store for milk. Unlike Julian, who'd run out of there so fast when Mitch went all catatonic, you'd have thought he hadn't just made a speech about "responsibility."

Allie was worried, antsy. She couldn't make herself sit. Mitch was typically a level-headed person, and normally she wouldn't have given a second thought to his state of mind but dropping a bomb — two bombs — like she just did could push a rational person over the edge. And, she reminded herself, he'd gone over that edge once before, not so long ago in Galveston.

Allie picked up her phone and called Murphy just as she began hearing Jamie fuss in the bedroom upstairs.

"Hey, Allie! What's up? Listen, I just got in my car. Can I —

"

"Murphy, it's Mitch," she blurted. "He's…I told him some things, and he just left…" She didn't know how to explain herself, and she didn't have the luxury of telling Murphy the whole story, even if she'd wanted to. Jamie's fussing was turning into a cry.

"He's really upset, and I'm worried about him. Will you just check on him, please?"

"Sure, but what—"

"I gotta go. Baby's waking up."

CHAPTER 31

"I've been looking all over town for you," Murphy said, exasperated.

Mitch was sitting on the edge of his back porch, drink in hand, staring out at the woods where all this had started. He felt like someone had died. Something had died. And he couldn't get it back.

"My house is usually a good place to look," he responded dully.

"I've been by here twice earlier this evening. How long have you been home?"

Mitch shrugged. Murphy sat down beside him. "How many of these have you had?" she asked, pointing at his drink.

Mitch shrugged again. She took the drink out of his hand, took a big swig of it herself and returned it to him. Even several drinks in, he could read the concern in her voice. "How'd you know?" he asked.

"Allie called me. She was worried about you."

"Worried?" he slurred, listing to the side before swaying his torso back upright. "She should've thought about that before she fucking fucked someone else and got pregnant." He looked at Murphy and saw the surprise register on her face. So Allie hadn't told her the whole story. Suddenly, he wanted to talk about it. "Didja know I might not even be Jamie's dad?"

In fits and starts, with a generous dose of expletives, Mitch recounted the life-destroying news Allie had dropped on him hours earlier. "You know whas the worst? All the fucking vagueness. She doesn't know if I'm Jamie's father; she doesn't know if she has HIV. What the fuck 'm I supposed to do with this information?"

"Jesus, Mitch." Murphy took his glass again, drained it and went back into the house, returning with two full glasses. They sat there for hours. She listened to Mitch yell, ramble and slur. She didn't offer any of her customary advice or point out how he was being an asshole. She sympathized, she made him drinks. It was only when Mitch woke up in the morning he realized she must've put him to bed at some point. He was still fully clothed, on top of the covers, and he had a ringing headache. His mouth felt like an ashtray, and he noticed a mashed pack of cigarettes on the floor next to the bed as he rolled to his side, trying to get up. *Was I smoking last night?* he wondered. Where had he even gotten a pack of cigarettes?

Mitch stumbled downstairs in search of some aspirin and water. There was a note by the coffee pot with a bottle of Advil on top of it:

Mitch,

'Had to go to work this morning. 'Hope you're not feeling too rough. Call me when you get up?

Love, M

Mitch popped three Advil, guzzled a glass of water, and started making coffee. It was already ten o'clock. He had a ton of work to get done, and for once, rental paperwork sounded appealingly distracting — better than thinking about everything he'd learned last night. He showered, brushed his teeth and began to feel a little less like human garbage. He sat down at his desk and immersed himself in work in a way he hadn't been able to since Allie left over a year ago. It was a relief to focus on something simple and concrete instead of his mess of a personal life. He let everything but the forms in front of him fall away.

About an hour into it, his phone rang, and he glanced at it. It was Allie. *Fuck her.* He thought and let it go to voicemail. A few minutes later, he heard a text come in. He reached a stopping point, got up from the desk to stretch and checked his phone. It was Murphy; he'd forgotten he was supposed to call her.

You OK? the text asked.

As well as can be expected, he typed back.

What are you doing?

Working.

Good. Can I come by when I get off?

Mitch knew Murphy was babysitting him, but he didn't care. It was nice to have something to look forward to at the end of what was sure to be a shitty, shitty day.

CHAPTER 32

Allie was dusting the shelves at the boutique; Jamie strapped to her back in the carrier. He was asleep for now. Her back was killing her, but he'd wake up if she sat down, so she filled the time cleaning. Shirley was off at some antique show a few towns over from Lime, and she was sure to come in with more stuff they'd have to find space for.

Mitch wouldn't take her calls, and even though she didn't really want to talk to him, she needed to. She'd called Julian twice and texted him several times. She hadn't yet resolved anything with him, either.

Fucking men, she thought. *Why couldn't they ever finish a tough conversation?*

Julian had been beside himself at the idea that he may have indirectly infected Jamie, and the thought that he might be Jamie's father seemed too big to process altogether.

She'd called her sister that night after Julian vanished in the air like he was so adept at doing, and Mitch had gone railing off into the night. Baby Jamie had been sound asleep. She remembered what Jamie, her sister, had said after she'd told her how things went: "Don't stick your head in the sand over this, Allie, and don't waste time beating yourself up, either. You've got a kid now. That's your priority."

"I know," she'd responded. "I hope he — they realize that, too."

"Not to be insensitive, but I read this thing that said babies often look like their dads, so the dads will realize the baby is theirs and take care of it. It's an evolutionary thing. So, who does Jamie look like?"

"I don't know. I keep staring at him, trying to figure that out. He just looks like a baby to me."

"I've never met Julian. What does he look like?"

"Kinda tall, thin, brown hair…"

"So your average white guy, just like Mitch."

"Yeah." Allie chuckled. It was kind of funny. But not really.

Life was fucking hard. And here she was dusting shelves, cleaning and working, with a baby on her back, and where were they? Off licking their wounds like it was their birthright because they didn't have boobs.

Julian was probably gone because, no matter how hard he tried to tell himself to stay and be responsible, running away was what he did as far as Allie could tell in the short time she'd known him. Mitch was giving her the silent treatment, probably off drinking and feeling sorry for himself. *Well, fine*, she thought. She'd do it herself. She'd take Jamie to the clinic and get him tested. She had the morning off tomorrow. She could probably borrow Shirley's car and be back by the afternoon.

CHAPTER 33

"Do you know how Julian got it?"

Murphy and Mitch were perched on his back porch again, this time with glasses of water, sans whiskey. Mitch had had quite enough of that last night. He'd been so angry, but today, as evening had come on and he'd no longer been able to distract himself with work, he'd sunk into a mixture of depression and desperation. He did not know what to do. "I don't know much of anything," he admitted. "I was so freaked out, I just had to get out of there."

"Are he and Allie, like were they dating?"

He shrugged listlessly. "I don't know, but I guess I need to stop moping around and get tested."

"But you wouldn't have it. You said your trip to Galveston was before Allie met Julian…Wait a minute. Did y'all sleep together after Allie came back?" Without turning his head to look at her, Mitch could feel Murphy's eyes scrutinizing him.

"Yeah. Twice. While she was pregnant."

"Christ, Mitch. I guess Allie's not the only one making bad decisions around here. What were you thinking? Didn't it occur to you she might've been with someone else? She was gone a long time. You would've slept with me if I'd let you."

Mitch sighed. "No, it didn't. Maybe I just didn't want to think about it. For so long, I've thought it would be her and me, together. It didn't even occur to me it wouldn't work out, even after she left. Then, she was pregnant, and it seemed like it was all going to be okay. I guess I just…ignored the stuff I didn't want to see."

"Still hanging onto that happy family with 2.4 kids, a dog and a picket fence, huh?"

"That's pretty much blown to hell now." In the next few moments of silence, which felt heavy with things that might be said, Mitch's thinking drifted away from his own sorry state of affairs to Murphy and all she had done for him. She had a daughter, family, a job, and here she was propping him up, not asking for anything in return. He felt a warmth in his chest and was even tempted to smile a little. "Hey, by the way, thanks for hanging out with me last night. I needed to get the poison out, so thanks for listening."

"We all need to vent sometimes, but listen, you've got to talk to Allie. You know that, right?"

"Yeah, I know. I just, the longer I put it off, the longer I don't have to think about finding out that little man isn't mine. Weirdly, I'm more worried about that than I am about HIV."

"Your name is on the birth certificate, Mitch. You've been taking care of him. In the eyes of the state, he's yours. Don't get so hung up on biology. Just talk to her. Stop thinking about it and talk to her."

"I know, but every time I think about it, I get so angry at her. I know it's not doing any good, but I can't seem to help it. She exposed me, our son, to HIV. I can't believe how careless she was."

"Is that what you're really angry about? That she exposed you to infection?"

Mitch closed his eyes. "No. It's that she slept with someone else. I know that makes me a hypocrite, but I can't seem to stop being angry about it anyway. We were together for five years, and she just threw it all away. It hurts. And it makes me wonder, did she even love me? Like ever?"

"You loved her, right? What were you thinking about when you kissed me? Did you think you didn't want to be with Allie anymore?"

"I was just…lonely, and I like you, and I wanted to feel someone else, something else."

They were both quiet for a bit while Mitch mulled over what he should do. "So I should just, what? Forgive her for everything?"

Murphy sighed and rubbed her forehead, "I don't know,

Mitch. That's not exactly the word for it, but just come at it with some understanding, some willingness to listen and maybe discover you get where she's coming from, just a little bit. It takes two people to make a relationship work and two to mess it up, too."

They sat in silence again, gazing into the woods where Mitch remembered chasing Allie into the trees so long ago. It had been eons. He had been a different person then. He had been so sure of himself and where he was going.

He shook his head to clear the heaviness and elbowed Murphy playfully. "You sure you didn't miss your calling as a psychologist?"

"Ten years of therapy oughtta count for something."

"You see a therapist?"

"I am a single parent with an MIA baby daddy and one of the most stressful, mind-fuck jobs in the world. Of course I do."

———

Allie had agreed to meet Mitch at her place during Jamie's morning nap on Saturday. He picked up two coffees on the way over — sort of a peace offering. He was nervous; it reminded him of the jitters before a first date. He felt all fluttery inside.

When he pulled up in front of Allie's house, a beat-up pick-up truck was parked at the curb. Mitch's sense of foreboding grew stronger as he traversed the walkway and pushed the front door open, a coffee in one hand and the other in the crook of his elbow. Allie and Julian were on the couch together. His hand was up her shirt, and his tongue was down her throat. Her hands fumbled at his jeans, trying to get the zipper down.

Blood rushed to Mitch's head as he stared at them uncomprehendingly; his face was hot and pulsing. Pain seared down Mitch's side as the coffee spilled out of the cup, now smashed between his arm and his side. "What the fuck?!" Mitch yelled, dropping the other coffee on the floor. Julian jumped up, his cock out, hard and waggling at Mitch, Julian's eyes wide and innocent-looking.

Anger and disbelief roared through Mitch's torso and up into his brain, expanding, feeling as if his head might explode. "What the fuck, Allie?!" he screamed again.

"Mitch, it's okay," Allie responded in a soothing voice. "Julian's going to take care of Zach now."

"What? Who the fuck is Zach?" Mitch was starting to feel unsteady on his feet. His vision was beginning to swim as if he were very drunk. He struggled to stay on his feet, to keep from falling over. He blinked furiously in a desperate effort to clear his eyes.

"Our son," she responded, still smiling.

"His name is James!" Mitch shouted, "It's James!" He stumbled and blinked and fought to regain his balance.

"Julian liked Zach better, didn't you, babe?" Allie looked over at Julian, who was still staring slack-jawed at Mitch.

Mitch looked down and saw, as his vision cleared, that, instead of spilled coffee at his feet, there were gray kittens — tiny, with their eyes barely open. The liquid dripping from his shirt was coalescing into them. There were four, no five, no seven. He looked up to see Julian walking toward him. His cock had grown larger and was waggling between his legs, beating each thigh in rhythm to his slow swagger from side to side. Mitch was afraid Julian would step on the kittens, as he didn't appear to notice them. He bent over, furiously trying to gather them into his arms, but they kept multiplying and slipping away.

Mitch looked up in horror as he saw that Julian's cock had developed a crack at its base and was in danger of falling off and crushing the kittens. Then, Mitch heard something. Someone was yelling, no singing…His eyes snapped open.

The alarm was going off, and according to the time, Mitch was supposed to meet Allie in an hour. He sat up and rubbed his eyes, taking deep breaths and looking around the room to assure himself of its reality while his heartbeat slowly returned to normal. *Jesus, Murphy and her armchair psychology would have a field day with that one*, he thought.

When he felt almost normal, he got up and showered the rest of the disoriented, groggy feeling off of him that the dream had left. He made some toast for breakfast, crammed it in his mouth, and hopped in the car. He decided not to stop for coffee.

When Mitch pulled up to Allie's, he about jumped out of his pants when he saw Julian's truck in front of the house. *No fucking way*. He jogged up the stairs and decided to knock on the door. Allie opened it within a few seconds. She looked harried. Mitch could see Julian standing behind her in the living room. His member was mercifully out of sight.

"Mitch, sorry. He just showed up like three minutes ago. I had no idea he was coming, honestly." Then Allie turned to Julian, "Julian, you have to go. We can talk later."

"Hi, Mitch," said Julian, raising his hand in an awkward, static wave. "Listen, I just came by to talk to Allie, but maybe it's best that we're all here. Please," he implored, looking at Allie and Mitch, "hear me out."

"Julian, please just go," Allie said with a sigh, which managed to sound both exasperated and exhausted.

"Actually, Allie," Mitch chimed in reluctantly, "maybe he's right. This involves all of us." As much as he didn't want to be in the same room with Julian, hearing his side of the story directly and not filtered through Allie was appealing.

"Okay," Allie relented, sinking into the armchair in the living room. "Fine." And when Julian and Mitch continued to stand, "Well, sit both of you. Come on."

Mitch and Julian were forced to share the couch, as there wasn't any other place to sit. Mitch wondered if Allie had taken the only other chair purposefully. Julian and he sat on opposite ends, as far away as two people could get on the same piece of furniture. Julian's leg was bouncing. He seemed agitated.

—————

"Listen," Julian began, "I've been thinking and thinking about this, and if you want me to take a paternity test, I'll do it." He glanced nervously at Allie, then Mitch.

"How big of you," Mitch retorted, but Allie and Julian ignored him.

Julian continued, "If he's my son, I'll support and care for him the best I can. But I've been sick a lot over the past year. I'm having symptoms." He looked back and forth between Mitch and Allie again. Mitch could tell he was trying to read their reactions.

"Oh, Julian," Allie said, "I'm sorry—"

He waved her off. "I don't want any sympathy. I just want you to know I may not be around for very long to be…useful as a parent." Mitch thought he heard Julian's voice break just a little, but he regained composure quickly, swallowing, and continued, "And you two have been raising him together; I don't want to force myself into that. So…what do you want to do? Just say the word, I'll do it."

Allie sighed deeply and scrubbed her face with her hands. "I think we need to find out who in the house is HIV positive and who is not first. I can only deal with one thing at a time."

Just then, Jamie began to cough and fuss upstairs, and Allie cocked her head to the side, listening. "He's only been asleep 45 minutes," she said.

"I'll get him," Mitch said, eagerly rising from the couch.

"No, I will. You stay put," Allie said. Mitch reluctantly deferred his escape from the awkward interaction and sat back down. Allie hustled up the stairs, and after a beat, Julian spoke.

"I'm really sorry about this, man." He shrugged, his hands pressed together between his knees, staring at his lap.

"Sorry about which part, exactly?" Mitch asked. Julian's shoulders slumped, and he stared into his lap. He looked much the way Mitch had felt all too often since Allie had first left. In the past 24 hours, Mitch realized he'd done a bang-up job of making Julian the bad guy. In his mind, Julian had manipulated Allie into sleeping with him, damn the consequences. Julian had been promiscuous and careless and had passed that on to Allie in the form of a virus. But seeing Julian now, he sure didn't seem like the villain Mitch had imagined. He looked miserable.

"Look, I don't want you to think…Allie and me, I like her a lot, you know? But we were more friends with benefits." He glanced up briefly, risking eye contact, then thinking better of it and returning his eyes to his jeans.

Sitting there, Mitch thought perhaps he understood Julian, just a little. He didn't know what his life was like or who he was much at all, but he could see the situation he was in. He could imagine how that might feel. *This is what Murphy was talking about.* For all of their sakes, Mitch could be honest. "Julian, do you *want* to be Jamie's father? Because I do. Very much."

———

Mitch was incensed Allie had decided to get Jamie tested without talking to him first, but it's not like he wouldn't have agreed to it. He decided not to bring it up; they had enough to worry about without him picking a fight over something trivial.

In the end, since neither Jamie nor Mitch were positive or "reactive," as the doctor put it, they all drove home with relief. Mitch and Jamie would both need to be tested a few more times to be sure, but the odds were, they were in the clear.

Driving home, Mitch felt as if he'd finally exhaled after days of holding his breath. He could see Jamie in the rearview, through the infant car mirror, trying to grab his toes while strapped tight into his car seat. Mitch smiled. Allie was sitting on the passenger seat, staring out the window.

"Well, that's a relief," Mitch said to her. She'd been quiet since they'd left the clinic. "Whatcha thinking about over there?"

"Oh, just…Julian," she said reluctantly. Mitch's shoulders tensed ever so slightly. "I'm just worried about him. I don't think he's got anyone to take care of him, and he probably won't stay put in Lime for long."

Allie sighed, and after a few silent moments, Mitch realized she wasn't going to say anything else, so he changed the subject…slightly. "It's kind of unusual he got HIV from a woman, right? I mean, I did a little research, and it's fairly uncommon —

"

Allie cut him off with a cynical laugh. "It's not that uncommon. And why do you assume he got it from a woman?"

Mitch mentally reviewed his scant knowledge of Julian's sex life and realized he basically didn't know anything about it. He'd assumed. Again. "Oh. Of course it doesn't matter," Mitch said, a bit flustered. "I mean, it does a little, scientifically speaking."

"What do you mean 'scientifically speaking?" Allie asked, narrowing her eyes.

Mitch sensed he was walking into a trap, but he kept going anyway. "Well, you're more likely to contract HIV from a male —"

Allie cut him off. "Mitch, it doesn't matter. Right now, we are not talking about scientific risk factors; we are talking about people. I don't know why you even have to go down that path."

They were both quiet for a while, and in that silent tension, Mitch's humbled thoughts about his own assumptive tendencies turned towards Allie's more distant past, and then he started feeling defensive. He knew he should let it go, knew that no good could come of bringing it up, but he couldn't help himself. "I met your ex, Chris."

Allie raised her eyebrows in challenge.

"Why didn't you tell me she was a woman?"

"Because it didn't matter."

"If it didn't matter, why didn't you mention it? You deliberately edited the pronouns out of any story you ever told me about her. That says it *does* matter, Allie."

"Maybe because I didn't want to have this exact conversation with you."

"And what is that supposed to mean? You think I'd have a problem with you being bisexual? Do you think I have a problem with *anyone* being bisexual or gay or whatever?"

Allie barked a sarcastic laugh. (Mitch wished she'd quit doing that; it pissed him off.) "That's exactly the problem."

"What do you mean?" Mitch asked, banging his palm against the steering wheel in frustration. He felt like he and Allie weren't even speaking the same language.

Allie turned to him, took a deep breath and began, with emphatic patience, to explain, "I'm not bisexual. I just like what I like, and I am who I am. You know, Julian, at least, seemed to get that."

That stung. She was fighting dirty, which meant she was really pissed. Mitch'd worked hard to push down his rumbling jealousy and didn't take the bait. "So you like both men and women?"

"Sometimes."

"Isn't that the fucking definition of bisexual?"

"Why," she asked, "Do we have to be put into categories and labeled? Why do I have to be heterosexual, bisexual, whatever? When I'm attracted to someone, sometimes that person is a man, and sometimes it's a woman. Sometimes, and I know this is going to blow your mind, Mitch, they could be neither or both. Sometimes I want fucking chocolate ice cream!"

Mitch brought the car to a stop in front of Allie's duplex. "Okay," he said in exasperation, "I give up, then. What are you?"

Allie flung the car door open and climbed out. She peered back into the car and yelled, "I'm just me, just Allie! Why the hell do I have to be anything else?"

Mitch wasn't sure what she meant, but it would've made a great exit if she hadn't had to untangle Jamie from his car seat and pull him out of the car. She planted him on her hip and slung the diaper bag over her other shoulder. Halfway up the walk, Jamie got a hold of a lock of Allie's hair and yanked hard. She flinched, and the bag slid down her arm, causing her to stumble. Mitch got out of the car.

"Let me help."

"I don't need your help!"

"Well, I want to, OKAY?!"

Mitch slung the bag over his shoulder and followed Allie into the house, where he plunked the bag down on the floor and left.

CHAPTER 34

Allie sat at the kitchen table, spooning pureed sweet potato and apples into Jamie's waiting "o" of a mouth. Every so often, she tried to sneak a little of the pureed peas underneath the sweeter food, but he responded by scrunching up his face and rejecting the bite down the front of his bib.

She was pondering the conversation in the car with Mitch earlier that day. She'd been defensive; she knew that. And she knew she hadn't responded in the most constructive manner, but she was tired of being forced into roles by other people. He meant well, and he didn't even see he was doing it. He was exasperating.

When she and Chris had been together, the community they'd lived in was accustomed to same-sex couples. When they'd held hands or kissed in public, most people didn't give it a second glance. Allie used to count herself lucky for that — to live in such an enlightened place. But as time went on, she'd started to notice other, more insidious expectations. There was the way people often assumed she was vegetarian or how they always thought she was athletically inclined — the puzzled looks she got when she declined to join the community softball team. There was the way a lot of people assumed she didn't like men, even for friends.

When she'd lived with Mitch, there were different assumptions. People didn't ask *if* they wanted to have kids but "when." People assumed their goals were the same bourgeois aspirations of young couples everywhere — buy a bigger house, fill it with kids and dogs, climb the career ladder. Mitch's goals lined up with that, but hers didn't.

No matter where you were, she realized, society had expectations for you to act in accordance with your assigned role. It wasn't that she didn't want those things; it was that she didn't want to be told she had to want them. The expectations made her feel trapped. And judged. They didn't leave room for her to figure out what she *did* want.

Allie shook her head and came back to the present. She smiled, seeing Jamie's mouth wide open in expectation of the next bite, which she held hovering on the spoon in front of him. Her phone rang from where it had fallen from her pocket into the couch earlier that day, and she let it go to voicemail.

When she remembered to check it later that evening, she heard Jen's voice from the clinic. "Allie, we've got your test results back. Give me a call."

———

Allie sat across the desk from Jen. She heard the rush of thundering water in her ears — an impossible sound. Jen's lips were moving, but Allie couldn't hear her. She hadn't heard a word past "HIV positive." Then, Allie began to hyperventilate.

Jen was around the desk in a flash, helping her put her head between her legs. Then, she cracked the door and asked someone on the other side for a glass of water. When Allie's breathing finally slowed, and she was able to sit up, Jen handed her the water. The clinician was now sitting in a chair on the same side of the desk as Allie. Allie couldn't remember her moving it there.

"Allie, listen. This isn't the death sentence it used to be. We caught it early. You're not symptomatic. We can start you on treatment right away. There's no reason you can't live a full, normal life."

"But…" Allie could barely think. "What about Jamie?"

"His test was non-reactive. We'll test him again in a few months, but odds are—"

"But how am I going to be his mother? What if I get sick? What if people find out, and he gets bullied at school? What if he grows up resenting me for it?"

"Allie, he's six months old. We've got a few years before you have to worry about someone stealing his lunch money or stuffing him in a locker.

"We operate with the strictest code of confidentiality, and you won't get sick, at least not more often than a non-HIV positive person, if we manage this correctly."

"I don't want to manage it! I want it to go away!"

Jen reached out to take Allie's hand, but Allie pushed it away. Jen straightened in her chair. "Look, I know this is excruciating to wrap your head around, but you're going to be fine as long as we start treatment immediately. It's not going away. You will likely be HIV positive for the rest of your life, and while that may come with some daily medication and few other precautions, you can count yourself lucky."

"Lucky? I have a life-threatening virus, I have a child whose paternity is in question, I have a sick friend and a stubborn Mitch and a bullshit job with no benefits. I have a half-written book that will probably never be finished. You want to know the best part?" Her voice was rising in pitch, bordering on hysteria. She thought she might start laughing, then crying, then never stop. "It's all my fault. I got myself here. I suck. Everyone is in this predicament because of me!"

Jen was quiet, and then she spoke in a calm and measured tone: "First of all, it's not all your fault. Partly? Yes, but these things don't happen in a vacuum of one. Second of all, you ARE lucky. I see people who are HIV-positive every day. Some don't find out until they have symptoms and are laid up in the hospital with pneumonia; at that point, it's a lot harder to manage. A whole lot of those people don't have support from family or friends. Many of them are a lot worse off than you are financially. But they keep going, and you will too.

As she drove home in the car she'd borrowed from Shirley, Allie thought about what Jen had said; she knew she was fortunate in a lot of ways. But there was still a lot of work to do, a lot of heartache to share, and it made her tired thinking about it. She realized she still had to call Julian and tell him about Jamie's and Mitch's tests. That, at least, would be some good news. She dreaded telling Mitch about her own situation, telling her sister, her mother.

Allie heard the phone buzzing on the seat beside her. She glanced down at it. Mitch. He was watching Jamie at his place. She was almost home, so she waited until she was parked at the curb and called him back. She might as well tell him now. He answered immediately.

"Allie. Murphy called me. It's Julian."

CHAPTER 35

Allie met Mitch at the Motel 6 just outside of Lime city limits. Police tape cordoned off room 118. There were uniformed cops everywhere – questioning a hand-wringing desk clerk who looked all of eighteen years old and several disheveled-looking guests. There were a few people standing around outside the rooms watching the show.

Mitch got out of the car and strapped Jamie to his chest just as Allie disentangled herself from her seatbelt and joined him. He could see the fear in her eyes, but neither of them said anything. Mitch began scanning the crowd for Murphy. Soon enough, he spotted her giving instructions to what looked like someone in forensics based on the gloves and equipment. When she'd finished, Murphy hustled over to Allie and Mitch, ducking the police tape on the way. Her eyes were focused on Allie.

"Allie, I am so sorry," Murphy said. We didn't know who else to call, so I called you."

"So," Allie gulped, "he's…dead?"

"Yes. It appears to be suicide.."

Mitch saw tears welling up in Allie's eyes. All she could manage in response was a shaky "Oh." He saw her swallow and blink.

Jamie began fussing, so Mitch bounced and swayed to pacify him.

"We'll talk later," Murphy said and then trotted back toward the police tape, ducking back under it.

Mitch looked at Allie. She stared at an imaginary point somewhere over his shoulder. "I never got to tell him. That you and Jamie are okay. He would've wanted to know that."

Mitch gave her an awkward side hug so as not to squish Jamie. As soon as Allie slumped into his side, Jamie quit fussing and was silent. "Let me drive you home," Mitch said.

He was momentarily distracted by the desk clerk who, finished with her interview, was stalking back toward the front office. She paused for a second and took in Mitch, Allie and the baby. Mitch could read the judgment on her face. Whether it was because he was the one carrying the baby or because who the hell brings a baby to a crime scene, he didn't know, but he met her gaze evenly.

"No, I'll be fine. I have to get Shirley's car back." Allie said. Mitch could almost see her walling off whatever complex emotions she was feeling about Julian in order to take care of the business at hand.

In the end, Jamie and Mitch followed Allie to her place, and they all went inside. It was almost 8pm, so Mitch fed Jamie his bottle and put him down for the night. He was still sleeping in Allie's room, though he was almost too long for the bassinet.

Mitch went downstairs, where Allie was reclining on the couch, head back, eyes closed, feet propped on the coffee table. Out the window, Mitch saw a car pull away from the curb. Allie looked up. "Shirley," she said, following his gaze out the window. "I told her I could bring her car back, but she insisted on walking over." Her voice sounded scratchy and hollow.

Mitch went into the kitchen and made Allie some tea. Apparently, she developed a taste for it while they'd been apart. He sat down beside her and put it on the table to cool.

"Hey, you okay?" he asked.

"Not really." Her voice wavered slightly, she didn't open her eyes again or look up.

So Mitch sat on the couch, leaned his own head back and waited to see if she'd talk. His own eyes were drifting sleepily closed when Allie suddenly spoke.

"I'm HIV positive," she said. Mitch sat up and looked at her.

"When did you find out? I thought—"

"Today, right before you called. That's why I asked you to watch Jamie."

Mitch realized he hadn't even thought to ask Allie where she was going when she'd called to ask if she could bring the baby over. He'd begun to get used to her comings and goings. He was always thrilled to spend time with the kiddo.

"Allie, I'm so sorry." It sounded lame to Mitch's own ears. "What does this mean? What now?"

"Jen gave me a couple of prescriptions. She says if I start treatment right away, I'll likely live a long, normal life," her tone sounding as if she were a solemn journalist reporting a fatal car accident.

"Well, that's good, isn't it?"

"Yeah, I guess so. Jen thinks it is. I guess I was feeling a little sorry for myself in her office, but she said it's lucky we caught it early. I know that. I know I'm lucky in a lot of ways, but why do I still feel so miserable?

"I've got a healthy baby, I've got friends and family to support me, I have a roof over my head. I'm asymptomatic, and I have you, who is still here, despite everything."

Tears began to leak from underneath her closed lids.

"Of course I'm still here," Mitch said softly. His heart both ached and swelled. "I love you."

Allie opened her eyes and rolled her head to look at him. "I can't imagine why."

Mitch leaned in close and kissed first one cheek, then the other, right where the tears were forming rivulets. They stared at each other, and Mitch could feel them leaning closer, feel her breath on his face. He heard his own heartbeat starting to keep time in his head, then he heard a knock at the door.

Mitch leaped off the couch to answer the door while Allie hastily wiped the tears off her face with the hem of her t-shirt. It was Murphy.

"Sorry I didn't call. It's been a long day." She looked tired, haggard. "Can I come in? Is this a bad time?"

"No, of course!" Mitch responded, perhaps with a little too much enthusiasm. "Want a drink?" Mitch bustled off to the kitchen and returned with three juice glasses of wine.

Murphy was seated on the couch, so he took the chair across from them and set the glasses on the table.

"Thanks," said Murphy, taking a large, grateful sip.

"At the motel, you said we'd talk later." Mitch could see the expectant look on Allie's face, mirroring his own feelings.

"He took a lethal dose of some painkillers. His name was on the prescription bottle. He must've taken them sometime yesterday evening. We're trying to contact his family. Allie, would you have any idea how to get in touch with them?"

"No. He didn't talk about them. I have no idea. But why? Why did he do it? Didn't he leave a note or anything?" Mitch could hear the desperation in her voice.

"He didn't," Murphy said. "Look, I know it's easy to get caught up in wondering why, but that's not a question we're ever going to be able to answer." Murphy's eyes were fixed on Allie, and there was a softness to them Mitch hadn't seen before.

"But…" Allie began, "Was it because of his health? Was it because of everything I told him, was it…"

"Allie, we can't know what he was thinking in his last moments. He was likely in a lot of emotional pain, but — and I can't emphasize this enough — it is not your fault. Feel sad for him, feel empathy for what he was going through, but do not take his death on as your responsibility. His life was his own."

Allie sniffled and nodded. Mitch was grateful Murphy was there to say the things he couldn't put into words. Murphy reached out and rested her hand on top of Allie's. She squeezed it and smiled sadly. "I better be going."

Mitch walked Murphy to the door, then returned to Allie. She was still in her spot on the couch, hunched over with her head in her hands.

"Hey," Mitch said, resting his hand on her shoulder. "Let's go to bed, okay? I mean, you go to bed. Can I stay here on the couch?"

"No." She shook her head, her eyes staring into Mitch's.

"Um, okay. I just thought I could get up with Jamie in the morning, and you could sleep in."

"I mean no, I can't stay here." She was crying now and starting to breathe loudly, almost hyperventilating. I can't. I can't. I'm sorry. It's all too much."

Allie was up off the couch and heading for the door before Mitch could process what was going on. She grabbed his keys from the coffee table and was gone. He heard her loud sobs as she tore down the front walk and motor revving and the screech of car tires roaring and fading in the distance.

Mitch stood in the middle of Allie's living room stunned, staring at the front door in disbelief. He walked over and opened it. There was nothing. His car was gone, and the night was silent save for the crickets. He closed the door and went back to sit on the couch. Not knowing what else to do, he sipped his wine.

CHAPTER 36

Allie drove. She didn't know where she was going, but panic had begun to brew when she found out Julian was dead, and it had come to a head as Murphy talked to her and Mitch in her living room.

Julian had gotten out — out of this mess they were all in, out of the confines of mundane existence. It made her feel even more trapped, highlighted in technicolor for her the fact that, as much as she loved her child, his existence bound her to Mitch whether she wanted it or not. Her HIV-positive diagnosis bound her to her past, and she would feel the guilt and see it reflected in Mitch's and Jamie's faces every time she looked at them. When she hit the interstate, she began planning.

I could go back to Galveston. But no, people would look for her there.

I could go to Jamie's place again. But she wasn't sure grown-up Jamie would be quite as sympathetic the second time around.

Actually, she probably would, but Allie didn't want her to have to be. She didn't want to feel the shame of washing up on her sister's doorstep again with nothing.

So she drove.

Maybe the West Coast. She began to veer through the Texas Hill Country in that general direction. Allie drove and drove, her mind racing while she simultaneously tried not to think about the implications of what she was doing. It was dark. Her eyes kept drifting shut of their own accord until she would jolt and slap her cheeks to keep awake. Around 2 am, she had to admit she could go no further. She was in the middle of nowhere, West Texas, which is more "nowhere" than most.

By the faint light of the half-moon, Allie could see the dark shapes of scrubby bushes and cacti and flat, flat earth stretching to the horizon. She pulled off and tucked the car behind a rare hill where she hoped it couldn't be seen from the road.

Slowly, sip by sip, Mitch finished his glass of wine, then Allie's. Then, he just sat, in a daze, unable to put together a coherent thought. Allie was gone. Again. Would she cool off and be back in the morning? In a few weeks? Never? Suddenly, he had an inkling of what Allie meant when she said she felt trapped. But – and now clarity was beginning to return to him – *Did he even want her to come back?*

He loved her, but how many more times was she going to do this? He'd rather live with a permanently broken heart than have it put back together over and over just to be smashed once again. But his heart wasn't broken, he realized. His heart was full. Jamie. No matter what, he and Jamie would be okay together.

Mitch felt something let go inside himself then. He inhaled, exhaled; his shoulders relaxed several inches. Around midnight, he climbed the stairs to Allie's room and fell asleep in her bed next to Jamie.

When Allie woke, with the light of a new morning streaming through the rear window of the car, her back was stiff from sleeping in the reclined driver's seat. She blinked her eyes and stared at the ceiling of the car. She reached out and turned the keys, which still hung from the ignition, to the on position and pressed the button to open the sunroof. Chilly air wafted down toward her as the heat her body had created in the vehicle escaped. She shivered.

A cardinal called its signature *cheer, cheer, whoop, whoop, whoop.* Allie could hear the occasional car pass, though she could not see them beyond her hiding place behind the hill. After a few moments, she raised the seat upright, cranked the engine and slowly eased the car back out onto the road.

————

Mitch awakened in Allie's bed. It took a minute for him to remember where he was, and then the previous day's events trickled back into his mind. Jamie was cooing to himself in the bassinet. Mitch could just see his little legs flailing above its edge. He lay there listening for a while, and when the baby began to fuss, he scooped him up to change his diaper and get them both breakfast.

————

Allie sat in a diner, not unlike the one where she'd lost her pack. That seemed like decades ago. She'd dug enough change out of Mitch's car seats to buy a cup of mediocre coffee, and she sat at the bar drinking it.

"Would you like a muffin or a croissant?" the man behind the counter asked.

Allie's stomach was beginning to rumble, but she had no more money. She'd left the house without her wallet.

"No thanks." Allie tried to smile at him and slumped forward on her stool, beaten.

"Here," the man said, pulling one of each from behind the glass case. "I always have some left at the end of the day, and my dogs certainly don't need any more leftovers. Do me a favor and take these off my hands."

"Thank you," Allie said, "I appreciate it." She sat up a little straighter as she took the food.

The man waved her off, a nonverbal "It's nothing." He went about his business with the other customers. Allie sat munching the banana nut muffin, then the croissant, looking out the window at the morning. No people. Just birds. The dawn had been bright, but it was beginning to get cloudy.

Allie sat and thought. Jen was right; she was lucky. But no matter how fortunate she might be, life still felt terrifyingly difficult right now. She heard thunder rumble across the hills outside.

She thought about the future, about her son, Mitch, her family. And her health. There were no guarantees. But then again, when were there ever? She realized she might not always feel lucky or even optimistic, but she did have one thing: determination. She would be there for her son and for her friends and family the best she could. She wished Julian had been able to do the same.

She gave the man behind the counter a faint smile and thanked him again before heading back out to Mitch's car. She got in, started the engine and drove toward home. The raindrops began to fall, slowly at first and then in a downpour, sheeting across the windshield. Allie turned on the wipers, squinted against the deluge and kept driving.

He fed them both bacon and eggs — mostly eggs for Jamie, who only had two teeth. Mitch didn't know if Allie was giving him anything other than baby food, but Jamie seemed to enjoy the eggs. Then, Mitch called the client he was supposed to meet for a showing at 10am. They were local and didn't mind the cancellation, but due to all the shit that had happened in his life recently, he'd had to reschedule a lot of things. He knew it wasn't good for business.

Putting his phone back in his pocket, Mitch noticed the kitchen floor. He'd only made three eggs, but it looked like there was a dozen worth of scrambled ones down there. He was mopping them off the floor, the wall and the highchair when he heard the front door bang open. Mitch pulled Jamie out of his chair and tucked the baby under his arm as he strode to the living room. He stopped short. There was Allie, standing just inside the open front door, with his car keys dangling from the four fingers of her left hand.

Epilogue

It had been six months since Allie left and came back, six months since Julian died. Mitch felt like the three of them — Allie, Mitch, Jamie — had settled into a tentative rhythm. Jamie had finally gotten comfortable sleeping at Mitch's place, much to everyone's relief, and he began moving seamlessly between his two homes. Mitch was beginning to see how this would feel normal for Jamie as he grew up. After all, what was Mitch's own idea of "normal" based on but what he had grown up with? With Jamie being a year old now, Mitch felt (mostly) comfortable with the plan to start him at part-time preschool in a few months.

Mitch noticed that, although he and Allie talked a lot, it was always about logistics – when were Mitch's showings, when did Allie have to work, when did she need time to write, when did he have to be out of town for a conference, how did Jamie sleep last night? Deeper conversations were non-existent; despite Mitch's yearning for emotional connection with Allie, neither he nor Allie seemed to have the bandwidth for it.

After Allie had come back that night, Mitch told her he understood…a little, anyway. He could see how she may have felt trapped. He reflected on their relationship and realized he had assumed she wanted the same things he wanted. When she had protested, he didn't take it seriously. Not until she actually left. In retrospect, he felt sheepish about all his assumptions.

Allie had said she came back that night for Jamie, that no matter how trapped she felt, she couldn't leave him, and she couldn't take him away from Mitch. That is something Mitch did fully understand. He was grateful he and Allie were in agreement there.

Mitch saw that his and Allie's feelings for each other were more complex, more ambivalent, than the unwavering love they felt for their child. Sometimes, when Mitch saw her, in those moments she didn't know he was looking, he still loved her. He was afraid, though, to let himself fully feel that love. He thought Allie loved him too; he glimpsed it sometimes in the way she looked at him or how she held on when they occasionally hugged, but he'd stopped reading too much into it — stopped thinking she wanted anything more than what they had at the moment.

Right now is good, he thought.

Acknowledgments

Writing a novel is a lonely endeavor; it's an island in my head that friends and family can't visit. So it's funny, as I come to the close of a project, there are so many people to thank. It turns out, though they can't visit my island, they can send care packages. Thank you to…

• my sister, Bonnie Coover, my first beta reader, despite her fear it would be terrible and she would have to tell me.

• my friends David Serafine and Rebecca Boswell, who both separately let me ramble about publishing until I figured out what I wanted. Dave also stomached a highly unedited version of this story and gave valuable feedback. Rebecca gave valuable help with the cover.

• my longtime partner-in-crime, Kelly Martineau, who struggles with the writing process, too and has often made me feel much less alone.

• my extended family, out into the realm of step-uncles and second cousins, who make up the bulk of my constant readers and take the time to respond.

• Michaela Dunn, editor extraordinaire, who held my hand through cutting the chaff and had a vital role in making a messy manuscript into a novel.

• my grandmother, Sue White, who told me, "Keep writing," back when my longest composition was a recipe for strawberry jam.

• my parents, Pat and Linda Coover, who raised me to stubbornly pursue the things I most want.

• my partner, Jason Garner, who tolerated my underemployment while I took forever to write and edit this book because he knows all too well what it's like to be an artist.

www.ingramcontent.com/pod-product-compliance
Lightning Source LLC
Chambersburg PA
CBHW020238010826

48973CB00006B/1571